To Maria & Colin
best wishes
Carol M Creasey

NOT JUST AN AFFAIR

Biography:
My Life is Worth Living!

Fiction:
Fatal Obsession

Not Just an Affair

Carol M. Creasey

UNITED WRITERS
Cornwall

UNITED WRITERS PUBLICATIONS LTD
Ailsa, Castle Gate, Penzance, Cornwall.

British Library Cataloguing in Publication Data:
A catalogue record for this book is
available from the British Library.

ISBN 1 85200 118 6

Printed in Great Britain by
United Writers Publications Ltd
Cornwall.

To the memory of
my father,
who always encouraged
me to keep on writing.

Chapter One

Amy was almost asleep when she heard her husband Peter return from the pub. She hoped that he hadn't had too much to drink. Not only did it make him bad tempered, but it seemed to bring out that nasty side of him, never seen by others, only her unfortunate self.

She had tried to talk to him about it, but Peter was very clever, he knew how to be charming when necessary, and as it was a side well hidden from the rest of the world, he always played it down, changing very quickly into a loving and devoted husband, so that she was left feeling bewildered, and almost wondering if she had imagined his raging outbursts.

She sighed as she realised just how much marriage had changed him. Was it her fault? What had she done to cause it? With everyone else he was a hail-fellow-well-met' sort of person. Even his mother, who must surely know him best, always referred to him as her good-natured and easy-going son.

Maybe it was an exaggeration to say that he abused her. She wasn't really sure because she'd never told anyone else. He didn't beat her and give her bruises, but when he had those blind rages, he would spitefully twist her arm, or clench his fist at her, and sometimes he had rounded on the dog and kicked or hit him for no reason. This had hurt her even more, which was maybe why he did it.

Dear Jasper had been such a faithful friend, her best friend really! Amy was an avid animal lover. It had hurt her to see the bewilderment and misery in his brown eyes, and the way he had cowered away from Peter. She'd been unable to control herself then from screaming at him angrily, "Don't be so cruel to Jasper! He's done nothing to you!"

But then his charming manner had returned immediately, and putting his arm round her shoulders, he'd said very contritely, "Amy, my love, I'm very sorry. I'm under such a lot of pressure at work. You know what the bank's like, it's really getting to me! Come here, Jasper. Good boy! I didn't mean it."

Poor Jasper, being the loving family dog that he was, had grovelled over to him on his stomach, prepared to risk another blow from his unpredictable master, just to gain his attention.

Amy was left feeling that maybe Peter was heading for a nervous breakdown, and wondering if she should make allowances for him, but her inner self argued back. He didn't have to be spiteful. The reasons for his rapid change of personality were so trivial, like being a few minutes late going out, or maybe the house wasn't tidy enough, although she always kept it clean. With two energetic children, aged nine and seven, it wasn't always possible to be immaculate, so why did he have to be so unreasonable?

Once Amy had even tried to talk to her mother about it, just to get advice on what she was doing wrong, but Susan didn't seem to take her words seriously. When she explained about his bad temper, and need for tidiness, her mother had given her opinion formed by her years spent with Amy's father, David.

"Well darling, all men can be difficult, don't expect them to be perfect. They're not, and neither are we. You are lucky with Peter because he's so easy-going, so if he's complaining, you must be neglecting him. Our role is to wash their clothes, keep their home clean and feed them. Can't you get yourself a cleaner, they're worth their weight in gold!"

Amy had looked at her mother in horror. She was so old fashioned! That may have been true when she was young, but this was the new millennium, and weren't women supposed to be equal? It was useless trying to get any backing from her very out of date parents. "Whatever would I do all day if I did get a cleaner?" she said grimly. She didn't go to work, so she'd have to spend her time keeping out of the cleaner's way. What a thought!

"There's always coffee mornings, or maybe join a gym,"

suggested Susan. "I belong to a Charity Group. We always need volunteers to help."

It was no good. Her mother couldn't, or didn't want to understand. Now that Amy was married, much against the will of her father at the time, Susan had to make out her life was happy, even if it wasn't true. Amy had been tempted to say to her, "And what about sex, Mother. Do I have to give into his demands every time he wants it, and if I don't, isn't that rape?" but she didn't say anything.

Her parents had given her the impression, whilst she was growing up, that sex had only been invented for the creation of children. She couldn't understand that. She had found her sex life very enjoyable in the early days with Peter. He had been gentle and tender when they first got married. Now she only endured it. But on reflection, was that really true? When Peter was acting normally he could be charming, tender and kind, which tended to make her forget his nasty side and many times, afterwards, she wondered if she had over-reacted when he was angry.

During his stable periods their love life was good. They could go along happily for months, but then something would trigger him off. Sometimes it was his drinking, but not always, and then she felt only intense dislike for him.

She could hear his step on the stairs now, slow and blundering. Well at least she knew what to expect. Should she pretend to be asleep? But that never stopped him. Once she had found it a turn-on, to be erotically woken from a deep sleep, but not when he reeked of drink.

The door opened, and he knocked against the dressing table as he passed it. She could smell the stench of beer and stale tobacco on his breath, and she prayed inwardly that he would clean his teeth before he climbed in beside her. "There she is, my little woman, lying there waiting for me."

His words were slurred, and she shuddered as he peeled off his clothes (it was all right for him to be untidy) and stumbled into bed. The fumes from his mouth were disgusting, and she lay there, determined to keep her back to him. If he tried to kiss her with breath like that, she felt she would pass out with nausea.

She felt his naked body press up against her back, his hardness amazed her. After all, he was well oiled! It also aroused her, and she felt the familiar stickiness between her legs, and a desire to

9

stroke herself. She didn't need to, even when drunk he still knew how to tickle her into submission, and to her great delight, his exploring fingers easily found the right spot. In spite of her disgust at his state, she felt herself succumbing.

She told herself that she had to be thankful that he was in a good mood after all that drink. She was becoming very excited now, and was unable to suppress it, so before she knew it, he was inside her.

This was lust, nothing more. It certainly wasn't an act of love. She knew she was allowing his body to satisfy hers. What was she, sex crazy? All she really wanted was romance and love, but it didn't stop her from enjoying it.

He continued to pump away inside her and she felt his weapon become bigger and harder. He was grunting like a wild bear, and in that wild moment she knew that she was about to enjoy a mind-blowing orgasm. When it came, it swept through her body like a tornado, her clitoris begged submission from his fingertips, and it erupted deep inside. He shouted passionately at her, and then she felt the second one coming, his movements became even faster, followed by his explosion.

After a few moments she moved away from him, feeling a bit disgusted with herself as she once again noticed the stench of his breath. He was snoring now, his eyes tightly closed and his hands resting lightly between her legs; those hands that just a few minutes ago had evoked such desire inside her. Laying there in a drunken stupor, he looked most unappealing.

She thought of the times when he had been drunk and bad tempered. Then her body couldn't respond to him. If he handled her roughly she seemed to tighten up, both in mind and body. This made him angry, and then it hurt; God how it hurt! Like being poked by an iron bar. How could this man evoke two very different responses in her? Was he mad or was she?

As she lay there listening to his snores, she longed for the romance from when they were first married to return. At that time he would have worn aftershave, always dressed smartly, and wouldn't have dreamt of getting into bed without cleaning his teeth.

Unfortunately, ten years and two children later, she had accepted that this was marriage, this was reality. Where had all her spirit gone? Squashed down by his bad temper, was the simple answer to that. But how dare he! She vowed, at that moment, with or without the backing of her parents, she was no longer going to allow Peter to bully her. She was fed up with trying to keep up appearances. If necessary she would leave him. Her marriage was just a sham and she'd had enough!

Chapter Two

Ian Wood walked slowly up the path to the small house that he shared with his wife Miranda and their two daughters, Linda and Sophie. He was hoping the girls would still be up. Life was such a bitch, he felt, and they were both so cute and innocent. He did so hope that they weren't aware of all the misery that was circulating around them.

As for Miranda, she was so wrapped up in herself she probably hadn't even noticed there was something wrong. He felt his misery so acutely and he didn't know how to put it right. If he'd still been in love with her, they could have talked about it, but he wasn't. She'd taken away all his sexual confidence, and he found it hard to forgive that. She'd made him feel less than a man and he'd lost his own self respect.

He had tried to convince himself that sex wasn't the only thing in life that mattered. He still had the girls, but he knew that at twenty-nine years old he should still be enjoying a happy and fulfilling sex life. It seemed that everyone else was bonking, and the worst thing of all was that he didn't care if he never bonked again. Had he become some sort of freak? The thought was disturbing.

There were two little faces flattened against the front room window looking for him. At least he mattered to them. His spirits lifted a little. Linda pounced excitedly on him as he opened the door, exclaiming, "Daddy, I got a gold star for doing good work!"

Sophie, determined not to be outdone, joined in too: "I ate all my dinner, even my cabbage!" She pulled a face to emphasise what an ordeal it had been, and he laughed. They could soon banish his blues.

He looked at them with fatherly pride. They shared his chestnut hair and brown eyes, even the shape of their faces resembled his family rather than Miranda's. They still had on their school uniforms; chocolate brown tunics with peach blouses, and he thought how well these colours suited them.

Miranda was standing behind them with that complacent, self satisfied smile on her face. She really didn't seem to realise that his feelings for her had died, and what was even worse, he didn't even feel sorry for her. Like a greedy leech, she had drained him of all emotion.

"Oh, there you are Ian. The girls wanted to see you before they got ready for bed. I didn't have time to cook you anything, but there's microwave meals in the freezer, or you can get a takeaway delivered."

Ian brightened inwardly. At least he didn't have to endure one of Miranda's charred remains, known as 'dinner'. Life could only improve now! She loved to talk, so virtually everything she cooked was forgotten whilst she was on the telephone, or reading magazines. Not that she would admit she had burnt it. She always assured him it was only well done, which was the best way to eat meat. Ian could now look forward to a tasty microwave meal!

"Have a nice evening," he said, almost mechanically, and then she stopped in her tracks as she remembered something.

"Can you ring Rachel and tell her that we don't need her to babysit? You didn't tell me what time you would be in!" she said accusingly.

Ian was filled with horror. The last thing he wanted to do was to ring Rachel. How could he face talking to her, a seventeen-year-old girl, after his humiliation the last time he had seen her!

Miranda, aware that his thoughts seemed to be elsewhere, as they often were, took charge of the situation.

"Ian, I don't think you're listening to me! If you forget, she'll come round anyway and you'll have to pay her!"

This time Ian did take notice. He couldn't think of anything worse than actually being confronted by Rachel. At least on the other end of the telephone she was out of sight and out of reach.

13

He wouldn't have to see that look in her eyes, that look that made him feel such a heel.

Miranda was thinking about her marriage whilst she was driving to her mother's house. After nine years together, and two beautiful girls, their marriage must be as solid as a rock, she felt. Ian would never leave her. She chided herself for even thinking about it.

She looked regretfully at her ample thighs, bulging defiantly out of her size eighteen trousers. Her trousers were getting too tight and it was difficult to drive. Not that Miranda felt there was anything wrong with herself. Most women put on a bit of weight after having children. Look at Mum, it was in her genes, she couldn't stop it from happening. She had been a large fourteen, rather than a small sixteen when they married. He hadn't minded then, so now he must realise she had a more mature figure; being two years older than him, she was now thirty-one.

He seemed to have been acting a bit strange since he'd been in hospital last year. He'd caught a mysterious virus, the doctors couldn't say how or from where, and it had attacked his testes. They tried various medications, but in the end the doctors had to remove one. Miranda couldn't see why Ian had made such a fuss about it.

Her mother had thought it was cancer and predicted that before long Miranda would be a widow, and the girls would be fatherless. Maybe Mum shouldn't have mentioned it to Ian when she visited him, but instead of being glad that it wasn't cancer, he just seemed to be so depressed and wrapped up in himself.

The doctor had assured them that with time and patience their love life could return to normal. First of all she had said nothing to him, preferring to ignore the subject, but as the days turned to weeks she could feel her frustration building. In the end she had to do something about it.

One night she cooked him a steak. That in itself was unusual, as Ian did most of the cooking normally. She bought his favourite bottle of red wine, believing that relaxation was probably the answer, and even put on her sexy black set of undies. She brushed her wavy black hair until it shone, and gave herself a liberal splash of perfume that was guaranteed to make her irresistible, before joining him in bed.

14

By the time all this had happened Ian had fallen asleep, but laying next to him with this unbearable throbbing between her legs, she knew she would have to do something. She turned to kiss him, allowing her lips to travel all over his face, and then she started to touch him. She had expected to feel his erection, but apart from flinching with pain when she accidentally touched his scar, nothing happened. His penis remained small and floppy in her hands, and resisted all her attempts to rouse it.

She worked on him until her patience was exhausted, and then she couldn't help snapping at him. "Don't pretend to be asleep when I feel like this! You haven't even touched me!"

He had opened his eyes and told her he didn't feel like it. He was tired. This hadn't helped her frustration and she had told him he was useless. Naturally she hadn't meant it, and he surely knew that? She had stormed off into the spare room alone, hoping he would come after her and try to put things right, as he would have done when they were first married. But he didn't, so she had relieve herself in the only way she knew how. She was left feeling fulfilled in her body but not in her mind, because it wasn't Ian. She felt angry when she realised that he was no longer the super stud she had married.

Ian picked up the phone quickly, determined to get this ordeal over with.

"Go and watch TV girls," he urged. "I'll be with you in a minute."

Rachel's mother answered, to his relief. He could give her the message maybe.

"Hello, Mrs Miles, it's Ian here. Can you give Rachel a message for me?"

"She's not here, Ian. In fact, she's on her way over to babysit for you."

That was what he didn't want. Now he'd have to see her!

"We don't need her now I'm home!" he said, in desperation.

"You could always try her mobile," said her mother, trying to be helpful.

"Thanks very much, I will," Ian replied.

He knew where her mobile number was. Miranda had it pinned up in the kitchen. When he tried to ring it went straight into answerphone. She obviously had it switched off. But why, she didn't drive, she'd be walking round? Why couldn't it be on?

The doorbell sounded and he knew it was her. Linda's curiosity was too much for her, and she left the cartoon she was watching and ran excitedly into the hall. Ian was glad that no one knew how stressed he was feeling, and he tried to keep his voice light. "I think it's Rachel."

"Daddy, you said you weren't going out!" said Sophie accusingly.

"I'm not," Ian reassured her. "Rachel's just popped in to see us."

As he opened the door he tried not to meet her eyes. He didn't want to see a hurt look because it made him feel guilty.

"I've just rung your mobile as I'm now in. Sorry to bring you round for nothing."

"It's not on. The battery's low," Rachel explained, adding: "I was coming round to see you anyway."

Ian's stomach lurched. He had to stop this now, even though it had not properly begun. Rachel's serious grey eyes met his, her adoration clearly showing, and he squirmed inwardly for the mess he'd got himself into. Why oh why had he got involved with her? He knew the answer to that. Not only was she very slim and attractive, with the longest legs he'd ever seen, but also, she was naïve, adoring, and most unlikely to tell Miranda.

He must be the only bloke in the year 2002 to find a virgin, especially a girl as attractive as Rachel. Her body was great. Although slim, she had lovely breasts, but to his great disappointment even looking at, and touching them, had not roused him enough to cause an erection.

He remembered stroking her long black hair. She had closed her eyes with rapture when he kissed her. She was an infatuated teenager, which was just what his bruised and battered ego needed; someone who would look up to him. But all that hadn't stopped him from failing miserably at something that for all men should come naturally, sex! How on earth could he get himself out of this situation?

To his absolute horror Rachel dissolved into tears as she said, "I'm going away to college soon, and I won't see you for ages. I love you, I can't help myself!"

"Ssh, the girls will hear you." He hastily handed her a box of tissues from the hall table. He had expected anger and recriminations, but not this. He must try to keep it all under wraps, and let her down gently.

She blew her nose and wiped her eyes, still gazing at him like an adoring spaniel. Her eyes looked even bigger when full of tears. Ian watched her put the tissue in the pocket of her jeans with trembling hands. She was certainly a very striking female, but he had only used her, and now he felt ashamed. He wanted to try and make amends.

"Come and have some coffee. I'll talk to you when the girls go to bed."

She nodded silent agreement and followed him towards the kitchen. As he passed the lounge he could hear the girls giggling as they watched Cartoon Network.

"Ten more minutes, you two, and then bed," he informed them. There was no reply, but he expected that. They probably thought that if they pretended not to hear him they could stay up later.

Rachel sat at the kitchen table whilst he made the coffee, and he tried to think of a kind way of letting her know that there was nothing between them, and there wasn't going to be. This was more embarrassing for him than her, if only she realised, and to have to talk about it, and relive it in his mind again, was pure torture for him.

He handed her a mug of coffee, noting the dejection in her eyes when she looked at him, her shoulders bowed in an attitude of defeat. She obviously did realise that the feelings were one-sided. He braced himself to speak. "I must apologise for what happened the other night when I took you home in the car. I didn't mean to take advantage of you."

Oh hell, that sounded stupid, like some old fashioned movie, and she just sat there looking at him, so he tried again.

"Well, that is, I know nothing much happened between us, apart from me petting you. But I tried to make it happen and I shouldn't have done. I am a married man and you are our babysitter."

Rachel spoke at last. "But it's my fault nothing happened. I told you I was a virgin, and it's true. I didn't know what to do. I know you didn't fancy me, but I don't just fancy you, I love you, and I have ever since I first met you!"

Now the tears flowed again, and Ian jumped guiltily as he

17

heard a noise by the door. It was Linda, as inquisitive as ever. She was very fond of Rachel, and she put her arms round her, which made Ian feel as low as a worm.

"Don't cry Rachel, what's wrong?" she asked, puzzled.

Ian tried to give Rachel a warning look, but there was no need. She returned Linda's hug and then regained her composure.

"I was just telling your dad how much I'll miss you and Sophie when I go to college. But never mind, I'll be home in the holidays to see you."

By now Sophie had also appeared, so Ian took the opportunity that now presented itself. "Come on girls, time for bed."

"Can we have a bath?" tried Sophie, eager to delay the inevitable.

"No, it's late enough as it is!" he said firmly.

Rachel managed a smile. "I'll help you to get them to bed."

After they had gone to bed, he sat down to try and explain things to Rachel. He owed it to her to tell the truth at least. "The reason why I didn't complete making love to you Rachel, was not because of you, but because of me. I couldn't. My mind fancied you but my body let me down. I'm impotent."

He then proceeded to tell her about his illness, the operation, and the devastating effect of it, both mentally and physically. He didn't really feel words were enough, but then no one else could possibly understand what it had done to him and how he felt inside.

The amazement on her face as the tale unfolded was apparent, and he felt relief at having now got it off his chest. He didn't need to tell her that he no longer loved his wife. That might give her the wrong idea. He also felt he owed Miranda a certain loyalty, so he would have to lie a little.

"In case you're wondering why I tried to make love to you, I feel you should know that I found you very attractive. I was tempted to have an affair with you, but it's wrong. I must stay faithful . . ."

Rachel burst in passionately ". . . I wanted my first time to be with you so I could remember it for ever!"

Ian looked awkwardly at her. Why were teenage girls so dramatic! This was not proving easy and he was feeling humiliated by it all. To have to admit he was a sexual failure was a nightmare. He fixed his brown eyes on her and willed her to

18

understand. "I know you think you love me, but believe me, one day you'll realise it's only infatuation. You don't even know the real me. When you go to college and meet a new boyfriend you'll find out what love is all about, and then you'll forget me and what nearly happened."

Rachel tried once more, tearfully sobbing. "But I love you so much. I'll try to help you make love. I'll do anything you want me to!"

What an offer! In his super stud days, Ian would have been tempted to avail himself of it, but right now he just wanted to escape from this tangled web of emotions he had created.

"No, Rachel," he said gently, but firmly, ignoring her tears. "I like you too much to lead you on. It would hurt too many people, especially my girls, and I could never leave them, please understand."

Rachel looked deep into those brown eyes that she adored, and then she turned to kiss the cheek of the man who had just ripped her heart to pieces. She knew there was no future, but these feelings were driving her crazy. If only she could get him out of her mind. She couldn't eat or sleep, or concentrate on anything. Maybe she needed to go away to stop herself from falling apart.

"I'll never forget you," she said huskily.

Ian returned her kiss, putting his arms round her briefly. He couldn't let her go away without showing some feeling. She was a sweet kid really, and had been good with the girls. "Take care, and come and see us when you're at home on holiday," he murmured.

"Oh yes, I will," she promised him.

As he stood by the door he watched her walk down the path. Six months from now, he reckoned, she'd have a bloke of her own, then he would be forgotten. Those long legs, curvaceous hips and breasts, would soon be appreciated by randy young college boys.

He had no desire to ever make love to Miranda again. If his marriage was loveless, then tough! He tried to pretend not to care. He couldn't, or wouldn't, make love. He wasn't sure which it was.

Chapter Three

Amy had decided that she would go to the party with Peter. Her plan to leave him would soon be put into operation, but she needed to confide in Gill, her best friend, and although tonight would probably not be the time to do it, she could at least make an arrangement to see Gill on her own soon

She realised that it wasn't going to be easy without the understanding and backing of her parents, but hopefully when they realised how unhappy her marriage was, they might change their attitude.

Maybe her brother Max could help. They had always been close. If the truth was known, she had to admit to herself, one of the reasons why she had kept quiet was because she didn't want to prove her father right. At the time, he had opposed their marriage, especially as Amy had only been eighteen. But Amy had thought she knew best. She had fallen heavily for Peter's charming and cheeky manner, which sadly had soon disappeared after they were married.

Daddy had thought that because Peter came from a less affluent background, that he might be after her for her money. This had made Amy very angry at the time. Didn't Daddy realise that not everyone can inherit a nice country house without having to work for it? Mummy and Daddy had been this lucky because Daddy's father was a self-made man, a city banker, and Daddy didn't even need to work because there was so much money floating about, he just devoted his spare time to becoming a local councillor, and doing good work for the community.

Peter's parents were both at work. His Dad, George, was working in the council offices, and his mother, Jane, was a part-time nurse. They lived in a three bedroom semi-detached house, so although they were not rolling in money, they weren't destitute either.

That was another of her parents' sins, they were snobs, and liked to move in higher circles; so much that they had put a substantial amount of money towards the house that Amy and Peter bought, making sure that Amy lived on the affluent side of town. Their house was detached like her parents', and David paid for the children to attend private schools. They had also done the same for Max, her brother, and his wife Anna. It might sound like generosity, but Amy knew that her father didn't want to look down on his children for being in a lower class than himself. If she was going to get divorced and give all this up, it would really put the cat among the pigeons, but she had decided she'd had enough, and if Peter had married her for her money, then he, too, was in for a shock.

"Come on Amy! Aren't you ready yet?"

She was interrupted from her reverie by Peter's voice. His mouth was twisted with annoyance and his eyes looked small and mean. This might be the start of one of his nasty tempers, but this time she was having none of it!

"You do nothing to help. You only look after number one!" she shouted angrily, and her eyes now flashed back at him. "Next time we go out you can take care of the children, and wash and brush Sarah's hair, and I'll get ready at my leisure!" They were walking down the stairs now, and as Amy's parents were in the front room looking after the children, his manner towards her immediately changed, just as she knew it would. He had to play to his audience.

"Well, I'm glad you're ready now," he said lightly, then poking his head round the lounge door, he smiled genially at her parents. "Are you comfortable in there. You know how to work the TV, don't you?"

David rose out of his chair, and shook his son-in-law's hand. "Of course. Young Paul is beating me at Monopoly you know."

"He will!" said Peter proudly. "He's got ideas of being an estate agent when he grows up."

21

Amy struggled to swallow down her bitterness. Peter was such a phoney!

She smiled fondly at her two children as she followed him into the room. It was sad that they would soon find out that their parents were not a happy couple, but she just had to leave him! As for Daddy, he had long since ceased to be over-protective towards her, believing that since they were married Peter had become part of the Lee family and was solid and respectable.

She bent over to kiss them, and then remembered Paul, at nine years old, would not want her to. He considered it sissy. She ruffled his blond curls lightly, and his blue eyes glanced briefly at her.

"Get off, Mum. Grandad's losing all his money!" he said excitedly.

He had inherited his father's blond curls, wide blue beguiling eyes, and lean long-legged frame. At the moment he didn't appear to have inherited his temper, being of a quieter disposition than his very feisty sister, Sarah.

Sarah looked up from the computer, which was usually a bone of contention between the children. Out of the two of them, she was most likely to get her own way, both from Paul and Peter.

"Mummy, I like your new dress, can I have something new Daddy?"

"You're always having new things," smiled Peter, ever the doting father, and he said aside to Amy's mother Susan: "She'll play these computer games all evening if you let her, so we say no more than an hour at a time."

Susan nodded her agreement, and Amy couldn't help thinking that she was usually the one who had to put her foot down over this. Peter was too engrossed in flicking round the millions of television channels that cable TV provided them with, to know what either of the children were doing, let alone how long they spent on the computer.

She smoothed down some imaginary wrinkles from the simple black dress that Sarah had admired. Usually Amy wore trousers, like most women these days, but going to a party was different, and she wanted to dress up a bit.

She wore her straight blonde hair in a very simple style with a fringe. Her eyes were a deep cornflower blue, big and expressive, and although she cursed her skin for being so fair and she couldn't tan easily, its very milky glow set off by the black dress, was a sharp contrast to the usual brown that most women acquired from a sunbed. She had a petite, slim figure, with superb legs, which were displayed to their advantage as the black dress was well above her knees. It was made of a silky material, which clung to her small but perfectly formed breasts, and was fitted which accentuated her tiny waist. She had only a light touch of make-up. It was all she needed, because Amy's beauty was in the simplicity of her appearance. She was a natural beauty.

Amy kissed her daughter's upturned face. Sarah didn't have Paul's halo of curls. Her hair was the same golden blonde, but she didn't have her mother's very blue eyes. They were grey, but not serious, they shone with exuberance. Underneath her pretty but fragile looking exterior, a strong character was forming. She was the naughtier of the two of them, the one who found it difficult to take no for an answer. Just like Amy had been with her father as a child.

Paul, surprisingly for a boy, was the quieter of the two, although at times, he took great delight in teasing his gullible sister. Amy loved them dearly, and so did Peter. That's what made it all so hard. He was never spiteful to them, and Sarah was the apple of his eye.

"We may be in quite late from the party," Amy reminded her parents, as she kissed them goodbye.

"No problem!" said Susan. "Enjoy yourselves, and we'll see you in the morning."

Peter was kissing Sarah, who had now forgotten her computer game, and she clung to him fussing that he was going out and leaving her.

Peter released her with good humour, laughing. "That's enough young lady! Now don't forget, both of you, when Nan and Grandad tell you it's bedtime, no arguing, just go!" He wagged his finger with mock sternness at them, and Sarah, determined to get someone's attention, turned to Susan.

"Nan, can you brush my hair and make it shine like Mummy does?"

"I'll try," smiled Susan.

Amy and Peter made good their escape, knowing that all would be well in their absence.

"It was good of them to come and baby-sit," remarked Peter,

23

as they closed the front door. His earlier impatience seemed to be forgotten.

Amy did not reply, she was thinking how well Peter performed in front of her parents; always the perfect son-in-law. Tonight he would have to curb it a bit. He wouldn't want to give David the chance of calling him a loud mouthed drunken idiot. He would too, because one thing David hated, was people who couldn't hold their drink.

Peter put his arm round Amy's shoulders in one of his rare displays of affection towards her. She could feel her bitterness towards him melting and she struggled not to succumb. This had happened so many times before.

He looked very handsome tonight. His unruly blond curls that refused to lie flat, and his eyes full of fun at this moment. Why did he have the power to make her forget his nasty side when he was like this? Amy felt her confused feelings again. Her life was like a roller coaster, and at this moment in time, she wanted to stay on it. Maybe she was mad, she didn't know. Or maybe she thought he could change.

Peter could be a real humorist, and no doubt he would be tonight. People always seemed to take an instant liking to him, and it seemed his charm was still working for her. It made her overlook everything else. She must still love him.

They had arranged to walk to Gill and Derek's house first, which was less than a five minute walk, and then they would all share a cab. They crossed the road and walked briskly towards Derek's house. It was a cold evening at the end of November and although only about eight o'clock, the street was deserted. The echo of Amy's high heels on the pavement invaded the quietness, and as they arrived at the gate a car swept round the corner with its headlights briefly illuminated, reminding them that they were not alone.

"Ian, why didn't you tell me that Steve and Mary were having a party tonight? I wouldn't have known if I hadn't met Mary in the town!"

Ian faced the accusing stare of Miranda, domineering as usual. He hoped he'd got out of this one, but no. Did he really have to go out with her?

"Oh, I just forgot about it." He tried to sound convincing, but now the girls were getting in on the act too. Sophie stood there with her hands on her hips, and at that moment she sounded just like her mother.

"But you've got to take Mummy. She's got a new dress to wear."

Ian shuddered at the thought of it. Miranda spent money like water. She was always buying clothes. Many of them hung in her wardrobe unworn. She didn't like to admit to her size, and they ranged from 14 up to 16 'because they would fit her when she lost weight'. Sometimes she would take them back, secretly, and get a larger size. He had tried to be diplomatic. If she wanted to convince herself that the dresses were at fault, and not herself, he preferred to let her get on with it. Life was more peaceful that way.

Three pairs of angry eyes flashed at him. He was definitely out-voted. He made one more feeble bid to get out of it. "But we haven't got a baby-sitter. Rachel's gone to college."

Miranda's voice became even firmer, if that were possible. "Yes we have, Mum and Gwen are coming over."

Ian subdued a sigh of disappointment. He knew he had to concede defeat. Women! Miranda's mother, and elder sister Gwen, who not surprisingly had never married, both weighed about sixteen stone, and were just as forbidding as she was. He stood no chance. He had jokingly referred to them with his mates at work as 'the heavy mob', but it was a joke that he kept private, because none of them would have been amused. As each day passed he could see that Miranda was beginning to catch up with them. If he looked at her mother, he could see what she would look like in about twenty years. It was not an appealing thought.

He went reluctantly upstairs. He wanted to go his own way, and not have to go out with her, but how could he make a stand in front of the girls? They would side with her against him and that would hurt. He couldn't bear the thought of losing their love. He knew his marriage was just a sham, but he comforted himself with the thought that one day, when the girls had grown up and gone, he would leave her, but it seemed a long time to wait.

25

b

Chapter Four

"Hello Amy, and Peter, darling. Come in and have a drink."

Amy hugged Gill as they entered the hall. Peter, being the joker that he was, insisted that Gill kissed him on the lips when it was his turn.

Amy took no notice. Jealousy was not in her nature. Derek came over and kissed her cheek too. He was not flirtatious like his wife, and Amy had always felt comfortable with him.

Gill was also dressed in black, but her dress had a low neckline and thin straps. She was not wearing a bra, and her nipples could clearly be seen through the thin material. Amy couldn't help thinking that Peter would never let her dress like that, not that she wanted to. He would say she was showing all her goodies on a plate.

Gill had a very extrovert personality, with her long and very black wavy hair, and big gold hooped earrings, she had the look of a romany gypsy about her. She could always be guaranteed to be the life and soul of any party. She seemed to make enjoying life her main aim, which was great when she was out, but Amy knew there was another side to Gill. Sometimes she suffered from depression. Why this was, Amy had not yet found out.

Derek was the complete opposite. Quiet, modest and unassuming. He had auburn hair and hazel eyes. He was good looking in a quiet sort of way, and he dressed soberly in a blue open necked shirt and denim jeans. According to Gill he was a wow in bed, the strong silent and sexy type.

"A glass of wine, Amy?" he enquired hospitably, his hand poised expectantly near the bottle.

"Yes thank you, Derek," she said smiling. He handed it to her and she turned towards Peter. His eyes were on Gill and he laughed loudly in response to something she had just said. Amy wondered what it was.

Peter took his glass of beer from Gill, smiling broadly. "You know my poison, whoops nearly spilt it on my jeans." He sat down carefully, brushing imaginary drops of beer from his navy blue check shirt which Amy had ironed especially for the occasion. The men preferred to dress casually, as they spent all day, and every day, in a suit at work. Amy and Gill, on the other hand, wore trousers all the time, so it was nice to feel a dress against their legs for a change, it made them feel feminine.

"Where are the boys; in bed?" asked Amy, surprised. It seemed very quiet.

"They're at Mother's." Gill's eyes gleamed with excitement. "We may be out all night, you know."

"Same here!" said Peter, enthusiastically. "Amy's parents are staying!"

Amy didn't want to stay out all night, but she said nothing. Drinking for hours on end resulted in a king-size hangover. She had learnt her lesson when she had a bad headache afterwards, but Peter never had. If he was in a foul mood on Sunday because of it, she would go out. Go anywhere with the children, and leave him to get on with it.

Gill was ready to go. She made it clear that the conversation was boring her as she swished past Derek, who was in earnest discussion with Peter about the previous day at work. Her cleavage quivered, doing its best to escape from the confines of her dress. Amy felt like an innocent schoolgirl with her high neck and long sleeves. Gill looked very seductive, she'd have all the men round her, especially with her nipples so prominent, but Derek didn't seem to mind. What an understanding man he must be.

Ian knocked at the door of the house, from which the sound of loud music could clearly be heard. Miranda pushed her way forward and he gulped awkwardly as her bulky frame seemed to fill the doorway. Why was she letting herself get bigger and bigger without doing anything about it? When he had married her she had been a pretty young woman with a good bust line, maybe a little overweight, but it hadn't worried him then. She was now losing her looks, because her weight increase had gone to her face; her cheeks looked puffy, and her eyes seemed to have disappeared into the folds of extra flesh around them.

Most of her trouble was the way she ate: everything with chips, and also lots of cake and biscuits. He wasn't happy about the sort of food she gave the girls either, and had told her so. They lived on junk food because she was too lazy to cook; or takeaway pizzas, anything really that Miranda didn't have to cook herself.

Steve welcomed them. He was surprised to see them, as Ian had told him at work they might not be able to make it. "Glad you could make it," he said, his freckled face beaming at them.

"We nearly didn't. Ian forgot to tell me, but luckily I met Mary!" exclaimed Miranda.

Steve did not pursue that, as unable to contain her curiosity, Miranda swept past him. Ian felt relief that she had gone, so he did not have to explain his convenient loss of memory.

He gave Steve the bottle of wine he was holding and also the vodka, which Miranda liked. She always drank it with orange juice, so she had added a couple of cartons of this to be sure. Miranda always looked after herself very well.

"Thanks, I'll get you a drink if you come through," said Steve. The doorbell rang again and he went to answer it, apologising to Ian for having to leave him.

Ian moved along the hall which was full of people talking, laughing and generally having a good time. Miranda was deep in conversation with Mary, the hostess, who was tiny, with hair cut short like a boy's, which had obviously been dyed as white as possible. What she lacked in height was made up for by her very heavy make-up, her eyes were particularly noticeable because she wore bright green eye-shadow.

"Hello Mary, how are you?" smiled Ian politely. It was a shame she'd made herself up so much. She had pretty doll-like features and she'd ruined them.

Mary gave him her attention briefly. "Fine thanks, Ian, food and drink are in the kitchen, feel free to help yourself." And then she returned to her conversation with Miranda.

28

He thanked her politely, realising he was a bit peckish. Miranda had eaten out with the girls, McDonald's or something similar, and as usual she hadn't given him a thought. He was well aware that time had moved on, and women no longer slaved over a hot stove to feed their men, but it would have been nice to be able to find something, either in the fridge or the cupboard, that he could have actually eaten! There was no bread or milk, and the fridge was full of half-eaten and unappetising leftover pizza. Normally he liked pizza, but this one had gone mouldy, and the whole fridge smelt nasty.

Miranda, by her own admission, had met Mary whilst out shopping this morning, but it hadn't occurred to her to actually buy some food, or to clean out the offending fridge. He had planned to get out a piece of steak from the freezer and cook it for his supper, before he had been coerced into coming here. She quite often went out to see her mother on a Saturday evening and he had been looking forward to his own space, but it hadn't worked out that way.

As he went into the kitchen he noticed the usual collection of men standing near to the table of drink. It was difficult to get through the crush. It was only a small room, maybe eight foot by six foot maximum. Steve had done the drinks to begin with, but with the doorbell continually ringing, Ian could see that he would be best to help himself.

As he poured himself a glass of white wine, he noticed the slops on the table where people had missed the glass. He looked for a paper towel to wipe it with but there was nothing There was another table, pushed tightly up against it in an effort to try and give more space, and this contained the food.

No one else, to his surprise, seemed interested in eating. Maybe they'd all had dinner, but Ian was, by now, very hungry, and he found a plate which he filled with goodies and then sat down to eat.

Mary came bustling in with a cloth to wipe the offending table. She was accompanied by Miranda, and Ian saw her eyes glitter when she saw the food.

"Mary, the food looks lovely. If no one else is going to do it justice, I will!"

Ian almost choked on his French bread. She'd eaten less than two hours ago with the girls. She hadn't spotted him yet, so he

29

took his plate of food and slipped quietly into the other room. If Miranda was going to eat her way into the centre of the table like her mother and sister did, then he didn't want to be around to witness it.

As he entered the room he noticed the sideboard, which was light teak, and the china cabinet which sported a display of model houses. They obviously liked old English cottages with thatched roofs, as there were many of them in various sizes lining the shelves.

Steve was talking to a group of people, some of whom Ian didn't recognise, and he called Ian over to introduce him. "Ian, come and meet Peter and Derek, and of course their lovely wives," he added hastily, after a playful poke in the ribs from Gill.

Ian already knew Peter a little from work. He had met up with him a couple of times whilst dealing with customer accounts. He seemed an agreeable sort of fellow, happy go lucky, a joker, and the life and soul of any party. Derek was quieter and more serious, he could see, but it was obvious his wife wasn't.

She was attractive, in a dark mysterious way, and he couldn't fail to notice a certain look in her eyes when they shook hands. She was intimidating, which made him feel uncomfortable and very aware of his failure in the bedroom department now. At one time he might have found her intriguing, even if she did offer herself on a plate, but not now, he had no desire for sex any more. She would have to look elsewhere if she didn't find her husband satisfying enough.

Peter was introducing his wife now, and she couldn't have provided a bigger contrast to Gill. Apart from her looks, which were blonde and petite, her personality seemed less brash, although there was a determination in her grip that he liked when he shook her hand.

He looked into her eyes. They were beautiful, big and innocent looking, and as deep blue as the sea. Her skin felt soft, and he was surprised to find that he felt as if he didn't want to let her hand go.

At a guess, he judged her to be in her late twenties, but she looked younger. The black high necked dress she was wearing showed off her slim waist and hips to perfection. The pencil slim skirt finished above her knees, and her lovely legs could clearly be seen. She was class, he could see that, and for a fleeting moment, he wished he could have met someone like her ten years ago instead of Miranda. He envied Peter, he was a very lucky guy.

Amy had expected Peter to dance with Gill. He liked to mix and her best friend was an obvious choice. She had been left with Ian, but although he was a comparative stranger to her, she felt comfortable with him. The first thing that had struck her about him was the sadness in his eyes. It was almost as if he had lost someone who was very close to him.

His hair was chestnut brown, and his eyes, those sad brown eyes, softened as he looked at her, and she could feel herself sharing his sadness. He looked so vulnerable she felt as if she should put her arms around him. She could sense that he was gentle and sensitive, not rough and ready like Peter.

He was a very handsome man with clear cut features, a strong nose, and a ruddy complexion. He was broad in the chest, but slim, no beer gut to spoil his stomach. She noticed the glass of wine in his hand. He was definitely not a man's man like Peter, propping up the bar all evening. She guessed his height to be about six feet.

If anyone had asked her how long she stood there looking at him, or how long her hand had remained touching his, she wouldn't have known. It was like she was under a spell. She felt as though she wanted to ease his sadness away, but why she felt like this she didn't know. He was a complete stranger.

"Peter's spoken about you to me, I feel as if I already know you." He smiled, thinking in no way had Peter done her justice. She was exquisite, in Ian's private opinion.

When he spoke to her, his sadness vanished almost immediately. His expression of softness was still there, and his face became friendly and relaxed. Had she imagined his misery? She couldn't be sure because it had been so fleeting, that look. She felt completely at ease with him and able to talk.

"Are you married too?" she asked lightly. She was sure with looks like that he must have an equally stunning wife. He could have his pick of women.

Ian tried to stop his face from darkening. The mere reminder of his past mistakes made him feel miserable. If he had thought that he had escaped from Miranda he was wrong, just like the proverbial bad penny, at that moment she turned up. He tried to keep his expression amiable as she approached. "Yes, this is

31

Miranda, my wife."

The magic of the moment had been cruelly shattered for him, he turned, struggling to sound casual: "Miranda, meet Amy, who is Peter's wife, and if you'll excuse me ladies, I'm going to get another drink."

Amy watched him go with bewilderment. Her sensitive nature had noticed the change in him. One minute she had felt comfortable talking to him, the next he seemed to have become withdrawn and distant. Had she offended him in some way? He couldn't wait to get to the drinks. Perhaps he was like Peter, and all men probably, only interested in drinking. For one brief moment she had imagined that this man was different.

Chapter Five

Amy was tired of listening to Miranda's voice. She had just endured what seemed like hours, but was only minutes, listening to her talk incessantly, mainly about herself and her children. Amy felt like saying to her, I've got a life too, and children, but it would be rude. She didn't feel as if she wanted to become too friendly with her, and was now looking for a chance to edge away.

Gill was the reason that Amy found herself suddenly free of Miranda. She paused, only to draw breath, and noticed that Gill was doing her best to engage Ian's interest at the other end of the room. Miranda was having none of this, and she left Amy very abruptly, explaining briefly, "I'm just going to see Ian."

Seeing Miranda stride up with determination written all over her face, Gill took the coward's way out, sidling up sheepishly to Amy. "He's very fanciable," she confided, "I could go for him, but I really don't know why he married her."

"You won't get past her," grinned Amy. I'm going upstairs to powder my nose. I'll be back soon."

She could see Gill was a little bit drunk, as she raised her glass at her in salutation. Not that she would put anything past Gill. She always flirted with men, and her clothes were very provocative. But it was none of her business really, and it had nothing to do with their friendship.

Amy slipped upstairs. The bathroom was free. She had eaten her lipstick as usual, so she needed to freshen it up. Her handbag was in the main bedroom, buried underneath the mound of coats, so she went to get it. As she pushed the door open, she heard a little moan as if someone was in pain but, as it opened, she was totally unprepared for what she saw.

The couple were on the bed, locked in a very passionate embrace, and most of the coats were now on the floor. The groans came from the girl, who was lying there with her dress, if you could call it that, it was so skimpy, undone to the waist. Her amorous lover had his hands, and his mouth, all over her breasts. They were both panting with passion, and it was obvious that they were totally in a world of their own.

Amy stood rooted to the spot, her embarrassment turning to rage. It was Peter. How dare he! She closed the door loudly, and she saw the girl's face for the first time. She didn't know her. She looked about eighteen and had a mane of red gold hair which was flopping all over her face. Amy felt hatred, and a jealousy that she never knew she had, take control of her body. She had been brought up never to air her dirty linen in public, but all middle class respectability gone, she screamed like a fishwife: "You whore! Leave my husband alone!" and plunging onto the bed, she pulled at her long tresses as hard as she could, feeling a slight sense of satisfaction when the girl howled with pain.

The female looking guilty now, as well she should, and tried to pull the apology for a dress around her boobs. She had moved away from Peter now, who was quite clearly very drunk. If he's yours, you're welcome to him. He's very drunk. He wouldn't leave me alone . . !"

Amy's look of contempt silenced her. Peter had finally realised it was Amy, but instead of hitting him she put all her spite into her next words, directed at the girl. She would sort him out later!

"I should put some clothes on if I were you, or I could send the men up one at a time to service you. You'd enjoy that!"

The girl's gasp of indignation pleased her, as she banged the door shut, ignoring Peter's drunken voice, pleading with her. "Amy, come back. It was only a bit of fun."

Amy's heart was banging with emotion and pain. I'll give him 'bit of fun!' she thought angrily. If I'd stayed much longer, I'd have seen him screwing her, and as for that bitch, she wasn't forced, she loved it all. What a naïve, idiotic fool I've been. Ten years of marriage, and I always thought he was as faithful to me as I was to him. If he could go upstairs at a party when he's with

34

me and try it with someone else, then how many others has he had when he's been without me?

Her emotional state gave speed to her feet as she ran down the stairs. She just wanted to get out of here, away from her cheating husband, and weep all the misery out of her system. Where was Gill? She burst into the kitchen, looking for her. Her fury knew no bounds. She was going to divorce the lousy scumbag and Gill must be the first to know.

Gill was talking excitedly to another man, whom Amy didn't recognise. Her eyes were bright, and her speech was slurred too. He, too, looked the same way, with his arm tentatively round her waist, he whispered something, and they moved away from the table, towards the hall. Amy felt vicious. She no longer cared about anyone else.

"Someone's looking for you," she said ominously to him. He was just another unfaithful jerk, and Gill was a fool to encourage him. He quickly slid his hand away from Gill, looking guilty.

Gill was leaning against the table. "It won't be Derek. He doesn't mind what I do," she said sarcastically, and the strange man went, much to Amy's relief.

Her anger was overtaken by the tears that she had struggled for so long to keep back. Her whole body shook as she sobbed. "He's cheated on me, here! I hate him. That's the finish of us!" Her sobs became louder, and she seemed heedless of whether anyone else could hear her or not.

Gill looked at her in amazement. The sight of Amy in such distress, had temporarily sobered her up.' What do you mean, cheated on you?" she asked.

And out it came, the confrontation in the bedroom, her fury when she realised it was Peter. She had expected Gill's face to take on a look of horror when she had told her, but to her amazement this was not so.

Gill interrupted her. "When you found them, did he actually have her knickers off?"

Amy looked at her, aghast. She wasn't at all shocked. "No, they hadn't got that far, but they would have done if I hadn't come in then," she said, darkly.

"It seems they were having a snog and a grope and you surprised them. The chances are he won't even remember it in the morning. It's certainly nothing to get upset about."

35

Amy looked at her incredulously. She could see now how different Gill's marriage must be to hers. She was the old-fashioned and faithful type. But she'd thought Peter was too. She felt the pain inside her again.

Gill laughed. "Get with it, Amy. This is 2005. I don't follow Derek around at parties. Just because we're married we don't have to be joined at the hip!"

Amy gasped with amazement. "You mean you wouldn't be jealous."

Gill smiled. She was enjoying the fact that she was shocking her. "No, if I'd caught him out like you did, I'd have joined in." Then she laughed, seeing Amy's face. "Only kidding." But Amy wasn't sure that was true, and she was fed up with not being taken seriously.

She turned away angrily, and the kitchen door opened to admit a very dishevelled Peter. His hair was a mess, his clothes all crumpled and his face flushed. His sense of drunken well-being had worn off and he knew he was in trouble.

He couldn't see why she had made such a fuss. He decided to pretend he couldn't remember, just to appease her. He put on his most innocent blue-eyed look, and ran his finger through his tousled curls in bewilderment, hoping it would win her over.

Gill was eyeing him too, her eyes travelling over his ruffled appearance. Peter guessed Amy had told her he'd been a naughty boy. Her eyes were bright and she looked very sexy, and although he had guessed she'd be more than willing, regardless of her friendship with Amy, she was a bit too close to home for comfort. He did love Amy, but the thrill of laying other women was like a drug to him and he couldn't stop doing it. He needed it, but he didn't want to lose Amy, or her Daddy's money.

Gill was feeling decidedly bitchy. She had wanted Peter for herself for some time. He looked sexy. His eyes appeared so innocent, but he had often flirted with her and given suggestive looks during the past five years. To her great disappointment that had been it, as far as it went. Now he was in trouble she couldn't help feeling a certain malicious satisfaction.

"Are you having a good time?" she said, just loud enough for Amy to hear. The thought of what he'd been up to gave her thrills of excitement. How she envied that girl!

Peter pretended not to hear her. His attention was on Amy. He didn't want her to run home and tell Daddy about him. He didn't want to be a villain in her parents' eyes. He flashed Amy his most ingratiating smile. "Amy, my love, I've been looking for you. I've had a bit too much to drink, can't remember much, but I would love to dance."

Amy faced him, her eyes flashing. "That's the last thing I want! I'm going home!"

"OK, my love, I'll ring for a cab," he said soothingly. He could see he was going to have to try another way.

"I'm not your love," she snapped. "Now that the bedroom's not full of writhing bodies, I'll go and get our coats."

He winked at Gill whilst she was gone. "I think I'm in trouble, but I can't remember why."

"You can remember!" Gill laughed. "Now tell me, was it worth it?"

He couldn't mistake the sexual come-on in her voice. "That would be telling." He laughed, fixing his eyes on her cleavage, which during the evening had worked its way further out of the top of her dress. He could almost see her nipples now, and she moved her shoulders seductively, enjoying his appraisal of her.

Other people were coming into the room now, so Peter decided to behave himself. "It's a shame we've got to go now, before the fun's started," he said regretfully.

"You've already had yours!" commented Gill, meaningfully, and he was spared further discussion when Amy appeared with his coat.

"Come on, we're off!" she said forcefully.

"We've got to wait for the cab," he reminded her. He'd always thought of himself as the boss in this marriage, but things were changing, and he didn't like the change. However, in this instance, he knew he would have to put up with it.

"I want to walk home. You need to sober up!"

But cunning Peter had a plan forming in his mind. He had to pacify Amy before they got home. If her father saw how upset she was he would want to know why, and Peter didn't want that.

"Ian has asked if we can share a cab with them as they're also ready to go now. You look tired too. Doesn't that seem like a good idea?" he asked, mustering every bit of tact he possessed.

Amy was still very angry with him, but she was also very tired. A cab home would be nice, if they were all going the same way,

37

so she capitulated. "I suppose so, if it comes soon."

"It will be soon," said Peter soothingly, inwardly exulting.

Amy glared fiercely at him. He wasn't off the hook yet. He needn't think by sweet talking her he would get away with it! Gill seemed to think she was making a fuss over nothing. Maybe fidelity was old-fashioned but Amy believed in it. The jealousy she had felt was amazing. She must still love him, but God only knew why.

Peter was relieved when the mini-cab arrived. Amy's anger was so unusual and he was worried she might make a scene. But luck was in for him. She said a very subdued goodbye to Mary. Steve was missing and so was Gill, but who cared nowadays what their partner got up to at parties? He would have to be unlucky enough to be married to someone who had old-fashioned ideals, which Peter knew he could never live up to. Peter couldn't imagine Amy cheating on him. Her parents had pumped her full of outdated ideas, in fact she was a virgin when they got married, something unheard of these days, and certainly the first one he'd ever been with. But when he thought about it, he had to admit to himself he wouldn't have been able to stomach her cheating on him. It was something his ego couldn't put up with, sharing his wife.

Ian was also glad to be going now. Miranda's voice had been getting on his nerves all evening, and when Peter had asked to share their cab, he had willingly agreed. Luckily for him Miranda's mother had not agreed to stay the night, so he had to be grateful for small mercies. He noticed that Amy looked flushed and her eyes looked as if she'd been crying. Could Peter have upset her? He seemed an easy-going chap. She looked as if she could be very sensitive.

As he glanced at her, he was surprised to feel a wave of sympathy sweep over him. He felt as if he wanted to put his arms around her and comfort her. He pushed the thought away. She was nothing to him. He was getting soft and stupid.

The car was here now, and as usual Miranda made herself known. The driver smiled at her, privately noting her size, and then opened the front door for her. "Would you like to sit in the front with me young lady. It's more comfortable."

"Yes, I don't want Ian squashing my dress," agreed Miranda, smirking with delight at this newly found attention.

The driver gallantly held her arm whilst she clambered awkwardly into the car, arranging her bright pink skirt over her knees. Privately he was thinking how nice it would have been to have the company of the blonde little piece instead, but being tactful ensured that he got jobs. Being a mini-cab driver wasn't much of a job for a redundant company director, but at least it was a job.

Amy sat wedged between Peter and Ian, and she could feel Ian's leg touching hers. There was nowhere he could move it and she didn't want him to. His warmth was somehow soothing and comforting, and her head touched accidentally against his strong shoulder. She could feel his breath close to her cheek, and there was a slight aroma of aftershave too, which she found pleasant. He seemed to have a calming effect on her, and she sat there with her eyes closed, savouring it.

They had reached Ian and Miranda's house now and the driver pulled up, leaving the engine running. Miranda got out first, and as Ian tried to follow after her from the back, he caught his foot and stumbled, but just as quickly regained his balance. Amy put her arms out without even thinking about it, in an automatic reaction to save him, and she felt it as soon as their hands touched, like a strong electric shock. It sent tingles through her inside and left her feeling breathless.

Ian smiled, and she wondered if he had felt it too, but his words gave nothing away. "Good night folks. See you again soon."

Did she imagine it or had his eyes looked meaningfully into hers when he said that. Why had her body reacted like that at the touch of his hand?

Amy and Peter said goodbye, and then Miranda, not to be outdone, said, "I'll give you a ring soon Amy. You can come round." Amy smiled back politely. How would she be able to get out of that one? Miranda was all right, but only in small doses.

As the car pulled away again, Peter looked tentatively across at Amy. She was sitting with her eyes closed and her legs stretched out in front of her in an attitude of weariness. He knew he must make a move now before they arrived home, when she would once again remember how angry she was. Her dear Daddy could well be up watching the late film now.

He slipped his fingers exploratively along the side of her leg, feeling the silkiness of her tights and her lovely soft legs. He felt her stiffen, but was confident in the knowledge that if she did stop him she would have to do it quietly because of the cab driver.

She stayed completely still, so he let his fingers stroke and play gently round her knee. He wondered if he dare risk going any higher. If she let him, then once he got inside her knickers he would have won. She would forgive him anything.

Amy lay back in her seat enjoying the feeling of well-being that Ian had created inside her. If only Peter were gentle like him, instead of loud and uncouth. And to add to his sins, he was unfaithful too. Her jealousy rose again, as she remembered that tart, laying there, revelling in his advances. Amy knew what it was like to feel like that, but she didn't expect to share it with someone else.

His hand touched her leg and she felt herself go rigid. If he thought he was going to get anywhere with her he was mistaken!

He stopped, sensing her reluctance, but then almost immediately, he started stroking her knee, and in spite of herself, she found it soothing. She kept her eyes closed as his fingers gradually stroked their way to the top of her thighs. He shouldn't be doing this really, with the driver so near, but the thought of that gave her an extra thrill and added to her delight, as his fingers stroked their way further inside her thighs.

He had reached the outside of her silky panties by now, they were so wet they clung to her. She wanted to sigh with pleasure, but she knew she couldn't, so with a supreme effort she managed to choke down her moans of delight, which inflamed her passion even more.

The aroma of Ian's aftershave lingered, and for a few blissful moments she allowed herself to fantasise. There was no harm in it. She imagined that the fingers that had now slipped inside her panties, were his, tender and gentle, touching her most intimate and sensitive parts, and she gasped as she felt her first orgasm rising. She wanted to scream and shout her delight as the tip of his fingers very gently tickled her clitoris. To hell with the cab driver! her body was reaching a crescendo, she wanted him, and she could no longer hide it . . .

Peter opened his eyes for long enough to see they were almost home. It was just as well, because his sexy little wife was getting herself all steamed up, ready for a frenzied bout of passion. He hadn't lost his touch with her. He slid his fingers reluctantly out of her panties and whispered, "We're almost home."

Amy came down to earth with a bang. The throbbing between her legs was driving her mad, and the disappointment of almost reaching a climax, unbearable. All she could think of was that she wanted sex, and she wanted it badly. By the time she had finished with him he wouldn't be fit to take on any other woman!

She sat there, not looking at him, feeling her passions flaming away inside her. Mercifully the car stopped, and Peter paid the driver off, whilst she stood and waited for him. She felt flushed and aroused, and couldn't wait to get to bed. He slid his arm round her as they tiptoed into the house, which was in complete darkness, and then he kissed her, long and intimately, flicking his tongue around the inside of her mouth, and still she was pretending it was Ian.

"You wait until my tongue touches your other lips," murmured Peter, and she almost swooned at the thought of it.

They fell into bed, and she didn't need any foreplay. Her body was wet and willing, and she mounted him, gasping with delight as she felt him inside her. She took control of him, commanding him to suck her nipples, which he did willingly. He was groaning and so was she, and she knew his climax was near, and she felt yet another wonderful orgasm erupting, about to take her body by storm.

Peter gave a shuddering gasp as his climax came, but Amy hadn't finished with him yet. She allowed him just a few seconds to recover, and then said boldly, "My other lips are waiting for you!"

Peter raised himself up. He was temporarily sated, but only too willing to see if he could give it to her again. He knew that if he did the job properly, she would give him the same treatment. Once she got her sexy lips on him, he was guaranteed another hard-on.

Amy lay there, allowing his lips to travel all over her body. He knew exactly how to satisfy her by using his lips and flicking his tongue everywhere. He made slow and unhurried progress down from her nipples, across her stomach, and as he approached her thighs, she felt another orgasm erupt. She had lost count of how many orgasms, but this is where woman reigns supreme. If she wanted him again, and was there any doubt? she needed to encourage him to get going again.

He used the tips of his fingers to stroke her very wet pussy, and he kissed the pouting lips of it long and lovingly. This drove her wild, so he gently opened them, and then kissed her little button-like clitoris, whilst she writhed and moaned in ecstasy. "Your tongue, I need your tongue!" she begged him.

"My randy little sexpot. I'll make you come like you've never come before," he panted. He stretched his body across hers, and her willing mouth closed over his huge erection. She used her lips to kiss the end where he was so sensitive, and then her tongue lapped across too. She was groaning as his tongue continued to tickle her protruding clitoris, her juices flowed yet again, and she felt him swell even more in her mouth.

He concentrated very hard on not coming just yet. Pleasure like this must be prolonged for as long as possible.

Even Amy had her point of no return, and as her exquisite feelings of pleasure once more erupted into a mind-blowing orgasm, her clitoris now sated, she writhed, as she pushed his tongue away, panting, "No, no more, screw me now, hard!"

This time Peter took control. He was confident he could do that without coming immediately, having already given his all less than thirty minutes before.

"Kneel you whore so I can shag you!" he said sexily, passion and desire taking over.

Amy was only too willing to comply. She may have been brought up to be a lady but in bed, the coarser the language, the more she enjoyed it. Even the thought that her parents were nearby didn't dampen her ardour.

She knelt across the bed, arching her back. She felt like a wicked trollop, it was lovely, she'd serviced him, and now he was going to service her, yet again. As he pushed it in she gasped with delight, and felt the muscles of her vagina tightening, milking it, squeezing every bit of pleasure there was to be had. His strokes were deep, and he groaned as she did, together they were ascending to the highest plane of enjoyment. His hands cupped her breasts and at the same time his thrusts became faster. She knew he was coming, but this time she was glad, because she felt as if the orgasm she was about to experience would blow her mind, just as he had promised.

They both shouted as they reached the height of their passion, shuddering as if they were in the middle of a volcanic eruption.

Such intense feelings had dominated their bodies, and now exhaustion took over.

Afterwards, when they lay together, totally sated, Amy kept her eyes closed, still imagining she was next to Ian. It was a lovely dream to keep in her mind, and tomorrow, when she woke up, it would be over, and life would go back to normal.

Peter glanced over at her but she was already asleep. That little bit of crumpet seemed tame in comparison to Amy. In spite of her posh upbringing, Amy was a very sexy woman. He had no complaints about her in the bedroom department. Maybe her jealousy at catching him out had stirred her up to give him that mind-blowing bout of passion. No matter what the reason, he wanted to repeat it as often as possible. With a contented sigh, he turned towards her back and put his arms round her, falling asleep almost immediately.

Chapter Six

Mondays, I hate them! thought Amy fiercely, as she piled the clean washing out of the machine and into the clothes-basket. A glance out of the window at the grey November skies, from which a fine drizzle was falling, confirmed her belief that there was no point in putting it out on the line. It just wouldn't dry. Thank goodness for her tumble-drier.

She was still smarting over the humiliation Peter had caused her at the party on Saturday. She had tried to understand her own feelings, sometimes her head was in such a jumble. Firstly she had felt like divorcing Peter because he was such a bully, and at that time, she had felt that anyone else was welcome to him.

But on Saturday, at the party, the jealousy and rage she had felt when she pulled that girl's hair, had made her realise she did still want him. Did she love him, or just desire him? She couldn't be sure, but she certainly didn't want to share him.

Peter had begged her to forgive him on Sunday. He had said it was a mistake, a one-off. It had never happened before, and would never happen again. Amy wanted to believe him, but she wasn't sure. She planned to go and see Gill, and have a talk with her. She couldn't tell Mummy and Daddy about it. Daddy would shake his head and remind her that he had thought at eighteen she didn't know her own mind when they married. He would also say that now she had made her bed she must lie on it, and Amy didn't want to hear it.

Peter had proved himself to be weak and easily seduced. But

her conscience was niggling at her too, telling her that in her mind she was just as bad. On Saturday night she had practically raped him, although he had been a willing party. But in her mind, it had been Ian, a man she knew nothing about, another woman's husband, and she had never been so turned on before! It was all because he looked so gentle, a man she would always feel safe with, but with hidden depths of passion she could sense. He wasn't hers to have. Whatever had come over her?

She'd put a casserole in the oven to cook slowly for tonight, the washing was done, and the house was clean and tidy. Tidy, that was, until the children arrived home with school books and bags all over the place.

She picked up the telephone, deciding to check if Gill would be there. It went straight into answerphone. She felt disappointed, but decided she should leave a message.

"Hi Gill, it's Amy . . ."

Her voice was cut short. ". . . Yes, I'm here, Amy."

"Are you OK?" Amy asked, concerned, "you don't sound it."

Gill sighed. "I suppose so. I just feel yuk."

"I won't come round then, if you don't feel like it."

"I'm not that bad and I would like to see you."

Amy brushed her own feeling of depression aside. Gill seemed to be like this after having a good time. Amy was used to her being an extrovert whilst out and then falling into a depression soon after. When Gill was like that her life seemed to stop, so she would need Amy's help to pick it up again.

Amy wondered if Derek gave her much support. Gill never said. She had confided to Amy that she took antidepressants, and Amy wondered why she needed them. She had never asked her, it wasn't really her business, but she was sure Gill would tell her if she ever felt the need to.

She had a couple of hours spare now before she needed to pick up the children from school. It was amazing how quickly the day passed. Because they were at private schools, they had to travel further to school but Amy didn't complain about that. David footed the bill willingly. He wanted his grandchildren to have the best start in life. Amy had been a little reluctant to accept, she wanted to feel independent, but Peter had thought it was a good idea, he had not had the same start in life, so on this issue Amy had been overruled.

45

David had more money than he knew what to do with having been left a great deal by his own father. Her parents' house was set in two acres of land, in a private road. The area was not one that many people could afford to live in, and Amy had grown up amongst this affluence without ever thinking twice about it.

Peter's colleagues from the bank were much like themselves. They had young families, a mortgage and an average lifestyle. Their houses were a little more modest because they didn't have Amy's Father to help them. David had helped financially with the purchase of the house, under the guise of buying it as a wedding present. Peter had been most eager to accept the lump sum that David had paid against the mortgage, leaving the balance easily affordable on his wages, and Amy hadn't argued that time. She was used to her father's extravagances.

She had decided that after ten years of marriage they could start to be more independent, and had even suggested to Peter that she could get a part-time job. His reaction had been one of horror. He didn't want her to work, he wanted her there, at home for him. But this made Amy even more determined that she would. Tough if he didn't like it! Of course he would have Mummy and Daddy's backing on that too, but she didn't care. Middle class wives didn't work, unless they had a proper career, like a barrister, or something similar.

Getting married at eighteen, and having her children so quickly, meant that Amy had only got as far as being a librarian; not exactly a career. Once she had met Peter, at sixteen, she had not wanted to go to university. She had stayed on at school for A levels, and passed three of them, French, Spanish and English, but had decided against a career abroad because she wanted to marry Peter.

Her parents had been devastated at the time, that their bright daughter wasn't going to university. They had tried to change her mind, but Amy was always self willed, and they failed. Her father also tried to stop her from marrying Peter, but Amy had told him quite frankly that she would elope. David, always worried about what the neighbours might think, finally capitulated. Amy now wished she hadn't been in such a hurry. Maybe Daddy had been right, if she'd had a career there would be something to go back to now, to claim her independence.

She had started an Open University course at home. When she

46

had finished it she planned to go back to work whether Peter kicked up or not. She was tired of being a stay-at-home wife. Gill worked three days a week in a shop and she said it helped to keep her sane. Life at home all day in an empty house was so boring, apart from the money being so useful too. Peter would have to get used to it!

She shut the door carefully behind her and walked round to the garage. Inside was her little red Ford Fiesta, her passport to freedom, or so she had thought when she passed her test. But this hadn't been the case. She mainly used it for shopping, and running about to pick up and drop the children at school.

She soon got to Gill's house, and by the time she had parked the car and reached the door it was opened by Gill. "I saw you coming," she volunteered.

Amy noticed that she had no make-up on and her dark eyes contrasted with the paleness of her cheeks. Her long black hair was rumpled and untidy, the only sign of her usual mode of dress was the low cut tank top she wore. Amy wondered why everything that Gill wore always had her boobs hanging out, even on a bleak November day.

"You really don't look well. Maybe I shouldn't have come." commented Amy, genuine concern showing in her eyes. She knew that sometimes Gill liked to shut herself away when depressed. Many a time she had come round to straighten up the house for her or do some cooking. Gill just let everything go when she was like this.

"No, I'm glad to see you. I've been on my own all morning," said Gill miserably. She wondered why Amy had to look so smart. The red trouser suit she was wearing looked really good on her, sort of classy. Gill felt even more of a wreck. She always showed her assets, knowing she had a good figure boosted her confidence, but seeing Amy dressed like that made her realise that showing her cleavage wasn't the answer. Amy had style, which Gill knew she lacked, and a bearing which came from within. Gill knew she could never compete. She shut the front door quickly, "I'm cold," she said, shivering.

"Well it's not surprising. You've not got much on," Amy remarked smiling, hoping to see Gill share the joke, but her face remained serious.

Amy had seen it all before. Shoes all over the floor, with coats just slung on top of them. Gill, as usual, didn't appear to notice.

"Come and have some coffee."

Gill led the way to the kitchen, and as they passed the lounge Amy noticed that too was in a state.

"I can run the hoover over whilst you make the coffee," she said brightly.

Gill usually let her, but today she seemed worse than usual, as if nothing mattered any more. "No, it'll get messed up again when the boys get home, and Derek never notices anyway," she shrugged wearily.

"Are you sure?" said Amy doubtfully. She couldn't help thinking how lucky Gill was to have Derek who didn't mind. Peter would have gone mad if she'd left their house in a state like this.

"I need a coffee!" said Gill firmly.

They entered the kitchen, which was large and well equipped. On a good day it looked smart with its wall units and cupboards of oak, but the working surfaces were littered with dirty dishes which Gill swept impatiently out of the way. She filled the kettle and plugged it in.

"Gill, you can't let everything go, just because you feel low!" said Amy, looking in horror around her. She couldn't sit and drink coffee in this mess, so this time she took the initiative. It didn't take long to load the dishwasher, or to wipe down the unit tops; about the same length of time that Gill took to make the coffee. Only when it was completed did she feel she could sit there and drink coffee.

"Thanks Amy," said Gill, handing her a mug of coffee.

Amy had been intending to confide in her about Peter. She wanted reassurance from an outsider who wasn't family, that Peter's behaviour on Saturday had been a one-off occasion. If anyone would know it would be Derek. He was Peter's best friend, and he would surely have told Gill.

Seeing Gill like this made her change her mind. Gill was too wrapped up in herself to want to discuss Peter. She must try to help Gill if she could.

"Gill, do you think those pills you take are helping your depression?" asked Amy, as tactfully as she could whilst they sipped their coffee.

"I'd be much worse without them!" said Gill quickly. She

48

knew why she felt down. She had left them off for a week without asking the doctor. She couldn't mix drink with them, and she'd wanted to enjoy the party. Now she was feeling the effects, as so many times before, but it didn't stop her from doing it. She knew she shouldn't play around with them, take them or ditch them was the answer, and she promised herself she would give them up soon.

"If you want to tell me anything, I'll always listen," said Amy softly.

Gill took a deep breath, her depression temporarily forgotten, she wanted honesty in her friendship with Amy. She was keeping too much misery to herself, and no one realised because when she went out she was play-acting, all because of Derek.

"Derek and I have a modern marriage, Amy. I never ask him what he gets up to and he never asks me. We have no jealousy, no rows, and we both love the boys." She didn't add that this was how it had to be. That was her secret. She couldn't tell it all to Amy. Every time she thought about it, her feelings of inadequacy welled up. She watched Amy's eyes as she studied her, hoping not to see disapproval there. Amy was her best friend, and although no one would have thought it, Gill was lonely and she needed a good friend.

"But do you love each other?" asked Amy pointedly. Gill's marriage sounded more like a business arrangement than a love match.

Gill looked defensive. Amy was getting too close for comfort.

"In our own way, yes," she hesitated. "If I tell you something very private, will you promise to keep it to yourself?"

Her eyes were pleading, and Amy couldn't help her own natural curiosity from rising.

"Of course you can trust me. I won't say a word."

Gill's voice faltered. Her usual bouncy manner was absent, and when she spoke the words came out slowly. "When I told you Derek was good in bed, it was a lie. We don't do it together. We can't."

Amy ignored the wave of embarrassment that swept through her. This was really personal stuff! She was amazed. Gill appeared to be very sexy; the way she dressed always showing her boobs, and she moved like a cat.

"You and Derek should talk about it. There are people who can

49

help you with this problem. Is he impotent?"

Gill swallowed hard. She couldn't be disloyal to Derek. She had told Amy enough and she hoped it would excuse her behaviour with other men. "After we had the boys he changed. He always seems too busy," she said, deliberately sidestepping the question.

Amy sensed her reluctance to say any more. It sounded a bit weird to her. It was at least six years since their younger boy Alan had been born. That was a long time to go. No wonder Gill was depressed. Maybe Derek had another woman. Somehow Amy's problems seemed less than Gill's, and she could cope with hers, whether she stayed with Peter or left him, she knew she would cope. No wonder Gill was always after other men. Who could blame her?

"Well keep your chin up, that's all I can say. You know where I am if you need me," said Amy. She glanced at her watch. "I can't believe the time. I've got to collect the children from school."

Gill felt a bit better now she had shared some of her torment with Amy. Maybe she would tell her the whole story one day, but not at the moment. Gill had only just recently found out herself and she still needed time to get her head round it.

As Amy drove to meet the children she thought about Gill's revelations. She could see a lot of things now, why she was depressed, why she flirted such a lot, and why she was on pills. She must love Derek or else surely she would leave him. Why didn't he fancy her any more? Whatever was going on in that household had temporarily made Amy forget her own anguish. She realised that when she looked at Gill's marriage, she seemed to be in a much worse position than herself. Maybe her own life wasn't as bad as she thought it was.

Chapter Seven

"Amy, is my tie all right?"

Peter's blue eyes looked innocently into Amy's, and he gave her his most beguiling smile. They were going to the bank's Christmas party. It was just a month since that fateful party and he had promised faithfully that this time he would behave. Amy had decided it was his last chance, and if he blew it their marriage would be over.

"Here. I'll straighten it." She retied the knot for him, and then stepped back to check that it looked right. "That's better."

Her eyes took in his immaculate grey suit and the crisp white shirt that she had made him iron. His black shoes shone, and he looked particularly handsome tonight. She wasn't going to tell him. His head was too big already.

She glanced briefly in the mirror at herself. She was wearing a wine-coloured velvet dress. The sleeves were short and the waist was fitted. It had a slit at the side of the straight skirt which showed off her shapely legs to perfection.

"Do you like this dress?" she asked him.

"You look fantastic!" said Peter, enthusiastically, but she couldn't help wondering if he would have said so if she hadn't prompted him.

Derek and Gill had gone away for Christmas, so they would not be there. Gill seemed to be on top of things again, thank goodness. The last time she had visited her the house looked as it should, but she wondered whether Gill and Derek would get any help to restore their love life. It wasn't really Amy's business, and as Gill hadn't mentioned it again, she didn't like to bring it up herself.

As she sat next to him in the taxi, her thoughts strayed to the last time they shared one. That night was a memory now. She couldn't understand her own behaviour, her lust, and her fantasies. She had tried to put it all out of her mind, but deep inside her, if she cared to admit it, she hoped she would see Ian tonight.

Miranda had kept her promise to ring, and after running out of excuses, Amy had met her one day to go shopping. It seemed Miranda wanted to make a friend of her, and she had asked for her help in choosing a new outfit for a wedding.

Amy had found her something smart in brown and cream. The colours did enhance her dark hair and very brown eyes, and Amy privately thought that if Miranda could lose some weight she could look very attractive, but Miranda gave the impression that she was very content with herself just as she was.

They had now arrived at the hotel where a special room had been provided for the Christmas party. Peter had explained it was a dance really, hence the need for the men to wear suits. Amy was glad about this. After the last party this would be a refreshing change.

Peter got out of the cab and paid off the driver. He then took Amy's arm and propelled her towards the door, whilst smiling pleasantly at the doorman. After checking the invitation card, the man directed them to the suite at the top of the stairs from which the sound of a band could clearly be heard.

They entered the room and Peter slapped someone on the back, greeting him like a long lost brother. Amy stood there, waiting to be introduced, and then she saw Miranda, waving frantically.

"Amy, we've saved a table so you can sit with us."

Sitting with Miranda meant seeing Ian. Even her chatter could be endured if necessary. She waved back. "OK, see you in a minute." And then turning to Peter she pulled at his arm. "I'm going to sit with Miranda. They've saved us a table."

"OK. I'll be over in a minute."

Peter's reply was not enthusiastic, but she didn't care. She walked over towards Miranda, who was seated at the table with Ian and two empty chairs beside them. There were groups of

52

tables all around, most of them full up. As was to be expected, so early in the evening, the dance floor was empty. Ian rose to greet her, his brown eyes showing friendliness and warmth.

"Hi Amy, how are you?" he asked politely.

"I'm fine thank you," she said.

She tried not to look at him too much, nor to notice the strange magic that seemed to flow between them. Was she going crazy? She didn't know. All she knew was that he was Miranda's husband and she had no right to think of him in any other way, but it didn't seem to make any difference.

Ian tried not to smile back at her too much. Strange things were happening to him, and it seemed to have something to do with Amy. She was such a pretty girl but she seemed to be unaware of it. She could cause a stir wherever she went. She had breeding too. After Miranda's brusque and overbearing ways, he found her personality a refreshing change.

Miranda smiled indulgently at Ian. He looked so handsome tonight in that dark suit. She had put on her new black skirt and white blouse for his benefit. The skirt made her feel elegant, and she was sure people must think they were a smart couple.

Ian gave her a watery smile in return, but she didn't notice. He turned towards Amy, who had by now seated herself next to Miranda. He was pleased for the diversion from listening to Miranda's voice.

"Amy, what can I get you to drink?" he addressed Amy only, and he couldn't help it if his eyes mirrored his adoration of her. She was a beautiful young woman, 'pretty' didn't do her justice.

"Thank you, a white wine would he nice."

Amy could feel herself blushing under his gaze. Peter never looked at her like that. She certainly couldn't say that he was flirting with her, not that she wanted him to she assured herself, glancing guiltily at Miranda, who was as ever full of her own importance.

"Ian, there's Clive. I think he's coming over to ask me to dance."

Ian looked at her in amazement. He somehow couldn't imagine Clive leaving the bar to ask Miranda to dance on an empty floor. Now if he'd been using a dance as a pretext to talk to Amy, then he wouldn't have been at all surprised. He knew his thoughts were disloyal but he couldn't help them. He decided to humour her. "Well if that's what he wants, then go," he said easily. He could think of nothing nicer than talking to Amy.

Miranda reacted haughtily. "But you know that I don't dance."

Ian was saved from having to reply by Clive's arrival. He was a man in his mid forties, with an abundance of dark hair which was just beginning to show signs of grey. He seemed to like to flirt with women but had never married and lived alone. This had caused speculation at work, but his private life was his own affair, Ian had decided, and he wasn't that interested anyway.

He was Ian's office manager, and he couldn't admit to being madly keen on him. There was just something about Clive's manner towards him in the office at times which made him feel that Clive didn't really like him.

"Good evening everyone. I hope you're all enjoying yourselves."

His gaze, as Ian had expected, rested on Amy more than anyone, and Miranda hastened to do the introductions.

"Hello Clive. Do you know Amy? Her husband works in office three, doesn't he, Ian?"

Ian swallowed his annoyance and said curtly, "Yes, that's right."

Amy shook hands with Clive. Miranda seemed to know everyone. One could almost imagine that she worked at the bank and not Ian.

"I'm pleased to meet you," she said. Peter had never mentioned him to her, but she didn't have to say anything more because Peter appeared and swept himself into the conversation in his usual lively way.

He wasn't going to let Miranda be in the limelight, so Peter led the conversation, with Miranda in hot pursuit. Clive too, was making a bid to say his piece, but Amy wasn't listening to any of it. She was watching Ian as he went up to the bar to get her white wine.

Ian strode over to the bar and got himself a white wine as well. He liked it dry, so he got one dry and one medium, then Amy could have the choice of either. Maybe he should get Peter a beer. They'd all been so busy talking he hadn't stopped to ask. He carried the two glasses of wine over first. Clive had now gone and Peter sat between the two women, looking very much like a caged lion.

"Do you prefer medium or dry wine, Amy?" he asked,

hesitating.

"Medium please," said Amy, which is what he had guessed, so he handed it to her.

"A beer for you, Peter?" he asked, turning hospitably towards him.

"Thanks mate, just what the doctor ordered!" replied Peter enthusiastically, as Ian went up to get it.

Even though he said it, Peter didn't really mean it. Going to get a beer would have been a reason to get away. Amy could talk to Miranda and he wouldn't have to. He'd much rather help his mates to prop up the bar, but Ian returned with the drink.

"Amy, what do you think of my new shoes?" asked Miranda as anxious as ever to steer the conversation back to herself.

"Very nice," murmured Amy, glancing at the low heeled court shoes Miranda was wearing. Miranda took one off for her to examine the quality, and Peter tried to drink his beer quickly. He found women's talk very boring. It was time he joined the others at the bar, leaving the women to talk about silly unimportant things like this. In fact he was very surprised that Ian was here at all. He could see the bar from where he was sitting and he spotted Steve, who raised his hand in salutation at them.

"Ian, Steve's waving at us. We'd better see what he wants."

Ian stood up, picking up his glass of unfinished wine. He too, wanted to join the other men, but he didn't want Amy to think he was bad mannered.

"I hope you ladies will excuse us, boring bank talk no doubt . . ." He gave a grimace as if he didn't really want to hear it, and Miranda cut in quickly:

". . . The dinner starts in half an hour so make sure you're back for it."

Ian could feel his anger rising. How dare she speak to him like a little boy in front of other people! This time she had gone too far.

"I would never have known that! Whatever would I do if I didn't have you to remind me?"

His voice was sarcastic and his eyes flashed with barely suppressed anger. Amy noticed immediately, she had been cringing with embarrassment for Ian at the way Miranda seemed to treat him. She could see, looking at Miranda, that his words had gone right over her head. She hadn't noticed the sarcasm. She

55

really must be so insensitive.

Amy watched them go off. Peter didn't glance back, but Ian did. She didn't know why his eyes softened when they looked back at her, but she told herself very firmly that although he was a very attractive man he was also Miranda's husband. Having a harmless fantasy was one thing, but giving off messages that she was available was quite another. Anyway, why would he look at her? Not everyone was as easily led as Peter, and she swallowed down her feeling of pain at the memory of it.

Later, when the meal was over, the dance floor gradually filled up with couples. Amy liked dancing, but Peter would take some moving. He hadn't overdone the drinking tonight, thank goodness. He knew, even when off-duty, bad behaviour would be a deciding factor when promotion came up.

Amy could see Miranda's lips still moving, but the music was loud and it drowned her voice. Amy found her feet tapping to a lively number. She turned to Peter, grabbing his arm. "Come on Peter, let's have a dance."

Peter was enjoying his after dinner liqueur, and the thought of shaking up all that Christmas dinner, which was nestling comfortably inside him, did not appeal to him. How could he get out of it gracefully? He suddenly had a flash of inspiration, and turning to Miranda, he remarked lightly, "Miranda, I bet you're a good dancer. Why don't you two ladies dance and we'll watch."

Miranda's eyes flashed with annoyance. Getting on the dance floor was not for her. She had no sense of rhythm, and deep down inside, although she would never have admitted it, she knew her weight was against her.

"No! I never dance!" she said shortly, and then in an effort to save herself from further embarrassment, she said pleadingly to Ian, "You're a good dancer, can't you dance with Amy?"

The same thoughts were going through Ian's head. Miranda had never objected to him dancing with other women at parties, she only wanted to chat. He felt the same way as she did about dancing with her. She was getting too heavy to trip the light fantastic these days. Amy, on the other hand, was like a slim little elf, but she was also Peter's wife so he mustn't look too eager.

Peter was only too pleased at the idea. He didn't have to worry about Amy flirting with other men. She wasn't like Gill. Whilst they were dancing he could disappear outside and smoke a cigar.

Miranda couldn't stop him, thank goodness.

"Yes, she's all yours, as long as you bring her back afterwards." He laughed in his easy way, knowing that his apparent generosity at lending his wife for a dance would sound good.

Amy bridled, and her eyes flashed. "You don't own me Peter, just because we're married! I'll decide who I want to dance with!"

She knew it was silly, cutting off her nose to spite her face. Of course she wanted to dance with Ian, but she didn't want Peter and Miranda arranging it as though they were like puppets. She wanted Ian to ask her himself. She got her wish.

"Will I do, Amy?"

His brown eyes looked so sincere, she gulped, trying to control her thudding heart. Of course he would do! It was like a dream. If only it had been a slow dance so that he would hold her, but she dismissed this thought from her mind as soon as it surfaced.

"Yes, of course." She could feel herself blushing, and he took her hand gently, leading her onto the dance floor. The music was loud so there was no chance of conversation. They turned and faced one another, and then danced without any contact, just like everyone else was. Amy felt disappointment flood through her, wanting to feel his hand touch against hers.

Ian wanted this dance to end. He preferred to jive, old fashioned or not, at least he would be in contact with her. She was moving her body to the rhythm, her hips swayed, and she was smiling, enjoying it. He privately admired her superb legs and slim body. She had spirit and a mind of her own. He liked that.

She was the sort of young woman who could really turn you on, but then he felt regret when he hastened to remind himself that no one could turn him on now. He was impotent and quite safe for any woman to be with.

The music stopped briefly and then the band struck up a very slow tune. He stood there, looking at her, knowing he didn't want this to end. He could feel a pounding in his veins, and he wanted to encircle that tiny waist in his arms and have those blue eyes gazing into his, but why he didn't know.

"Let's take a slow one now." His voice was soft and intimate, and Amy felt herself melt into his body. The moment was romantic, the lights were low and his cheek was near. She could

57

smell the pleasant musky aroma of his aftershave, and her hair brushed against his chin. She looked up at him and their eyes met, and she knew at that moment, that safe within his arms was where she wanted to be.

Ian had a strange feeling inside him as he held this beautiful young woman in his arms. She appeared to be fragile, but yet tough, soft and vulnerable, and she evoked a feeling of tenderness inside him which he knew shouldn't be there. Her body was warm and he could feel the softness of her breasts against his jacket. He could also feel a stirring in his loins that hadn't been there for a long time. He closed his eyes, imagining what it would be like to kiss those pert lips of hers.

His thoughts moved on. They were x-rated he knew, as he fantasised about slipping that dress off her and touching those beautiful breasts. He visualised those beautiful little buds with erect pink nipples, and how lovely it would be to worship them with his mouth and his hands. My God! He was getting an erection, a proper one, he'd forgotten what it was like!

He caught his breath in amazement. She was as intoxicating as wine and had made him feel like this just by being in his arms. The music stopped and with it the rapture of the moment passed too. The important figure of the director of the bank went up on stage to draw the raffle, and Ian and Amy were left standing there. Regretfully he took her back to her seat, not wanting to look at her too closely in case his face betrayed his feelings of passion.

He remembered his manners as she sat down, "Thank you for the dance," he said, his eyes briefly meeting hers.

Miranda commanded his attention.

"Ian, I've lost my earring somewhere on the floor. Can you see it?"

Her words were wasted on him. He hadn't heard her and he didn't want to listen. His heart was full of Amy and the feelings she had aroused in him. Feelings which had been dormant but were now threatening to drive him crazy. There she sat, sympathising with Miranda, acting as if nothing had happened. Well maybe nothing had happened, it was all in his mind and that was the only place it could be.

The rest of the evening passed in a haze for Ian, and he had no further chance to be close to Amy. He saw that look in Miranda's eyes on the way home and he knew what she wanted. He pretended to be unwell, telling her he felt as if he had a cold coming, which gave him the excuse to sleep in the spare room.

Once in bed, he allowed his mind to wander, remembering Amy's beautiful body so close to his and how she had made him feel. He had the stirring of an erection, but it wasn't enough. Try as he might to imagine it was her delicate sensitive hands stroking him, he couldn't maintain it to reach a climax. He tossed and turned, feeling frustrated and unfulfilled, grieving that his sexual feelings had temporarily returned but, it seemed, there was nothing he could do about it.

Chapter Eight

"Thank you very much for asking us, Miranda. I'll check with Peter and come back to you . . ."

". . . Just tell him, like I do with Ian! See you about eight, bye for now."

Amy put the phone down with mixed feelings. Miranda never took no for an answer, and short of being rude, she didn't see how she could let her down lightly. Amy didn't want her dominating her life. She seemed to want to make a friend of her, but Amy found her too overpowering and her talk, mainly about herself, was very boring.

If Amy was honest with herself, the only reason she put up with her was because of Ian. Although she had told herself frequently, since the bank dance, that she was not really attracted to him, it hadn't stopped her thinking about him. She had mixed feelings about spending an evening sitting opposite him at a dinner table. If his brown eyes were looking into hers, then it certainly wouldn't help matters at all.

Peter was slumped on the sofa watching television, with a glass of beer in his hand. Paul and Sarah had gone to a birthday party, and they only had each other for company. At one time it would have been an opportunity to do something together for a couple of hours, he could video the football, but Amy wasn't sure she wanted to. A nice walk on her own with the dog appealed more to her.

"Peter, that was Miranda on the phone. She's invited us for

dinner. Do you fancy going if Mummy and Daddy can baby-sit?"

Peter's eyes didn't leave the television, and he muttered absently. "If you like, I don't mind."

Amy glanced at him in amazement. She had been expecting him to refuse because Miranda got on his nerves. Had he heard her? This wasn't the Peter she knew. "Are you sure?"

Peter's good humour deserted him, there she was yaking away, interrupting one of the best goals ever scored. He jumped off the settee. His intention was to grab her arm fiercely and force it over her mouth, just to show her who was boss, but he was stopped by the look in her eyes. Anger flashed, where there had once been submission there was no more. She was no longer afraid of him. Like all bullies he was a coward, so he sat down again.

"Go away and arrange it. I want to watch this in peace." His voice had an edge but he only sounded irritated. He could sense the change of power. She was standing up to him. Gone was the fear in her eyes and he didn't know why. For the first time in ten years Peter was unsure of himself. He wasn't master in his own home any more and he didn't like it.

Amy felt a feeling of triumph inside herself. Peter no longer scared her. He wasn't her whole world any more. She no longer felt the need to put up with his bad temper, not after what he'd put her through. Her ideals had been shattered, and she could feel herself changing. It was up to him if their marriage was going to survive and it certainly wasn't going to if he bullied her. It was up to her to decide if they were going out or not. She made her decision, and then took the cordless phone away from the noisy television set and into the kitchen.

"Hello Mummy. We've just had a sudden dinner invitation. We wondered if you and Daddy were free to baby-sit."

"Yes, I'd love to. Daddy's away on one of those dreadful conferences."

Amy never understood why her Dad needed to go to all those meetings. He didn't actually work, but it had been explained to her that he owned companies and so he had to go to the conferences. They always seemed to be at the weekend, so it left Susan alone.

"Do you want to stay and have dinner with us tomorrow? We won't be in that late, but you know you're always welcome to."

"No, don't worry dear. Max and Anna are coming over

61

tomorrow. Daddy might even be back in time too."

"Yes, of course . . ." Amy then remembered that they had been asked too, but had to say no because Paul was having a friend round for the day, and it had already been arranged. ". . . I spoke to Anna yesterday. She said her sickness is much better."

"Yes, thank goodness, I was like that with you," said Susan, sympathetically. "I've never forgotten it."

"Do you want to be picked up tonight?" asked Amy, although she knew what the answer would be.

"No thank you. I'll drive, of course," said Susan firmly, and Amy didn't argue. Her mother was always independent.

"Thanks a lot Mummy, we'll see you later then."

As Amy put the phone down, she reminded herself that she must invite Max and Anna round soon. The days seemed to fly by but that was no excuse. She had always been close to her 'Little' brother as she called him. He might be six feet tall but he was three years younger than herself, and he had married Anna only last year. Now they had their first baby on the way and Amy was looking forward to being an aunt.

She walked back into the room where Peter was watching football. He smiled uncertainly at her, sensing her mood. No, she didn't want him with her, grumpy misery that he was! She picked up Jasper's lead and the dog heard it and came to her. She patted his head. "Come on, boy." She put his lead on and strode out, not even bothering to tell Peter where she was going.

"Ian, I've invited Amy and Peter round tonight for dinner." Miranda looked at Ian. She never asked him if he minded. She made arrangements and told him afterwards, but this time he didn't mind.

Since the Christmas dance, Amy had dominated his thoughts no matter how much he tried to forget about her. He did want to see her even if her husband was in tow. Oh, how Ian envied him!

He admitted to himself that he was very attracted to her. She made him feel as if he still had male feelings, even if he could only enjoy them in his mind.

"What's on the menu?" he asked Miranda. She wasn't renowned for her cooking.

"Well, as I'm dieting, I thought we could start with tinned

grapefruit, then chicken with salad and new potatoes, and then for dessert we could have strawberries and cream.

Ian breathed a sigh of relief. Miranda would have bought a cooked chicken, prepared salad, and even the new potatoes she bought from the supermarket would be cooked and ready to eat. All she had to do was put it on the table. Tonight he would look forward to his dinner for a change, and to seeing Amy.

Miranda noticed how he seemed to brighten up. Maybe they should entertain more often. She was always inviting people but most of them seemed too busy. She had noticed a change in Ian, she was quite worried about him these days. Since that operation he had lost his sex drive and he showed no interest in her at all. There was nothing wrong with her, so it must be the operation, Miranda decided. Sometimes he slept in the spare room, and she was fed up with it, maybe she should take him back to the doctor.

She busied herself preparing for the evening, confident that Peter and Amy would come. She had bought everything ready prepared so nothing could go wrong. She didn't usually spend much time doing housework but she would today. She would send Ian out with the girls so she could get on uninterrupted.

After they'd gone out she took out the hoover and polish. She didn't enjoy cleaning at all. Often she left it for Ian but today she would make an effort. She huffed and puffed when she tried to bend and stretch. Her size did not help her when she tried to be active. The furniture had a rare treat when it was polished until it shined, and she sat back with a look of satisfaction on her face. Now Ian could see what a competent wife she was.

Peter stood in the shower, soaping his body and enjoying the feel of the hot water running down him. He was deep in thought. He had his own reasons for making a friend of Ian. He was a useful bloke to know in many ways.

Only last week he had fixed the car for him, saving an unnecessary trip to the garage and more expense, which he could afford if necessary, but Peter was tight. He didn't spend money if he didn't have to. Tonight he would take Ian a bottle of vodka as a thank you. He didn't particularly like the stuff himself and there was one left from last Christmas which was untouched. That would save buying anything. Yes, it was well worth keeping in with people who were useful to you, so he was even prepared to suffer Miranda to further his own ends.

He reached for the towel and rubbed his hair vigorously, and then his body. Amy's attitude today had taken him by surprise. He had expected it after the party when he had been caught out, but she was still acting bold. He could sense that she had changed towards him, but she must still love him, surely? He didn't want a life without Amy, or her daddy's money. But she wouldn't leave him. Peter knew Susan and David well enough to know they wouldn't want that. They liked to keep up appearances. His future was safe enough.

As he walked through to the bedroom he noticed that Amy had her red jersey suit on, which always looked good on her. She was very lovely, but he couldn't let her know that she was gorgeous enough to attract anyone. He had no intention of losing her.

"I'm going casual tonight," he announced, getting out a pair of black jeans. He teamed them with a black check shirt, which he wore outside his jeans, and he wore black trainers. This relaxed mode of dress made him feel less like a bank clerk.

Amy was looking at him carefully, noting his mood. He must turn on the charm because Susan was downstairs with the children. He smiled ingratiatingly, asking, "Are you ready?" he knew he had to.

"Yes," was all she said as she picked up her bag.

When they went downstairs Sarah ran out of the lounge, her face alight with curiosity.

"Daddy, where are you going?" her tone became almost a whine as she tried to win his attention. Peter bent to kiss her, and Amy noticed how gentle and good humoured he sounded.

"I'm taking Mummy to dinner with friends. Doesn't she look nice?"

Amy wasn't taken in this time. He really played to his audience. Susan was beaming at her wonderful son-in-law, or so she thought, but Amy knew it was an act. He was known as good tempered Peter and it was a joke. He was nothing like the Peter she had married at eighteen, the boy who had been so in awe of her parents.

"You've seen me in this suit lots of times, Sarah," she said, brushing off his apparent admiration.

Susan joined in too: "Peter's right dear. It does look very nice."

Amy looked at her mother. If only she wouldn't bury her head in the sand. Peter was a bully, and today she had not let him intimidate her. He no longer scared her. She had decided she was going to try talking to Daddy about it. She would have to make him believe her because whether they liked it or not, if Peter didn't treat her better, she was going to ask Daddy the easiest way to get a divorce.

Chapter Nine

David sipped at his drink whilst waiting for her to arrive. The hotel had been carefully chosen as usual, several miles away from the town he lived in. He didn't know the staff and they didn't know him.

One telephone call and his evening had been arranged. He swallowed nervously, feeling the excitement inside him. He had asked for a blonde, and young, he had stipulated that too, as young as Susan had been when they first met. But Susan had changed towards him after Max was born. Sex had become a dirty word to her, and he had still been a young man with needs and passions which plagued his body.

He had seen the advertisement for the escort agency, and as he was in desperate need of female company to soothe his damaged ego, he had rung them. Girls were provided for company, he was told. He could take them for a meal but he mustn't expect anything else. This was part of the excitement of it all, because some of the girls took a lot of wooing to get them into bed. They were high class whores, but David was a rich man and could afford to give into their demands.

In return, he was given a night of unbridled passion, fulfilling all his needs. If they were acting they certainly did it well and this helped to restore his ego. He liked to think he was still attractive to women now. At the age of fifty-four, he still had a full head of thick brown hair, his eyes were steely blue, and he had kept himself lean and healthy by playing golf and swimming at his private club.

It was all very discreet with no strings attached. He had been living like this for over twenty years now, and long since ceased to feel any guilt about it. After all, his marriage was intact. Susan had no idea, nor had Amy and Max, and he wanted it to stay that way.

He did love his wife, so one could say he was happily married, and it was particularly important right now because his name had been put forward as a potential leader of the local Conservative party next year. He couldn't afford to have any scandal touching him.

The door opened, bringing with it a gush of cold air and a young woman with long straight blonde hair. She hesitated, and he noticed how tall she was. She was wearing a blue silk trouser and top set which looked good on her. Her eyes were almost as blue as Amy's, and she had a look of innocence, which totally belied her profession. He stood up smiling. "Are you Jenny?"

Her blue eyes studied him briefly, she seemed to approve, and then she smiled, which made her look even more attractive. He liked her high cheekbones. She had a classy look about her.

"Yes, I am. You must be Charles Turner . . ."

"Indeed I am, what can I get you to drink?"

"A dry Martini, please."

He signalled to the waiter. This girl was lovely, and after a very special meal, he would have the pleasure of making love to her. With all his past experiences, he knew how to arouse a woman and satisfy her, and in return, she would do the same for him. He could feel his senses tingling at the thought of it. If she proved to be good, he would ask for her on a regular basis and they could ascend the dizzy heights of ultimate pleasure together often.

Ian could sense that Amy was as unhappy with life as he was. She had sat there all evening whilst Peter and Miranda had done most of the talking, replying when spoken to, even smiling at times, but he could still sense there was something wrong with her.

Peter had told a few jokes in his usual bluff and hearty way. Even Miranda had stopped her chattering to listen to them. Amy didn't appear to be listening, her eyes had a faraway look in them, but Peter hadn't noticed. He was the life and soul of the party.

Ian had noticed though. She looked sad, as though something had made her miserable, just like at the party when he first met her. Maybe she wasn't happy with Peter. He felt again that desire to hold her in his arms and comfort her, to stroke her hair and tell her he could make everything all right again.

But he couldn't, could he? He told himself sternly to stop being stupid, but the voice of his conscience was getting weaker and he knew it. As he watched her helping Miranda to clear the table, she was smiling with her lips, but it didn't reach her eyes. Those eyes haunted him, big deep pools of loneliness, and how he longed to drown in their depths.

Every time he saw her it got worse. The desire to ease her misery, whatever it was, was getting too strong to ignore. She had left the room now and he poured Peter a brandy, trying to keep his mind on what he was doing.

"How's the car going?" he asked, in a desperate attempt to dismiss her from his thoughts.

"Great, thanks to you. Since you cleared the blockage she goes like a bird," commented Peter, enthusiastically.

Miranda appeared with the coffee pot. "Any more coffee for you two?" she enquired.

"Just a little. It's very nice!" declared Peter.

"Leave the dishes, Amy. I'll do them tomorrow," called Miranda, glancing towards the kitchen as she spoke.

"You won't stop her. She never sits down for five minutes," laughed Peter.

Ian saw his chance. He managed to smile at Miranda, and she glowed back in response. "Miranda, you've done all the preparations so I'll go and help Amy to clear up. You sit there and tell Peter about when you broke down in the car on the motorway." And then he added encouragingly: "It's a very amusing story!"

Peter didn't look amused, but Ian didn't care. He wanted to get out in the kitchen with Amy, and he knew Miranda could be relied on to keep the conversation going.

He walked through to the kitchen and there she was, diligently stacking dishes in the dishwasher. This new gadget was Miranda's pride and joy. Ian had budgeted very carefully to buy this for her. It was for his own benefit too, because most of the time Miranda didn't wash up, she left it for him.

Amy turned as he entered the room, her eyes registered surprise, and he noticed again how beautiful they were.

"I've come to lend a hand," he said very humbly, and she smiled, and this time the smile reached her eyes.

They shared a companionable silence as they worked together. Ian rolled up his sleeves and washed the things that couldn't go in the dishwasher. Then he wiped down the kitchen units with a soapy sponge. He was just about to put the remains of the salad in the fridge, when Amy asked him: "Where does Miranda keep the cling film."

"I'm not sure." He wrinkled his brow, and opened one or two doors to try and find it.

"I've got it," said Amy, her head triumphantly emerging from the cupboard under the sink. Her hand touched his as he handed her the bowl, and he felt tingles of anticipation going up and down his spine. Right or wrong, he knew he wasn't going to know any peace until he kissed her.

He didn't think about the risk he was taking. Her face was near, her eyes looked into his and he saw her lip tremble. At that moment he knew instinctively that she felt the same way, he bent towards her and his lips met hers.

His kiss was gentle and tender. She was like a precious flower which needed to open up in the sun. He sensed her vulnerability and it stirred his protective instincts. Her lips were even sweeter than he had expected, and he closed his eyes, savouring the moment for as long as he could.

But inevitably it had to end, and she pulled away guiltily from him as he had expected her to. He said, softly, "Thank you very much Amy, for your help. I love your company."

She blushed, and he found it quite entrancing. Her voice was shaky. Had he stirred her in the same way that she had stirred him?

"After all the hard work from Miranda preparing it. I thought it was the least I could do."

Ian didn't want to think too much about Miranda. He could hear her voice coming from the next room and it seemed there was no escape. Well, he'd come this far, and he knew that his dearest wish was to make love to Amy, but he wasn't sure that he could.

If all he could do was to become a friend to her, he would settle for that. He just longed for her company, and to ease her sadness, whatever the reason for it. He whispered gently to her. "Amy, I must see you again! Please will you meet me at lunchtime on Monday at Wolseley Park?"

He felt he already knew this woman inside out. Her reaction was exactly what he had expected. She raised her eyes and they were full of guilt and uncertainty. She whispered hoarsely, "No, don't ask me, we both know we shouldn't!" and then she escaped from the room, and he was left standing there knowing that she was trying to fight her feelings, whereas he had given in to his.

Amy was sick to death of Peter tonight. He positively grated on her nerves. She'd heard his silly jokes so many times before, and his attempts to be such a mate to Ian annoyed her. He was a user, always keeping in with people who were useful to him. He was so false and she knew he would drop Ian as soon as he ceased to be useful to him, and she didn't like the idea of Ian being treated like that.

She hadn't intended to think about Ian. He hadn't appeared to be drunk, but what other reason could there be for his behaviour, first kissing her and then asking to meet her. The thing that worried her most of all was that she wanted to meet him too.

His lips had tasted like wine, and she had felt the need to wrap herself in his strong arms and tell him about Peter and his bullying ways, and how she had finally, after ten years, got up the courage to stand her ground. But that was disloyal, and until now she had never wanted to be disloyal, but she could feel herself changing.

There he sat, slumped on the taxi seat, snoring like some drunken old tramp. He was so uncouth. His breath positively reeked of brandy and he'd even managed to spill some on his shirt. Well just let Mummy see what a drunkard he could be, she thought triumphantly when he staggered out of the car and into the house.

Susan was spared that ordeal because he made a quick dash for the downstairs shower room when they came in. Amy fully expected to hear the sound of vomiting, but when he emerged he had taken off the offending shirt and wrapped himself in a towelling robe.

He yawned convincingly. "Goodnight Susan, I'm off to bed. Thanks so much for coming over."

Amy glared at him, but he appeared not to notice. She

addressed her mother. "Were the children OK?"

"Yes, but Paul coughed a bit, and he complained of a sore throat . . ." said Susan anxiously, ". . . I nearly rang your mobile, but he went off to sleep quite quickly."

Amy felt quite guilty. She shouldn't have left him and then none of this would have happened, and her feelings wouldn't be in such turmoil. However, her common sense told her different. This attraction towards Ian had been growing ever since she met him, and her feelings for Peter were diminishing every day.

As for Paul, it wasn't the first sore throat he'd suffered and it wouldn't be the last. She would keep an eye on him tomorrow, and if he didn't improve he would have to stay off school and that would put pay to any temptation to meet Ian. But that would only delay the inevitable, and she wondered how long she could deny this craziness inside her which threatened to dominate her life.

After Amy had seen her mother's car drive off, she followed Peter up the stairs to bed. She was feeling very weary now and couldn't bear the thought of him anywhere near her tonight, and for the first time wished that they slept separately. As she entered the bedroom she could see that he was already in bed. He was disgusting! His body smelt sweaty and his breath reeked of stale brandy. She undressed quietly, hoping he would fall asleep whilst she was washing and cleaning her teeth, and then climbed into bed.

His hands moved over her body, but this time she was having none of it! Her hands came up and she pushed him away, hard, shouting, "Leave me alone, Peter!" Her voice even surprised her, and she waited for his wrath to descend on her, at the ready to face up to him.

Peter couldn't believe it. She'd pushed him away! He was used to having his way with her whether she wanted to or not. His temper snapped, and he cursed her. "You're supposed to be my wife. Show some feeling, you bitch!"

He pulled her body towards him. She couldn't mean it, he was a sexy stud. She was only teasing him! But then her knee in his groin left him in no doubt that she didn't want him. He doubled up with a howl of pain as Amy jumped out of bed and left him on his own. For the first time in his life Peter couldn't cope. After years of bullying, the worm had turned, he had lost control of her, and he now realised that no longer would he be able to control her with his displays of anger. Whatever would he do now?

71

Chapter Ten

"Have a nice day at school and work hard!"

"Yes, Mummy."

Amy smiled as she watched Paul stride through the school gates with his sports bag in his hand. He had football today, which he loved, and as his sore throat had now gone there was no reason to keep him off school.

She put the car into gear and drove off slowly towards Sarah's school, glancing cautiously around her to make sure the road was clear.

"It's your turn, now, Sarah."

Sarah looked hopefully at her mother but Amy was not to be swayed.

"I hope my throat will be all right," Sarah said ominously.

"Of course it will. If it isn't you might have to miss swimming tomorrow." Amy pointed out, knowing how much Sarah loved to swim.

"Well, it might only hurt for today," said Sarah.

And Amy laughed, knowing her daughter's acting ability. Today she had maths, not her favourite subject, and tomorrow was sports, which she did love.

They had arrived at her school now, and Amy indicated and stopped. She had to jump out quickly to get Sarah out and as she opened the door, Sarah exclaimed excitedly.

"Hurry up Mummy, I've just seen Amanda."

All thoughts of being ill now forgotten, she barely had time to kiss Amy goodbye, as she ran to catch up with Amanda. Amy was relieved that it had been that easy to get her to school after all. If Paul complained of being unwell she knew it would be true, unlike Sarah, who was a born actress, and it appeared that today she had decided to copy her brother to get some attention.

Amy went home. There was washing waiting to be done as usual, and the house needed cleaning after the weekend. Whilst she busied herself, she thought about Saturday night. Peter had said nothing to her, but he knew something was very wrong. She had always forgiven him his tempers before and given in to his sexual demands, even when she didn't want to, but now, after ten years of it, she'd had enough and he could see it. Where did they go from here? If he couldn't change, and that seemed unlikely, they would have to part. The only thing that held her back from doing this was the children. Peter loved them too, and in fairness to him he had never been violent towards them. How could she justify depriving them of their father? But on the other hand, how could she spend the rest of her life married to a man she was beginning to despise?

Her dog, Jasper, was lying on the mat, supposedly asleep, but with one eye on her. She had taken him out already this morning when she went for her early morning jog, but he knew she normally gave him two outings a day, and being the canine charmer that he was, he would wait patiently for the next walk.

The telephone interrupted her thoughts. "It's Gill, Amy. Are you coming round today? I haven't seen you for a while."

It seemed to be the ideal solution to her problem. Going to see Gill would stop her going to meet Ian. She could avoid temptation. But she didn't want to avoid temptation. She had wrestled with her conscience all morning, and now she wanted a friend to confide in, but not just any friend, she wanted him. Her voice was contrite, but firm.

"Sorry Gill, I can't make it today. I've got an appointment I must keep. We'll have to make it another time."

"Never mind."

Gill's voice sounded disappointed, but Amy stifled any feelings of guilt. For once in her life she was going to do what she wanted, and to hell with everyone else!

*   *   *   *

d

Ian knew she would come, even though she had said no. It would be hard for her because she was decent and loyal. Affairs these days were often undertaken lightly and then referred to as a mistake, when it came out, but Amy would not be like that. She had old-fashioned values and he liked that about her.

Something was bothering her and her own husband didn't seem to notice. Maybe it was Peter, who knows? Even if she only wants me as a shoulder to cry on, I don't mind, he thought. A lovely young woman like her should be enjoying life.

Of course it was a rash thing to ask her to do. Wolseley park was a few miles off the beaten track from where they lived, but there was always a chance that someone might recognise them.

He sat in the car waiting for her to arrive. Normally Miranda used it and he got the train to work but he had told her he needed it to go and get something. As her birthday was close she had immediately assumed that it was for her benefit. His income wasn't enough to run two cars and he often wished, now that the girls were older, Miranda would get herself a part-time job instead of sitting around all day reading women's magazines. That was the trouble with Miranda. She didn't live in the real world.

He dismissed her from his thoughts as Amy's red Fiesta arrived in the car park. She was driving slowly and he saw the black shape sitting in the back, which astonished him, and then he realised it was a dog; she had brought her dog.

As soon as she stopped, he sprang out and went to see her. Jasper barked furiously even though his tail was wagging.

"Hello Amy," he said, smiling. "What a lovely dog! I bet he's not as ferocious as he sounds."

Amy laughed. "Well, he's very protective of me, but I expect when he realises you're a friend, he'll lick you to death."

Ian laughed too, and suggested, "Let's go for a walk."

Amy smiled her agreement. She got out of the car and put Jasper on his lead, then handed it to Ian to hold whilst she put her coat on.

Ian knew he must be crazy, as he was wearing only the jacket of his suit and it was such a cold day. But walking next to her, he probably wouldn't even notice it. She walked briskly and he fell into step beside her. Once Jasper realised Ian wasn't going to hurt Amy, he became a friend. Amy let him off the lead and he began

74

to explore, his tail wagging nineteen to the dozen.

"Look at him, he'll wag it off," laughed Amy, and he smiled back at her, noticing how bright and sparkling her eyes were. She seemed much happier than on Saturday, and he was glad, her unhappiness had touched his heart.

They walked for about fifteen minutes, not meeting anyone at all this cold day, and then they returned to the comparative warmth of the car. Amy put Jasper in the back of hers and then brought out a thermos flask and some sandwiches.

"Come and sit in my car," said Ian hospitably.

"OK," agreed Amy. Holding the thermos up she enquired, "Have you eaten yet? Here's some soup and sandwiches."

Ian hadn't given a thought to eating. He had only been concerned about seeing her, and when he did the last thing on his mind had been food. Now she had mentioned it, he realised he was very hungry.

"Well, only if you have enough," he said gallantly.

"Of course there's enough. I couldn't drink all this!" said Amy, as she poured it out.

He sat there, slowly drinking the steaming liquid. It was warming him nicely inside. To follow were roast beef sandwiches, which tasted delicious, and he couldn't help comparing her with Miranda. She was very capable and she seemed very happy. Then it hit him in a flash. She was happy when Peter wasn't around . . . so it was him. She was unhappy with him for some reason.

They sat there quietly, and he was enjoying her company. She was undemanding and relaxing to be with, but at the same time, he found her attractiveness disturbing. He glanced at his watch, realising he only had a few minutes left before he must return to work. If he wanted to keep on the good side of Clive, he needed to be punctual. Was there time for her to open up her heart and tell him her troubles? He decided to find out.

"You seemed unhappy on Saturday night. Call me nosey if you like, but I wondered if you needed a friend to talk to about it."

He looked straight into her eyes as he spoke and he saw the pain there, and then the anger. Her words came tumbling out as she explained about Ian, his tempers and spitefulness, and how she had finally, after ten years, plucked up the courage to stand up to him.

He felt a rush of pity for her and then anger towards Ian, that he could abuse such a lovely wife. What a fool the man must be not to appreciate what he had!

"I shouldn't be telling you this. Peter is your friend. But my parents will find it hard to understand and so will everyone else, and I needed to tell someone," and then she added: "Peter always seems so good natured."

She was looking miserable, and he marvelled at how the mention of her problems had destroyed her happy mood so quickly. His arms went instinctively round her, she didn't try to resist, and he held her comfortingly against him, cursing himself inwardly for opening his big mouth and causing her even more distress. Then he felt her body shake and the tears came, but they were tears of relief at unburdening herself at last, and he continued to hold her until they stopped.

She made a supreme effort to control herself, and he found his handkerchief and gently wiped her tears away. Her lips were near and the closeness of her body was affecting him again. Those lips made him feel dizzy with desire and the temptation was just too great.

As his lips met hers it started with a gentle kiss, but then he could feel her responding and those irresistible lips tasted like fire. His body felt on fire too, and he could feel his sex impulses coming to life. He wanted her, oh God, how he wanted her!

In the madness of the moment he forgot where he was, and as their lips continued to fuse, the desire to stroke and explore her beautiful body became too much to bear. He kept one arm round her, his other arm freed itself, and his fingers stroked their way down her soft neck.

She was still wearing her coat which was undone at the neck, and underneath she wore a jumper with three buttons down the front. He slowly undid the buttons, longing to see and feel her breasts, and still her lips clung feverishly to his.

His hands had found her bra now and he undid it, and those little buds felt even more beautiful than he had imagined. Finally their lips parted and she lay there panting whilst he stroked her, delighting at the sight of her erect nipples.

He couldn't stop worshipping her body. She was beautiful, all woman, and his dearest wish was to make love to her. He really felt as if he could. The throbbing between his legs was driving him mad, and he felt as if he would burst through his trousers.

"No Ian, what are we doing?"

Amy surfaced, her eyes were bright and her cheeks very flushed. She was having an attack of conscience. Ian didn't feel guilty, she was bringing him to life again, sexually, but he wanted to respect her wishes.

"Amy, I'm so sorry! You have such an effect on me that I just can't keep my hands to myself. You are so lovely. Please forgive me."

His brown eyes pleaded for her to understand, as with feverish hands she tried to put herself in order.

"We're both married," she said primly, and suddenly he knew he couldn't let her go just like that.

"Yes, and we're both lonely, that's why this is happening," he said sadly. "If you want me to, I'll get in my car and go away and we'll forget this ever happened, and I promise I'll never come near you again . . ." He saw the misery in her eyes that his words had caused and inwardly exulted. She didn't want that to happen. ". . . Or if you want someone to talk to you could meet me again, same time, same place, and I promise faithfully I will never lay a finger on you again unless you want me to."

Amy had by now fastened up her coat buttons and she turned her face towards him. He could see it in her eyes, because they betrayed her, no matter what she said.

"Well, if all we're going to do is talk, then I suppose it's all right," she said, opening the car door. As she got out she spoke again: "You'd better go, you'll be late for work."

Ian groaned when he looked at his watch. He was going to be about half an hour late, but it had been worth it. He'd have to think up a good excuse for Clive whilst he was driving back, and in the meantime all he could do was long for tomorrow.

77

Chapter Eleven

Amy was trying to convince herself, every time she met Ian, that there was no harm in it. They talked a lot and that was all. It was almost like she'd dreamt that he'd kissed her that first Monday, and when she thought about how intimately he'd touched her, she felt flushed with embarrassment, or excitement, she wasn't sure which.

She found Ian easy to talk to. She had told him about Peter's rough and uncouth ways, and then she admitted that she didn't even love him any more. "If I want to divorce him I'm on my own because my parents will not give me support," she said sadly. "Daddy didn't want us to marry in the first place, but now we'll be expected to stay together because of the children."

"You won't find that easy if you don't love each other, and the children will be upset anyway," pointed out Ian, feeling a bit of a hypocrite. Wasn't that exactly what he was doing?

He stroked her hair as he spoke, and she closed her eyes, enjoying the gentle touch of his fingers. It was difficult to control the feelings that were running amok inside her. She knew by now that she didn't just want him as a friend, she wanted him to make love to her and her body tingled at the thought of it.

Meeting him like this was doing her head in! If she was a bad person, then so be it, because she couldn't help it. Even the words unfaithful, cheating and anything else that described her, failed to douse her desire.

Amy raised her head, and his eyes, so expressive, looked

deeply into hers. "Please kiss me," said a voice which she could hardly believe was hers. When it came, his kiss took her breath away, and she could feel herself, once more, rising to the dizzy heights of expectation. When he finally released her, his hands moved slowly from her shoulders to his lap, and she felt disappointment flood through her.

She looked at his hands lying idly in his lap, those hands which she longed to touch her.

"I want you," she said desperately. "I thought you felt the same way, but you confuse me."

Ian took her soft hand and stroked it gently. It was time he explained to her.

"I want to make love to you as much as you want me to. I can't help how I feel either . . ." he took a deep breath, ". . . but I can't make love to you, Amy, or any woman, I'm impotent."

How he hated that word! But he had said it now and he felt better. Admitting the problem to her had taken all his courage, and her reaction was exactly what he had expected.

"Ian, I'm sorry. I didn't realise." And she continued to hold his hand, and there was no expression of contempt, nor amusement on her face, only concern for her own misunderstanding of the situation.

Prompted by her sympathy, his explanation came tumbling out: his illness, the very painful but necessary surgery and terrible after effects, the loss of desire for sex and his belief that he could no longer father a child. He even told her about Rachel, whom he had turned to rather than his own wife for help, and spurred on by her understanding, he admitted that he hadn't made love to his wife for over a year, and since their one ill-fated attempt, he had no desire to.

Because he felt so close to her, he said something that he could never have said to Miranda, not even at the beginning of their married life when he thought he had loved her.

"Amy, I thought with you recently my feelings were coming back, but I'm not sure. You turn me on, but I need help . . ."

He buried his head in her shoulder, feeling humiliated, but there was no need to. Amy spoke firmly, but tenderly, as she kissed his brow. "I will help you."

"I can't do it in the car. I need to spend the night with you somewhere comfortable where we can relax."

This would be difficult and Amy knew it. Lunchtimes were easy, but finding a reason to be away overnight would not be. She wasn't used to lying and deceiving, but somehow she would do it, she knew she would. There was a feeling deep inside her, driving her on, which she couldn't control, and her desire to make him feel like a man again was so strong she just couldn't deny it.

Peter didn't like the way Amy had changed towards him and he wasn't sure what to do about it. She had ideas about being independent and it seemed as if he no longer had the power to stop her.

First of all she'd had that ridiculous idea about getting a job, and when he'd told her flatly she couldn't, what had she done, taken up an Open University course. But it didn't end there. She was planning to take up a career because she said she was getting left behind since computers and modern technology had arrived. Even though her parents had backed him, she had defied them all, and he knew that it was only a matter of time before she did it.

Peter didn't want that. He had hoped to keep her at home, at his beck and call, but now that the children were older she seemed to want to go her own way and she wouldn't take any notice of him. She'd always been self-willed, first defying her father to marry him, Peter hadn't minded that, but it was another thing when she defied her husband!

It wasn't just her desire to get a job that bothered him, she was getting too many friends and that made him feel pushed out. There was Gill. He wondered if they discussed him when they had their cosy little chats. She couldn't say anything nasty about him. Wasn't he hard working, a good provider, and he loved her? What more could any woman ask for? He paid no heed to the little voice inside him that argued with him, saying that he had done very well for himself when he married Amy and her money.

She'd also become friendly with Miranda, but he guessed she wasn't that keen on her. Miranda could be very tiresome and Amy would be too polite to tell her so. Apart from that, Peter wanted to keep in with Ian who had proved himself to be a useful friend to have.

Thinking of Ian reminded him that he had invited Ian and Miranda round this evening for dinner, and Amy didn't know yet.

He ought to give her a ring and make sure she had something reasonable for dinner tonight, steak or something similar. He wasn't giving her much notice, but Amy was a fine cook, he knew she wouldn't let him down, and he always kept a good stock of wines and spirits.

He dialled their number and the telephone rang out relentlessly. He frowned, wondering where she could be and why the answerphone wasn't on so he could at least have left a message. Next he tried her mobile but that was switched off. Where the hell was she, and why was it switched off?

If he'd been alone he would have banged his desk with anger, but he remembered he was at work, amongst people who knew him as long suffering, good natured, Peter.

"Problems," enquired Steve, noticing his perplexed frown.

Peter gave an easy laugh. "Only women problems. That wife of mine is out again. I'll have to catch up with her later."

"I know what you mean," said Steve, grinning. Peter smiled affably at him as he replaced the receiver, although inwardly he was seething. Perhaps he should try Gill. But when he did Gill said she hadn't seen her for a couple of weeks. Miranda was next, but she was out. He could feel his anger rising when Amy's mother also confirmed that she hadn't seen her for a week. It was no good ringing Max, he had taken Anna away for a holiday abroad, so Amy couldn't be there.

Now he was on his own, Steve having left the room, and he could finally give vent to his anger. He banged the telephone receiver down as loud as he could in frustration. Damn her! Where was she? Out with her dratted dog, no doubt. When he saw her she would know about it. How could he organise a dinner party when he couldn't even get hold of her!

Amy came out of the dentist, glad to have got away with just an inspection. She was just in time to pick up Paul from school. Sarah was going to tea with a friend and would be coming back later.

"Did you have a nice day at school today?" she enquired, as he got in beside her.

"Yes Mummy. I haven't got much homework. Can I take Jasper to the park with Alan when we get home?"

Amy looked fondly at him. He might resemble Peter in looks,

81

but he didn't have his spiteful nature. He loved the dog and could be trusted to look after him carefully. Not only that, she felt that Paul was safe with Jasper for company.

"Don't let him get muddy and covered with grass like last time," she scolded, laughing.

Paul grimaced, remembering his fate, and Jasper's afterwards, had been a hot bath, much to their mutual disgust.

"I won't take him in the stream," he promised, and Amy smiled. She didn't really mind because the bond between him and his pet was very strong.

Whilst she was driving, she thought about the recent events in her life. She had promised to spend a night with Ian soon, and she meant it, but for the sake of appearances they must cool the lunch-time meetings. Brave words, but she was missing him so much!

In an effort to inject some normality back into her life she planned to visit Gill. She hadn't been round for at least two weeks, and she hadn't seen Miranda at all. She couldn't bring herself to see Miranda any more. She now admitted to herself that her meetings with Ian were not innocent, they were about to embark on an affair and her conscience couldn't handle seeing Miranda. They were playing a dangerous game but somehow she couldn't stop.

"Mummy, look! Daddy's in," exclaimed Paul in surprise, as they pulled into the drive and saw his car.

"Oh yes," said Amy, trying to remember if there was a reason for it. Peter had been buried in his newspaper this morning so she hadn't bothered to tell him she was going to the dentist. She parked her modest little ear behind his gleaming BMW.

Paul jumped excitedly out of the car. Going out was on his mind and it would only be allowed whilst there was daylight.

"Don't forget your bag," reminded Amy. Paul picked it up dutifully. Normally he wouldn't, but he was in a hurry to go out.

As she entered the kitchen she saw Peter, grumpy as usual. Paul had gone upstairs to change into his jeans, so he didn't see his father glowering at her. She wondered what had rattled his cage this time.

"You're home early?" she said enquiringly.

"Why do you have a mobile when it's always switched off?" he snapped, ". . . and where are the children?"

"Sarah's gone to tea with Amanda and Paul's getting changed," she said, trying to sound reasonable. He was trying to pick a fight and she could feel herself bridling at his attitude. She had probably forgotten to switch her phone back on after the dentist, but so what, she didn't have to be reachable every minute of the day!

Peter moved swiftly, pushing her against the wall and pinning her hands back with his. When in a temper he looked menacing, and Amy felt the all too familiar fear inside her.

"Where the hell have you been today!"

His arm was hurting hers and she felt anger for all the times she'd been treated like this. She'd put up with it to save her marriage but not any more, she had the courage to fight him. He was a monster!

"Let go of me you pig! I went to the dentist. Not that it's any of your concern where I go. You don't own me!"

Peter's hand released its iron hold and he gaped at her in amazement. It wasn't working any more and now he felt at a disadvantage. He used to see fear in her eyes, but nowadays all he saw was defiance. Like all bullies he was a coward, so he released her and stepped back, coughing awkwardly.

"If you'd left the answer machine on I could have left a message," he said, but this time he said it quietly.

Amy could feel triumph inside her. She should have stood up to him years ago. He was just a bully, all wind and waffle!

"I was late going out," she said, determined not to sound apologetic. "Anyway, what was so urgent that you had to reach me?"

"Ian and Miranda are coming to dinner tonight and I wanted to make sure you had enough food in," he said, feeling very out of his depth with her.

"Well you're lucky, seeing as you leave it so late to ask me!" said Amy sarcastically. "I have some steak in the freezer and I've made a trifle." Her voice was calm, which made him feel even more ridiculous.

Inside her heart was pounding. Thank God Peter couldn't see. She would see Ian tonight and she must hide her feelings. She would also have to face Miranda. No one must guess! It would be hard but very necessary. Peter had flared up over nothing today, but if he found out about Ian some people might say he'd be justified in his anger. But even knowing this made no difference to her intentions.

Chapter Twelve

"I'll see you on Sunday evening. Have a good weekend." Peter kissed Amy and the children as they stood at the door watching him go.

"Will you bring me back a present, Daddy?" tried Sarah, and Peter laughed at her impudence.

"I'm going on a training course, not a holiday," he reminded her, smiling. Then he capitulated a little. "We'll see if you're both good with your mother. I might bring you a small souvenir from Bristol."

Paul joined in. "Can I have a pen, Dad?"

"I'm not making any promises!" said Peter, adding firmly: "I must go now or I'll be late!"

Amy did not return his smile. He had noticed a certain coolness about her lately and he could only put it down to last Friday. How was he to know she'd been to the dentist if she didn't tell him? It was true she'd come up trumps at the dinner party. She'd cooked steak in pepper sauce, with new potatoes and vegetables. As well as this, she'd also done a prawn cocktail to start off with, and her trifle had been delicious too.

They'd washed it all down with a bottle of red wine, followed by a sweet wine with the dessert, and then he'd opened a bottle of malt whisky to round the evening off.

He'd even managed to talk Ian into looking at the lawn mower. He didn't want the expense of buying a new one, or hiring a gardener, and Ian had been faithful to his word. He had arrived on

84

Sunday morning and repaired it, just before Peter had been due to leave to take Paul to football. He'd offered him a beer but Ian had declined because he was also in a hurry.

Amy's coolness allowed him freedom from any small pangs of conscience that he might otherwise have suffered. He had tried to make love to her that night after the dinner party, but she had declined, saying she was too tired. In this instance he hadn't tried to assert his superiority over her. She hadn't been in awe of him earlier in the day, so the chances are she would have stood up to him again. He could sense her change towards him. Maybe it was PMT. He hadn't noticed it before but, like all women, she was difficult to understand at times, and he didn't feel inclined to work at trying to understand her.

Peter felt he could go away without any pangs of conscience. During the day he had to attend the seminar, but the nights were his own and, as Jessica was going too, he had no doubt it was going to be a bonking good weekend. He had some unfinished business with that red-headed lovely, which had been interrupted by Amy at the party. He knew he'd been a bit indiscreet that night, too much lager, but that girl was tempting and he couldn't wait to get her knickers off.

He started the car and strapped himself in, aware of his unsuspecting family watching him from the door,

"Bye everyone," he said, as he pulled away.

He reckoned it had been a good idea to use the car because the bank had reimbursed the train fare, and he was expecting Jessica to pay half towards the petrol. Oh yes, I've got it all worked out, he thought smugly.

He drove quickly towards her road, knowing that she would be waiting at the window of her flat and when she saw him she would come out looking pleased to see him. After Amy's coolness it would be a refreshing change.

Ian was still marvelling at how lucky he'd been that Miranda had opted to take the girls away for the weekend at exactly the same time as Peter was away on a training seminar. Miranda was accompanying her mother and Gwen to visit an elderly aunt in the country.

Miranda said Aunt Agnes wanted to meet her great nieces, and so the heavy mob were preparing to descend upon her and eat her out of house and home. He had no desire to go because he knew he was hopelessly outnumbered. He hoped, fleetingly, once again, that Linda and Sophie would not grow up to be like the female side of the family, whom he found to be a formidable bunch.

Even if he hadn't had Amy on his mind, he wouldn't have gone. On his mind was putting it mildly! She was dominating his every thought and move. He was experiencing a mixture of emotions; elation that she wanted him and fear that he might let her and himself down, and it was driving him crazy. He knew deep inside it wasn't merely sexual attraction, just being with her seemed so right that he couldn't feel guilty. He felt as if it was intended.

He knew that he had to be content with only seeing her on Saturday night because she didn't think she could risk Friday as well, he would just have to be lonely tonight, sit there and think about her, and play the dutiful husband when Miranda rang to say they had arrived safely.

He would miss the girls of course, but they were close to their mother, he couldn't deny that, and if they did split up he knew he would lose them. This thought made his heart ache, and he couldn't help wondering if it would have been any different if they had been boys. But, he chided himself, he had two lovely little girls and in his eyes they were unique.

He had really pushed the boat out for Saturday night and he knew Miranda would go mad if she knew. He'd booked a room at Selsey Park Hotel, which was about fifteen miles away from their neighbourhood. Normally he wouldn't have stayed in such affluent surroundings, his earnings didn't warrant it, but these circumstances weren't normal.

Amy came from a wealthy family and she lived in a big and comfortable house. This was the sort of life she was used to. He didn't do this consciously to impress her, only to provide her with what he felt she would expect.

Selsey Park Hotel was set in several acres of beautiful grounds, containing a golf course and just about every other leisure facility that anyone could want. The rooms were de luxe, with luxury furniture and fitted carpets, telephone, cable TV, video and radio. You name it, they had it. The food was served on silver platters and the waiting staff wore evening dress.

Ian was determined not to appear out of his depth, and had his evening suit out and ready to wear. They could dance and dine in the main dining room if they wanted, or eat in the privacy of their own suite. Ian planned to go along with whatever Amy wanted to do, and he would make sure that he arrived looking smart, because in this place they didn't let just anyone in.

He had decided to pay the bill with cash so as not to arouse Miranda's suspicions when the credit card bill came in. He felt once again in his pocket to make sure the wad of notes was secure. He had already paved the way with Miranda by telling her he was drawing out three hundred pounds from their joint account to buy some parts for the car. She had believed him when he said that if he paid by cash he would be given discount, and as he usually did his own repairs to save garage bills, the story sounded convincing.

He looked around the empty house which seemed so lonely without the girls. Miranda, as usual, hadn't left it very tidy. She'd gone out in a hurry, and the girls had left their toys all over the bedroom floor as usual. He picked them up, putting them in the toy box in the corner. There, at least they could walk through to their beds when they came home without tripping over Barbie dolls. He made a mental note to rebuke them for it when they returned. They were as untidy as their mother.

Looking at his watch, he could see it would be at least two hours before they arrived and Miranda would ring him. If only he could have seen Amy tonight! He brightened. At least he could talk to her on the telephone, even just hearing her voice would be soothing. He picked up the receiver and dialled her number.

Amy took great pains with her appearance that Saturday evening. She was going to Selsey Park, for the first time, and she had heard just how nice it was. No one in jeans would be allowed inside it, not that she wore jeans at night, and tonight she would be dressed in a black cocktail dress which was right for any occasion, and as the weather was cold, she planned to wear her grey imitation fur coat.

She remembered when Daddy had bought it for her last birthday. He had wanted to buy her a real fur, he could certainly afford it, but Amy had been adamant. She was too much of an animal lover to want a real fur coat, and he had respected her wishes. Peter had thought her mad, but then he didn't share her love of animals.

She ran her fingers over her black tights to check there were no holes or snags in them, and when she was satisfied, she put them on. Her black patent shoes would look best with them, and she slipped them on and glanced in the mirror at herself. Her high necked dress needed some relief at the top, so she chose some chunky gold hooped earrings and a necklace that matched. That looked better, she felt.

Her hair was getting longer now. She was tired of short bobs. She brushed it until it shone with health. Her eye-shadow was a deep shade of blue, carefully chosen to accentuate the colour of her eyes, and their reflection stared innocently back at her as she applied her lipstick. But she wasn't innocent, was she? She was being a bitch to Miranda for fancying her husband so much. She really didn't understand herself, but something was driving her on and she didn't seem to have the power to stop it.

She sprayed herself with perfume. The label guaranteed it would knock men out, and she hoped it would rouse his ardour. If it didn't, she would, and she felt no embarrassment about what she would do.

Her local library had supplied her with a book about male impotence and how to overcome it. She hadn't dared to bring it home in case Peter saw it, but she had spent three hours at the library reading it from cover to cover. It had been enlightening, and she now realised how sensitive he would be. It could also cause him pain, and a fear of failure. It would need all her patience and understanding, and even then success might not be achieved tonight. After knowing only Peter it would be quite a delicate experience but one she was determined to cope with.

Paul, Sarah, and Jasper, were with her parents tonight, and she had told them she was at a dinner party at Gill's and might stay overnight. It was a lie she had to risk because she couldn't think of anything else. Her parents never saw Gill, and if her mother, or the children, should innocently let slip to Peter, then she would have to take a chance and use her as an alibi. She was sure Gill wouldn't let her down, but she hoped not to have to put her to the test. Derek was also away on the seminar, so he wouldn't know anything either.

She had packed her suitcase containing overnight things, including a red satin slip. It usually hung in her wardrobe unused, but now she had a reason to wear something to stir his passion. Peter didn't need to be turned on, in fact sometimes she felt he was oversexed, but she hoped that this bright shiny creation would arouse Ian and stir his sexual appetite.

She switched the answerphone on, hoping that if Peter telephoned he would think she had gone to bed early. A quick glance around her confirmed that she had left the house in a tidy state. It seemed rather cold and lonely without the familiar presence of the children and Jasper, and she had no desire to stay there alone.

Amy had planned to return after lunching with her parents on Sunday and picking up the children. She intended to ring them in the morning about the time they woke up, just in case they tried to ring her at Gill's.

Her heart was doing somersaults when she weighed up the risks she was taking. The more she thought about it, the more she realised Gill must be pre-warned. She had only held back before because this new experience was sacred to her, and she wanted to keep it private, but common sense must prevail. Gill must be told as much as she dared to tell her.

She quickly dialled Gill's number and it rang out for quite a while before she answered it. Amy rushed on as soon as the familiar husky voice announced the number.

"Gill, it's Amy. I've phoned up to ask a favour please." She was dreading having to say it, but there was really no choice.

Gill sounded a little distant. "Well, make it quick Amy. I'm otherwise occupied, if you know what I mean."

Then it hit Amy with a flash. Of course, Derek had gone too. Gill was making hay whilst the sun shone. She must have someone there. Amy said hesitantly. "I'm going out tonight and Peter doesn't know. I wanted to keep it a secret, and I wondered, if anyone asked, would you say that I came to dinner with you and stayed the night."

Now she did feel guilty, knowing that Gill must realise what she was up to, and there was a momentary silence whilst Gill digested her words.

"Well I never!" Gill's amused voice came over the telephone

89

line. "It must be a man Amy, who is it?"

Amy could feel herself flushing and the blood was pounding in her head. She couldn't tell her that. Oh no, she mustn't expose him! She spoke slowly and reluctantly. This hadn't been a good idea, but what other choice was there?

"I can't tell you his name, Gill, he's married. Will you give me an alibi?"

Gill was knocked for six. So goody goody Amy was at it too. She would never have believed it of her. But there again, maybe she was paying Peter back for his behaviour at the party recently. Well good luck to her.

Gill had a sexy stud to share her bed tonight. Her parents had agreed to keep the boys overnight after taking them to a pantomime, and she was desperate for a night of unbridled passion. Maybe this time, with Brian, she would forget about Derek. He certainly had the looks and physique, and he didn't have a wife. He was divorced.

"Amy, your secret is safe with me. Have a lovely time!" Her voice drawled with sexual undertones, and Amy flushed again at the other end of the phone. Why did Gill have to cheapen it?

"Thanks Gill, I'll be in touch next week," she said awkwardly, and was relieved to be able to put the receiver down.

She couldn't criticise Gill's behaviour because she was no better. But somehow she felt, before this even got off the ground, if it ever did, that fate had thrown them together and it was useless to try and fight it.

She glanced around her once more, picked up her overnight bag and headed for the door, firmly squashing down any feelings about changing her mind. He would be sitting in the car at the end of the drive waiting for her now, and she was going with him, no matter how wrong it might be.

Chapter Thirteen

Amy felt flushed and happy. She had just shared an exquisite meal with Ian. They hadn't gone to the dining room, preferring to savour this brief time they had together. So they dined in their room, feeling content with each other's company, in their own private little world.

Ian looked at her sitting there. She had such a glow about her. She seemed a poised and confident woman. He sipped his wine slowly, his brown eyes surveying her with such tenderness. Peter was a fool, in his opinion, a crude ignorant fool who didn't know a lady when he saw one. Perhaps he wasn't quite a wife beater, spiteful and immature in his behaviour by the sound of it, but certainly not deserving to have a wife like her.

Ian wanted so much to make love to her and cherish her, he only hoped he could. If he could have a very small part of her life, a few stolen hours every so often, it would give some sort of meaning to his life. He would settle for that rather than nothing at all.

He had been careful to have only one glass of wine, knowing that it might help him to relax, but any more than that might make his impotency worse. He couldn't bear to fail her and himself. This thought kept him sober.

Her blue eyes looked back at him. How he loved the way they held his, beguiling and full of warmth. Her mouth was soft, her lips moist, and unable to resist any more, his lips found hers and his arms went round her.

She returned his kiss with such passion it made his head spin, and when their lips eventually parted, he moved to put his glass on the table. He needed both hands to be free. Who needed wine with intoxicating lips like that to kiss anyway?

They were sitting on the bed now and he sought her lips again, whilst his hands stroked her beautiful neck. She shivered with delight, and her response thrilled him so much that he could feel the stirring of an erection.

Amy tried to take things slowly, trying to remember what she'd read in the book. Lots of kissing and touching, plenty of stimulation without worrying about the outcome, and relax and enjoy it. Well she was doing that all right, but Ian was in such a hurry to get her dress off, she couldn't slow him down.

As soon as his feverish hands had unclipped her bra she felt those dizzy thrills running through her, and she gasped with delight when he looked at her naked breasts, and then unable to contain himself any longer, his hands touched her and then his lips. She shuddered with rapture as her first orgasm ripped through her when his lips fastened on her erect nipples.

She was panting now, longing to be naked for him, wanting to feel his sexy mouth all over her. What a night this was going to be!

She had to make his pleasure as intense as hers, she knew that, and then they could share the joy of their sexual union together. She tried to detach her mind from what he was doing to her, but it was hard, her body felt on fire, and he had now removed all her clothes and was murmuring his appreciation of her beautiful nakedness.

Amy tried to leave the heights of paradise to concentrate on him. Her hands stroked the bulge in his trousers and then fumbled impatiently with his zip. Momentarily closing her eyes in rapture as his sensitive hands parted her thighs and gently stroked the very moist centre of her clitoris.

Her hands closed over his throbbing penis and she heard him gulp with pleasure, which spurred her on even more, wanting to make him feel the way he was making her feel. She worked on him with both hands, one of them rubbing his pulsating penis whilst she used the other to stroke the sensitive tip.

"No, No, enough, I'll come!" he groaned, and she eased up, and in return, his fingers teased her erect clitoris until her body shook with a mind-blowing orgasm, and she had to beg him to stop.

"I need you now!" he gasped, and she moved swiftly whilst he was ready for her. His voice was soft and sensual.

"Kneel, it'll be deeper," and she felt another thrill at the thought of it. She groaned as he entered her from behind. It felt fantastic, and she felt as though she was on her way to heaven.

"Oh, please no, I'm coming already!"

Even as he spoke those passionate but desperate words, she felt him explode inside her, his erection dying a very rapid death. She squashed down her disappointment. She had yearned for that wonderful final orgasm that they should have shared together and her body felt cheated, but she would never tell him. That would be so selfish!

Ian moved quickly away from her, his head buried in his hands, and to her amazement he was crying, something she had never seen a man do before. She put her arms around him, saying gently, "Thank you, that was lovely, I've never been touched like that before."

Ian's brown eyes, wet with tears, met hers. "Don't be kind to me, I'm a freak! You need a man who can make love to you properly. I've made such a fool of myself and let you down badly!"

"Don't be so hard on yourself," said Amy calmly. "You are gentle and considerate. I'm not used to that. We can get it right with time and patience."

Her words were sincere, she cared about his feelings of failure so much that it swept her disappointment aside. She kissed his wet cheek gently, feeling moved by his show of emotion.

Ian's brown eyes looked beseechingly into hers. "I still feel I let you down by coming too soon. I want to try again later. I had so much more love that I wanted to give you."

Amy stared at him. He had said 'love' not 'sex'. Was it a slip of the tongue? Whether it was or not, she vowed to do her utmost to make tonight memorable for both of them.

"Don't worry about it," she soothed him. "I'm going to take a shower, and then I could think of nothing nicer than going to sleep with your arms around me."

"Anytime," he murmured, and after she had taken her shower, he came into the bathroom, handed her a towel, and then took her place under the running water.

Amy didn't bother to put on her satin slip, she slipped straight between the silky sheets, and when he got in beside her, she could feel the fresh aroma of his clean body next to hers. Her longing for him rose again and her body was alight with thrills. "I'm not a super stud, Amy, as you've found out, but God I can't get enough of you. Please help me!"

She gulped as his mouth moved down her naked body and it sent her wild with desire. All thoughts of modesty were cast aside, lust reigned supreme, and the craving to do something for him just had to be satisfied. She wanted to turn him on and make him feel as he had never felt before.

"It's your turn now to be kissed," she gasped, and she very gently used her tongue and her lips to tease him into life again. His tongue continued to drive her wild, and she felt triumph when his flaccid organ sprang to life once more with her gentle but sensual stimulation. He was panting again, and she sensed that the point of his passion was reached, so she climbed on top of him and took control. His hardness inside felt wonderful, and this time they would make it together, she was determined.

She moved up and down on him, and this time they started their ascent to paradise together. He was creating feelings inside her that she had never experienced before. Her body merged with his and they became as one person. She could feel a lot more than lust for this man. Warmth and love, caring and sharing this wonderful expression of their feelings moved her so indescribably, in a way that lovemaking with Peter never had.

When her orgasm came it was at the exact moment that he exploded inside her, and the joy that she felt that he had finally conquered his impotence moved her to tears. "Thank you!' she sobbed. "You made me feel fantastic!"

Ian's confidence was growing, as she had intended it to. He felt a warm rush of emotion inside as he gently kissed her lips, and said fervently, "Amy, I've never felt like that before! What have you done to me? I feel complete for the first time in my life. You've given me everything, my virility, my self respect, and I owe it all to you!"

Amy stroked his hair tenderly. She could care for him so easily. But where would it lead. For one wild moment she wished they could just up and run away together.

"Please don't cry Amy, you mean the world to me! You've made me a man again. I love you! You're my life, and I can't let you go back to your ungrateful husband!"

As she gazed back at him, her own words didn't surprise her.

"I love you too," she murmured softly, and she felt relief in admitting what she had felt inside from the moment she had first met him. This was not just an affair.

Chapter Fourteen

Amy found it very hard to leave Ian that Sunday morning. They had shared a wonderful night of perfect happiness, and he had stirred her emotional feelings so deeply, that she felt she would burst with joy. She was in love, there was no use denying it, but they both had another life to go back to, and they shared the same concern for not wanting to hurt their children.

Ian had opened up fully to her, finally unburdening all his sorrows. He told her that he was so moved by these feelings of love for her, it was so totally different from anything he had ever experienced before. Not only did he no longer love Miranda but he doubted if he ever had. With Amy it was a lot more than just passion, it was feeling complete, caring and needing one another so much.

"You're like a breath of spring after her, Amy," he said warmly. "When we make love you care more about me than yourself. You were made to be loved, so gentle and loving. I just want to go on learning everything about you and enjoying the wonderful things you do."

Amy knew what he meant, and she was not embarrassed. She kissed him gently and looked him straight in the face.

"Ian, I feel so close to you, and I want you to know that I'm not a tart. You are the only other man I have had sex with. I hope I made you feel as wonderful as you made me feel. You bring out the vamp in me, and I love it!"

"Well that's honest. You wanton woman!" laughed Ian,

hugging her to him, and Amy quipped back:

"Yes, I'm want'n, but I'm not gett'n."

"Once more, if I can," he promised; and with her gentle help once again he was able to make love to her, and to their delight it took him longer to climax, adding to their mutual pleasure.

When it was over he held her tightly. "I could think of nothing nicer than spending my life in penile servitude to you," he said grinning, and Amy laughed too. Not only did she love him, he was also fun to be with, unlike Peter.

She had come down to earth with a bang when she realised she had to return to her less than idyllic situation at home. The thought of Peter's hands on her after Ian was abhorrent to her, even if he was her husband. But how could she stop it happening without arousing suspicion?

She was now plagued with jealousy at the thought of Ian returning to Miranda. He still shared her bed, even if they didn't make love any more. But how long would Miranda tolerate such a situation? The more she thought about it all, the more of a mess it was, but they had both known it would be and that hadn't stopped them. She wondered how long she could keep it from Peter. She wasn't used to lying and cheating, and now she had finally made love with Ian, because in her mind that described it exactly, she did pity Peter.

Did he love her or was she a mere convenience? Was he outwardly going through the motions of marriage but quite happy to lead separate lives? Somehow she doubted that, he was too possessive, even about friends like Gill, so maybe he did love her in his way, but it wasn't in the same way that Ian loved her, and it was the respect that Ian gave her that she craved.

He kissed her yet again, tightly holding her hand. Oh God, this was hard! Amy tried to be strong.

"I love you so much Ian, but I must go and fetch Sarah and Paul. If I don't get to my mother's soon it will look suspicious."

"Yes my love, I know," said Ian sadly. After a night like that he had to face the rest of the day alone, as Miranda and the girls weren't due back until about six o'clock. Having discovered such happiness with Amy he was dreading being alone.

"Amy, this is tearing me apart! You must let me see you tomorrow!" he cried passionately, his eyes mirroring the desperation of his love for her. The thought that he might lose her

97

was gnawing away at his inside like a virulent sickness.

"Of course you can! That's what will keep me together. I can hardly wait!" cried Amy, just as passionately. She was trying desperately to keep everything on a normal plane, but it was hard when her heart was telling her she wanted to spend the rest of her life with him, not just a few stolen hours.

She very reluctantly released herself from his arms, feeling the tears prick at her eyelids. She vowed to be strong, otherwise she would never leave him.

"Bye my love, until tomorrow, and take care."

Ian watched her walk up the drive, turning back to wave to him before she went inside. Oh how he longed for her to come back and kiss him again! But she wouldn't, she hadn't let him drive inside in case of nosey neighbours. After picking up her car she would drive to her mother's and have lunch and then return with Paul and Sarah. If only he dared to ask her to leave Peter for him.

In an ideal situation they could be together with all the children, but he knew Miranda wouldn't part with the girls, and they probably wouldn't want to leave their mother either.

He had nothing to offer her except love. She came from an affluent background, and he was married to a woman who spent everything he earnt. What chance was there for them? But he needed her so much. She was like a drug to him. She had re-awakened all his desires. Thanks to Amy, he could feel and love again, and he couldn't bear the thought of Peter touching her, even though, as her husband, he had every right to.

He told himself very sternly to pull himself together, he was no good like this. His trembling hand put the car into gear and he drove off. Maybe going home wasn't the answer. He would pop round and see Mum.

"So long Jessica, see you at work." Peter winked at her as she got out of the car. He felt absolutely shattered, but it had been fun. Jessica would keep her mouth shut, he was sure, having already had a taste of Amy's wrath.

Amy had a bearing about her that made you feel really low when you upset her. He'd suffered it too, so he had every confidence that their weekend would remain a secret. He had to admit, regretfully, to himself, that although he was only thirty-one, he was having trouble burning the candle at both ends. Jessica had kept him busy all of Friday night, wanting orgasm after orgasm, and making sure that he also enjoyed himself. But that's where woman reigns supreme, he thought enviously. He'd managed three climaxes of his own, and that wasn't bad after all that drink, but she seemed to have one after another, with the eternal zest of a very sexually active eighteen-year-old.

They had probably slept for less than two hours, and he had staggered down to breakfast and tried to tank himself up with black coffee to relieve the hangover, and also in an attempt to awaken his tired brain.

The seminar had passed in a haze. He hadn't learnt a thing this weekend, other than how to satisfy Jessica, and although he had started to feel a bit more with it by Saturday evening, the sexy little cow had started on him again, and this time, to his immense pride, he'd managed to screw her four times, and once again they had spent most of the night working up to it and there wasn't much time for sleep.

Thank goodness the seminar had only been a résumé on Sunday morning, and he'd managed to plead feeling a little unwell. Jessica had passed him her notes, which he'd read out to the instructor, who seemed quite pleased that he'd written down so much, even though he wasn't feeling great. Thanks to her he'd got out of that one nicely.

They had set off for home after lunch and the randy little bitch had only wanted him to stop the car in a deserted part of some woods they passed on the way. What did she think he was? The trouble was, she wouldn't take no for an answer, and whilst he was driving she'd unzipped his trousers and started on him. He felt quite proud to see it standing up yet again, and she certainly was a tease with her hands and her mouth. It hadn't taken him long to decide to pull off the road, and she kept him on the boil until he stopped the car.

It had been very quick. They hadn't even made it into the back seat. He'd taken her kneeling on the front seat, doggy-fashion, and she loved it. Her squeals of joy as he burst inside her were further heightened when she explained afterwards that she had looked out of the window and seen a man walking his dog, who had stood still, knowing what was happening, and watched.

She just didn't care. She was totally uninhibited, and Peter had to admit, regretfully, that a weekend was quite enough, fun though it had been. He just wouldn't be able to live at her pace for long. What was he turning into, a boring married man?

Thank God he'd had that vasectomy operation after Sarah had been born. His in-laws had been impressed by his caring attitude towards Amy, but Peter, as usual, had his own motive. He could sew his wild oats occasionally without any fear of little Peters being born.

Now that Jessica had gone and he was alone again, he just wanted to go home and see Amy and the children. He hoped her coolness had passed. When he stopped to think about it, he had missed her, and if Jessica hadn't started to get into his trousers as soon as she'd come to his room, he would have found the time to telephone and say that he had arrived safely. It was all her fault.

Derek would keep quiet, even though he'd seen them together. He was a dark horse himself, but he didn't appear to cheat on Gill, which was surprising.

Maybe he didn't realise that she did it to him. Peter had sensed her availability for years, but resisted so far, knowing that she was a bit too close to home. Nevertheless, he enjoyed flirting with her, and Derek never seemed to mind.

He turned into the drive and saw Amy's car parked there. She must be getting tea. Everything was back to normal and he could now resume his role of loving husband and father.

"Hello Mum, how are you?"

"Better now I've seen you."

Janet Wood couldn't disguise the pleasure in her eyes, and she hugged him warmly. "Come in son, I've got the kettle on."

Ian strode into the small flat. It seemed even smaller since he'd moved into his own home. Not that Mum needed much room these days with himself and Robin both married, but he hadn't forgotten those years at home, how she'd struggled on her own to bring them up. She had gone to work to do so and he'd been a latch key kid, not that he blamed her for that, with an absent father who made no contribution towards their welfare. She had done the very best that she could to keep a roof over their heads, and succeeded, and he had a great admiration for her.

He hadn't been round to see her for a while, and they both

knew why. He watched her making the tea, wondering if she would mention it. How long had she had that old brown teapot she was filling? Years! And the old carpet and shabby furniture were all an indication of her lack of money. All this had made him determined to buy his own home when he got married, and small though it might be, it was a palace in comparison to this.

Janet paused whilst pouring the tea. "How are the girls?" she enquired.

"They're fine!" said Ian warmly, and he felt guilt rush through him. "I'll bring them round to see you soon."

Janet's face changed from its severe expression when she smiled. "I'd like that, make it soon!" and once again he felt guilty.

She wouldn't mention Miranda, and over the years that had been the cause of all the trouble. He'd tried to understand that his mother had really had a rough deal in life. She'd been abused by her husband and it had been a relief when he left. Then she had found out he never was her husband when he was jailed for bigamy. Ian couldn't remember much about him, only that he was a tall man with dark hair, a naval seaman, who had left when he was about four.

Robin had more memories because he had been seven, and most of his mother's ill treatment had been when she was defending Robin. Even as a small child, Robin was one of those people who got under your skin, and as he became older, he became worse. He was cocky and arrogant, a born womaniser, married to a long suffering wife. But despite that, his mother wouldn't have a word said against him. She had loved them both with the fierce possessive love of a woman who clings to her children because they are all she has.

She hadn't wanted either of them to marry, but they had both realised that they must break away from her before it became too late. Robin, as the eldest, had been first, and his wife, Caroline, had been wise, she had made a friend of Janet, taking her out in the car, getting shopping for her and making sure that she invited her over regularly. When the children came along, Janet would frequently baby-sit, and this was a good arrangement on both sides.

It hadn't been like that with Miranda. As soon as Janet met her, she disliked her on sight. Miranda couldn't do a thing right and Ian found himself in the middle of two warring women. He found

101

that the more Janet denigrated her, the more he felt that Miranda was being victimised. It made his love seem stronger and eventually he had left home to marry, and his mother had refused to come to the wedding.

This had grieved him deeply, but he was determined that Janet was not going to rule him. He visited her on rare occasions, always alone, until Miranda became pregnant. He had told Janet very strongly then, that unless she was kinder to his wife, her grandchildren would grow up without ever knowing her.

Janet was stubborn, but she did want to see her grandchildren, so a very shaky relationship developed, so shaky that the two women were frequently falling out. Unfortunately, he was now beginning to realise that all the things his mother disliked about her were true. She was lazy, untidy and self centred. He'd wished a thousand times that his mother had kept quiet at the time instead of pushing them together even more. Their marriage had been a fatal mistake, but it might never have happened if she had let him find out for himself.

He pushed these uncharitable thoughts out of his mind, remembering that Janet was a lonely woman, and spoke confidentially to her.

"Mum, I've come round to tell you something very private and I need your advice."

Janet looked up in surprise. Ian asking advice? She'd been trying to give it to him for years but he'd never listened. Why the sudden change now?

"I'll try to help if I can," she said gently.

"To put it in a nutshell Mum, I don't love Miranda any more. You were right about her. I've met a girl that I do love. She's married with children, but I want to spend my life with her. She comes from a wealthy family and I've nothing to offer her. It's all such a mess!"

He covered his face with his hands, and Janet sat quietly sipping her tea, trying to absorb these startling revelations. It would be so easy now to say, 'I told you so,' but that wouldn't put things right. Maybe she should have left him to find out before they got married, instead of doing her utmost to prevent their marriage. Ian shared his mother's stubborn nature, so she should have realised that her efforts would be fruitless.

It was true that she'd never liked Miranda. She had always got under Janet's skin, so self-centred and spoilt, and she'd also committed the sin of taking Ian away so that Janet now had to face life alone. But now her own conscience nagged at her. Like it or not, Miranda was the mother of Linda and Sophie, her delightful granddaughters, and she owed her a loyalty.

She remembered back to Ted, her own philandering husband, his tempers, his violence, and then the poverty and the struggle to survive when he went. Thank God Ian wasn't like him! He had always been such a gentle boy with lovely manners, unlike his brash and boastful brother, whom she loved in spite of all his failings. She loved them both, but Ian had turned out the best, definitely. Robin's problems, she felt, had been the result of his ill-treatment by his father.

She was very proud of Ian. If he left Miranda, Linda and Sophie would suffer the loss of a very good father, and Miranda would probably never let her see them at all. It would be such a tragedy! She put down her empty cup and spoke firmly to him.

"Well Ian, you know I've never liked Miranda, so I can't blame you for finding someone else, but don't even think about leaving your girls. They need you, and you owe it to them to keep your home together!"

Ian looked at her incredulously. He had expected her to be over the moon that he wanted to leave Miranda, and had definitely expected her to support him. He was beginning to think now that the girls would suffer more if he continued with this loveless marriage, because that's what it was. A good clean break now seemed to be the answer, but his mother's opposition to it made everything even more complicated.

Maybe she was right, but he knew that he didn't want to make the best of things. He wanted Amy, selfish or not, the way she made him feel was something he just couldn't do without. His life had been ripped apart with this feeling of emotion. Well it looked like he was on his own, once again without his mother's support. He thought about it on the way home and decided, even if he was, he still had to do it, but it didn't stop the ache in his heart from persisting.

103

Chapter Fifteen

David rose from his chair, as the girl with the long, blonde hair entered the bar lounge. He knew instinctively that it was her.

"Sally?" he asked, smiling.

"That's right," she said, gripping his outstretched hand, and returning his smile.

"Would you like a drink?" he enquired hospitably.

"Yes please, scotch on the rocks," she replied.

He could see that this one was a harder nut all right. She didn't have the warmth and air of naïvety that Jenny did, but she would do for tonight. No doubt she would be good at sex, like they all were, at the end of the evening.

He would miss Jenny, but he had to make a change now, before she ruined his future. She had started to get serious, and that wouldn't do, professing to love him and asking him to leave Susan for her. He was flattered of course, but if any hint of his other life got out, he could forget his chances of becoming an MP.

So he had finished it, no more meeting her, and as she hadn't known his real name, or where he lived, chances are she would never track him down. The agency wouldn't give her any information either, he was confident of that. He'd made a change in the venue, another hotel where no one knew him, and another change in name in case Jenny knew Sally. But the agency said it was highly unlikely and they would do everything to keep his identity a secret.

David had slipped them some extra money for this service, but there was a small regret inside him for the loss of Jenny. They'd had some memorable times together, mainly because she reminded him of Susan when they had been young.

"Waiter, can you bring us some drinks please?"

The man took their order, and David pulled back the chair for her to sit down at the table opposite him. She had good skin and very even teeth when she smiled. The cream dress she was wearing showed off her tan, and she was tall and slim.

"Do you smoke?" she enquired, taking a packet of cigarettes from her handbag.

"No thank you!" said David, and his eyes must have shown his disapproval. It was the one thing he abhorred, a woman with breath that smelt of stale tobacco, and being touched by nicotine stained fingers. He shuddered at the thought of it.

Sally was quick to spot his reaction, and her response was immediate. "You're very wise, and I'm trying to give up anyway," she said brightly, putting the unopened box back into her handbag. She didn't want to lose this date because she needed the money, so she would just have to suffer a night without a puff, at least until they'd parted company. He was a nice looking, mature man, and she was assured of a first class meal inside her tonight. Judging by the hint dropped by Moira from the agency, that wouldn't be the only thing inside her.

Still, he had to pay extra for that, and he didn't look like the back of a bus. His clothes were expensive looking, so who knows, he might reward her well with a good performance. She thought of all the bills mounting up and the threat of eviction hanging over her. Yes, she would certainly give him a good night if that's what he wanted.

The words of his mother were still ringing in Ian's ears when he went to bed that night. There was one more thing he had to understand about his body, and he had to put it to the test. He had to know whether these sexual feelings were for Amy only, or whether now that his sexual confidence had returned he could still make love to his wife. His mother believed he should stay with his children, and the only way to make his marriage last was to bring sex back into it.

It was a brave thought, but when he looked at Miranda, and

105

then thought of Amy, he just couldn't do it. Amy was unique, and he was totally in love with her. Even the knowledge that Miranda was the mother of his children could not spur him on to try and make love to her. How long could his marriage survive without love?

He found out the answer that night. He went to bed early feigning an upset stomach. Endless excuses to avoid intimacy, and he knew it would annoy her as this was becoming a habit now. He drifted off into a rather troubled sleep. He was with Amy, but she was crying and begging him not to leave her. He held her tightly to him and then he felt her hands, those wonderful sensitive hands, stroking his penis, and to his great joy it responded and surfaced proud and erect.

Then she was gripping it and panting, guiding it between her thighs, and at that moment when he entered her, he knew it was not Amy, it was Miranda, and he awoke with a start.

She was moaning with delight, which was not surprising after such a long time, but he felt dead inside. All he could think of was that he was being unfaithful to Amy. He felt sick and disgusted with himself.

Miranda was so far gone with her own enjoyment that she didn't seem to notice, but that was how it had always been. She took everything but never gave anything back. He could feel his erection dying and she chose that moment to tell him that she loved him. "I'm coming, I'm coming!" she declared passionately.

Miranda's body chose that exact moment to erupt into such a powerful climax that she didn't even notice. She was still shuddering with delight when his flaccid manhood escaped from her cavernous depths, and she hadn't even noticed that he didn't climax. He was still horror struck that he could have mistaken her for Amy in the first place.

He now knew there was only one girl for him. That little episode had proved it. He vowed to himself that whatever happened to him in his future life, if he couldn't make love to Amy, then he didn't want anyone else at all.

Amy was relieved that Peter hadn't made any sexual demands on her last night. His weekend at the seminar had obviously made him very tired and she wasn't sorry. In fact he had been so pleased to see them all, that he played on the computer with the children with the new game he had bought as a present for them, right up until it was time for their baths and bed.

He had been warm and kind to Amy too, which was unusual, telling her to sit down because she looked tired, and making her tea. He wasn't usually so caring, and she accepted his ministrations awkwardly. His gentleness made her guilt even harder to bear. If he had treated her in his usual rough way, she could have told herself that her love affair with Ian was fully justified, but this time he didn't, and even as they went to bed, he told her with absolute sincerity:

"I know I'm a bit of a loud-mouthed rough-neck at times Amy, but I don't mean it. I really love you and the kids."

Amy was stunned at his confession, the first time in years he had ever owned up to being less than perfect, and what a time to do it! It was almost as if he had sensed something. But he couldn't, she reasoned with herself. She had told him she had gone to dinner with Gill and stayed the night, expecting jealous and sarcastic comments, but there were none.

She'd also told him that the children and Jasper had been with her parents, before they did. His reaction had been very reasonable.

"I'm glad you went out for a change. I'm sure it did you good," he said warmly, and this made her feel so uncomfortable. This was so unlike him.

At bedtime he had done no more than sleep with his arms lovingly round her, and she hadn't stopped that. It was almost as if he was clinging on to whatever there was left.

How many times had she stirred this cup of coffee whilst she was engrossed in her thoughts? It was Monday morning, the start of another week, and she could hardly wait for lunchtime when she would meet Ian.

She felt that magic feeling surge through her at the thought of him, the man who now dominated her life and robbed her of all reason. When she was in his arms everything else faded into oblivion, and no matter how short the time was that they spent together it was so precious.

How lucky Miranda was to wake up next to him every morning! She really envied her. But Miranda didn't realise how lucky she was, because if she had, their love affair would never

107

have happened.

The telephone interrupted her reverie and she went to answer it, hoping it wasn't Ian having to cancel their meeting. He didn't usually have the car, but Amy would pick him up in hers, just far enough away from the office for them to remain undetected.

It was Miranda, and she couldn't keep the jubilation out of her voice.

"Amy, I've got something wonderful to tell you. Do you remember that I told you that Ian and I had marital problems after his operation last year?"

"Yes," muttered Amy. How could she possibly forget? She could feel a cold hand clutching at her heart. She knew she had to listen, but she didn't want to hear what had made Miranda so happy.

Miranda rushed on excitedly. "It was last night. He touched me, and he hasn't done that for such a long time."

Amy felt the pain, like a very sharp knife, stabbing away at her heart, but still she had to listen. "Go on," she said quietly, her eyes were filled with tears. No matter how much it hurt she had to know.

"One thing led to another. I touched him and he was ready for me, if you know what I mean, and then it happened, we made love."

"That's good, now you can be close again," said Amy, desperately trying to conceal her emotions. She felt as if she would be sick. How could he go straight from her back to his wife, after all he'd said? He was just a phoney! She'd fallen in love with a phoney, that's all he was!

"It was quite a relief, I can tell you, after more than a year," laughed Miranda.

"Yes, it must be," agreed Amy, but inside her emotions were raging. Hurt and anger were seething away and she couldn't wait to get off the telephone to give vent to them.

"I've got to go now, Amy. I've booked some theatre tickets so we can go out tonight, and I need to ask my mother to baby-sit."

"Goodbye," said Amy curtly. Miranda wouldn't notice. She was too wrapped up in her own happiness.

Amy sat down and wept. How could she have been such a fool to give her heart away like that? She had helped him to regain his sexual confidence, and now Miranda was reaping the benefit.

Amy had helped to repair his marriage and shatter her own.

She felt as if she loved and hated him at the same time. Her jealousy was so strong that she felt positively sick inside. There was only one way out of this, and it would take all her self-control. She wouldn't meet him today, or ever again. She must put him out of her mind, count it as a lucky escape, and never see him again.

She left her mobile at home and switched off when the time came to meet him. If he left her messages, she would ignore them, and she took Jasper for a walk in a completely different place, so that there was no chance of meeting Ian. If he did have the car at the last minute, she was sure that when she didn't turn up, he would drive to the usual rendezvous to see if he had misunderstood the arrangements. She knew that if she stayed at home she would be hoping that the phone would ring, and that would be no good because then she might weaken.

The grey and forbidding March day totally matched her anger and melancholia, so she put on a warm hooded coat, and found a deserted park.

"It's just you and I, Jasper," she told him, and he wagged his tail in response.

Whilst she was walking she tried not to think about these things, but it all kept coming back to her. Was her jealousy making her unreasonable? Ian had a perfect right to make love to his wife. Amy was only his 'bit on the side'. She didn't like the thought of that, but it was true.

An affair with him was all she could expect, because she wasn't prepared to give up her children for him, nor did she expect him to give up his. Realistically speaking, as far as they were both concerned, to keep up an appearance of normality, they would have to submit to sex with their married partner once in a while. What had hurt Amy so much was the knowledge that so soon after sharing such a wonderful night of love, and declaring their true feelings for one another, he had turned to Miranda.

According to her it had been quite sensational, and this hurt her again after what she had shared with him. Who knows? Maybe he had decided to go back to Miranda and wouldn't have even been there to meet her today.

She strode even faster, fighting back the tears, which once again, threatened to fill her eyes. She was not going to think about him any more. After a glimpse of heaven, her life felt even more meaningless.

Maybe she owed it to Peter to try again too. If she made him stop bullying her, and she had once, life might be happier. But he would have to change. He stifled her. She needed to be allowed to have friends, hobbies and outings, without his unreasonable jealousy. Well Peter was never going to change that much, and it didn't alter the fact that she had fallen in love with Ian.

"Come on Jasper, let's go home," she called, and her faithful pet turned and followed her back towards the car.

Ian was longing for lunch-time to arrive so that he could see her and hold her. The girl of his dreams had now become a reality. Amy had proved to him that he was a man on Saturday night, and now he felt a complete person. He felt as if he couldn't get enough of her because the feelings she aroused in him were indescribable.

The morning seemed to take forever to pass and he tried very hard to concentrate on his work, but he could think of nothing except Amy. When at last the time arrived, he was intent on getting round the corner as quickly as possible, to the place where she would be waiting for him.

"You're in a hurry today, Ian!" remarked Clive.

In his haste to leave the office, he had knocked over a chair.

"Sorry," he said apologetically, stopping long enough to pick it up.

"Don't be late back," Clive reminded him. He'd noticed that Ian's lunch hours were getting a bit longer lately, although he had made up the extra time at night, so he couldn't have him for it. Anyone would think he had a bit on the side, he was so eager to get away. He certainly wouldn't be rushing off like that to meet his wife!

Ian left him musing at his desk. Clive's time was his own because he was out of the office quite a bit. Maybe one day Ian would be in that fortunate position. He didn't aim to stay a lowly bank clerk all his life!

He closed the office door gently, trying to make it appear that he wasn't in a rush. He pressed the lift button and tapped his fingers impatiently on the window sill. He was in a rush, and every moment that passed was wasted because he wasn't with her. He looked out of the window, across the blocks of offices, thinking that she was sitting in the car, only two streets away, waiting for him.

Thank goodness, the lift was finally here! He got in and was relieved to reach the ground floor. His impulse was to run, but he had noticed Clive's quizzical look a few minutes ago. If anyone else at lunch saw him running, they might wonder what the panic was too, so he walked briskly across the road and through the car park.

One more road to cross and she would be there, parked discreetly round the corner. They still had about fifty minutes to spend together, and he must try to be back on time after Clive's pointed remark. Mustn't arouse any suspicions.

His smile of happiness froze on his lips when he turned the corner and her car wasn't there. Amy was never late because she knew how short the time was they had together. His mind was filled with panic. Surely she hadn't had an accident?

He told himself to calm down and stop being ridiculous. She had probably got caught up in traffic and would be here soon. She hadn't rung his mobile, which he would have expected her to, so he rang hers but it went straight into answer mode. That in itself wasn't alarming because she might have left it at home. As much as he loved her, he knew she was scatty, and frequently forgot her mobile when in a hurry. This time it did matter, and he did need to reach her.

Next he tried her home number, but the only response was the answerphone. He didn't dare to leave a message in case Peter played it back later. Now he really was worried. Something must have happened to her on the way to meet him and he felt sick inside at the thought of it. There was no way that he wanted to go back to work and spend the afternoon worrying about her, but what other choice was there? He didn't have the car, and he wouldn't know where to start looking for her.

He paced up and down, nervously waiting for a while, and then glanced at his watch, only twenty minutes left now. He spent the next ten of them hanging around, just in case, but he knew she wouldn't come now. If only he knew where she was!

Eventually he decided to go back to the office. She could still ring his mobile until Clive came back and his lunch hour ended.

There might be a perfectly reasonable explanation for all this. He did hope so, because he feared that either she'd had an accident, or she had decided to go back to Peter.

He got back into the office with five minutes to spare before the others were due back, and as he sat down his extension rang. Hope flooded through his heart, and he picked it up quickly. His hope turned to irritation when he heard Miranda's voice.

"Hello Ian, it's me. Mum and Gwen are coming round to baby-sit tonight because I've managed to get us some theatre tickets. Can you get home early?"

His heart sank. Going out with Miranda was the last thing on his mind. Because of last night she thought everything was back to normal. How could he take her out and act normally when all he could think of was Amy?

This time, for the sake of peace, he would go. He wasn't ready at this moment to stand up to Miranda, her mother and Gwen, all together.

"I'll be in by six," he said gloomily.

Miranda couldn't hide her delight. "That's wonderful. We could eat out too."

"We'll see." Ian was non-committal. He really didn't care at all.

"You were great last night," said Miranda. "So great that I've got a confession to make." – Ian wasn't really listening. He was still worrying about Amy – "I told Amy, in confidence of course. I'm sure she'll keep it to herself."

As soon as Amy's name was mentioned, it hit him with a blinding flash, the realisation why Amy hadn't met him. She knew, and judging by the way Miranda would have told her, she would believe it was all over between them. He had quite a different story to tell, but Miranda, as usual, had got in first.

"You shouldn't have told her!" he cried angrily, and then to cover his anguish, he added: "I shall be embarrassed next time I see her."

"She won't mention it, I know," laughed Miranda. She was so elated that she hadn't even noticed his angry tone.

"I've got to get on with my work now," Ian said curtly.

"See you later then," murmured Miranda.

Her voice sounded so bright. She was so totally wrapped up in her own personal happiness, that she had no idea how he felt. If he wanted to be spiteful he could have told her that last night had meant nothing to him. She wasn't Amy and never could be.

All thoughts of work had vanished from his mind, and if he was putting his job in jeopardy then he couldn't help it. Tough! Amy was his only thought. He had no doubt that his dear wife would have upset her with a detailed and exaggerated description of their sexual encounter the night before. All he could hope for was that Amy would listen to his explanation.

He tried to ring again, but she still wasn't in, and he could feel his frustration building up inside. As he put the phone down, Clive, and other members of the office, came in.

"Ian, you're back before us!" said Clive in amazement, seeing him already seated at his desk.

"Yes, but I'm afraid I will have to go home. I don't feel well. I hope it's not 'flu."

He didn't feel guilty for lying. He had to see her at all costs, and soon. Even Clive's suspicious look did not make any impression on him.

"I'm sorry to hear that Ian, it must have come on very suddenly."

Ian blew his nose loudly. "Yes it did, so I came back early from lunch, but I really don't feel well enough to carry on."

"You'd better go home then, but let us know if you're not coming in tomorrow."

"Yes, of course."

Ian put his papers in his briefcase and reached for his coat. He didn't rush it, mustn't appear too eager. He turned to Clive as he was leaving. "I'll try to make it tomorrow if I feel better."

"OK old chap," remarked Clive with feigned sympathy. There was nothing wrong with Ian, he was sure. Later today he was going to ring and find out if anything else was going on. His eyes narrowed as he thought of what he suspected Ian was up to. If he did have a lady friend, a quick bonk at lunchtime was one thing, but he wasn't going to be allowed to do it all afternoon in the bank's time, that was a bit too much!

Chapter Sixteen

Gill was fed up. Brian had not come up to her expectations. His handsome looks and lithe body were a turn-on, for sure, but his sexual performance had been very disappointing. No wonder he was divorced!

She needed to talk to Amy, but Amy was neglecting her. She hadn't been round lately, one excuse after another, and as she'd supplied her with an alibi, the reason was clear, she was having an affair.

When Gill had got over the initial shock, she had felt pleased. Amy couldn't criticise her if she was up to it herself. After her recent revelations to Amy, Gill had wondered whether admitting to being unfaithful had been wise. If she had explained about Derek, maybe Amy would have understood, but her loyalty, and her love for him were too strong for her to unburden herself to anyone.

If only Amy would come round, they could have a laugh and compare experiences, but she hadn't. She was too busy with 'him' and Gill couldn't help wondering who he was, and how Amy had met him.

She had rung her several times, but Amy wasn't there. Gill envied her because obviously her lover was good if she saw him so often. Why couldn't she find someone like that to keep her satisfied and happy? Derek didn't want her. He had his own pursuits and she never interfered with those. She couldn't really!

It had been the worst shock of her life, after having two

children by him, to learn that her husband preferred men. But that was her secret. She wasn't going to humiliate herself to Amy or anyone else by admitting that she had been rejected by Derek, who favoured his own sex. That heartbreaking knowledge had precipitated her eternal quest for physical satisfaction. She could stay married to Derek and they could both lead their own lives. He was always very discreet. She couldn't fault him on that. He had a partner of long-standing, who lived about thirty miles away, so no hint of his other life was likely to follow him around.

It wasn't as if he looked that way, he wasn't effeminate in looks or gestures, just a very quiet man. No one ever knew anyone else's hidden depths really, and she had certainly been fooled by him when she fell in love.

Gill had never got over the shock, hence her continual need to project her sexuality. She had never stopped loving Derek either, even though the thought of his other life filled her with uncontrollable jealousy. There was also the worry that he might leave her for his 'friend' too. Sometimes she wondered if seeking help would be the answer, but then she realised it would make no difference. No amount of talking could change Derek back into a heterosexual male, and she marvelled how he had fooled her at the beginning of their marriage when their sex life had been so good.

Well it was Monday again, and she decided to try and get hold of Amy to find out who her stud was. But once again, all she got was the answerphone and she replaced the receiver in disgust. Ringing her mobile was a joke. It was on answerphone, and although she left a message she knew that by the time Amy got it, it would be too late for her to come round today. She was peeved that Amy was neglecting her, and more than a little jealous. When she did track her down, she was going to tell her off!

Amy took Jasper home before doing the school run. She decided to have a quick cup of tea, and whilst the kettle was on, she checked the answerphone.

There had been two calls but no messages. Her mobile had one from Gill, asking if she was coming round today. It was too late now, but she'd have to see her soon. Gill was her alibi. She must impress on Gill that Peter must never find out what she'd been up to.

After she had made some tea and sat down to drink it, the doorbell sounded. She looked out of the window but couldn't see a car in the drive. That's funny, she thought, it must be someone on foot whom she couldn't see, because they were standing right in the doorway. She opened the door with Jasper at her heels, but he didn't appear to be particularly upset by the intruder, and then she knew why.

Ian stood there, and his desperation showed in his eyes. "Amy, please let me explain!" he begged. "I love you and only you, no matter what you think."

She had intended to shut the door on him, to tell him to get out of her life and never come back, to say that she was going back to Peter and that she didn't need him, so he would feel as hurt as she was, but she said nothing.

His brown eyes seemed to have a hypnotic effect on her. The way he looked at her with such tenderness was melting her hostility. She tried, in vain, to be unmoved by his obvious distress. She could at least save her face by putting on an outward show of indifference, even if her heart was beating like crazy at the sight of him.

"What is there to explain, Ian?" she said coldly, and she saw the remorse in his eyes. So it was true. The wind gave a howl of indignation, as if echoing her thoughts, and Jasper gave a growl of retaliation.

Amy patted him gently. "It's all right Jasper, it's only the wind," she said soothingly, and when she turned back to Ian, who had still not replied, she said, as casually as she could muster. "You'd better come in. It's cold out there, and I don't intend to stand and freeze on the doorstep."

She knew she was taking a chance by asking him in, anyone might see them, but it didn't stop her. She just had to know if his feelings were the same as hers.

"Why aren't you at work?" she asked, puzzled, as he followed her into the lounge.

"I came away early. I just couldn't stay after you didn't turn up," he said miserably, his eyes mirroring his adoration of her.

Amy was now very confused. He took her hand in his, and she didn't snatch it away, so he went on to explain the situation.

"Amy, I know Miranda told you I made love to her, but that isn't strictly true, and I can imagine how you felt when on the same day I had told you that I loved you . . ." He paused, seeing her lip tremble. So she did care! ". . . Please understand, she woke me from a dream, and initially I thought it was you. When I realised otherwise, my body didn't respond. It was you that had made me back into a man again, and now I know my failure to make love to her before was not only because of my illness, but also because I no longer wanted to, because I don't love her."

She couldn't doubt his sincerity. It was written all over his face. His voice went on pleadingly.

"I got nothing from it Amy, nothing! I only want you from now onwards, and if I can't have you then I won't have anyone."

Amy had said nothing up until now, but she was very moved by his words. Maybe she was a fool, she didn't know, but she believed him. However he couldn't be allowed to get away with this too easily. He had told her he loved her yesterday morning, and she believed him, but somehow he had led Miranda to believe that he still loved her too.

"Well you can't have us both Ian," she said haughtily. "Who is it to be?"

"I'll leave her right now! It's you I want. I can't live without you, please believe me!" he implored her. As if sensing that this was the right moment, his arms came round her, his lips found hers, kissing away all her misery and unhappiness.

They clung to each other, conscious of the huge risk they were taking, but unable to stop themselves. They had only a few precious minutes left together, and for Amy there was an urgent need to erase the memory of Miranda with Ian from her mind. They both knew, as they feverishly removed each other's clothes, that the love, and the emotional satisfaction that they shared together, was the only thing that mattered.

There, on the rug by the fire, Ian made love to her. As he took her, he declared his undying love, and wished, once again, that he had something more than just his love to offer her. When they reached those dizzy heights of ecstasy together, Amy felt her tears flow, tears of happiness for the way he made her feel, and relief because she was the one he loved.

Clive looked at his watch. It was seven o'clock. He had a perfectly valid reason for ringing Ian, so why not? If he was cheating on his wife, then tough! What little he knew of Miranda, and knowing her a little was quite enough, gave him the impression she would react with a great deal of anger if Ian was up to anything.

He was more than a little jealous of Ian. Ian was fifteen years his junior, full of get up and go, good-looking, and probably destined to get on in life. Lately his mind didn't seem to be on his job. He did his work, but not with the same meticulous care as usual. Instead of delivering a far superior performance than the other office members he was just average.

He had been a few minutes late from lunch once or twice but had made it up at night, so really Clive didn't have much of an axe to grind. In fact, if it had been one of the others going off sick, he probably would have overlooked it, but as Ian showed promise for the future, and Clive knew he could be in line for his job, he decided that Ian must now reap whatever he had sewn.

Head Office were trying to persuade Clive to move down to Cornwall and be a Finance Manager for the branch there. He didn't want to go and he was convinced it was only to make way for Ian. Bob Martin seemed to think that the sun shone out of his backside! If Bob thought that he was over the hill at forty-four, then he could think again!

He sipped his pre-dinner whisky whilst he dialled the number. Soon his Indian curry would be delivered. He didn't recognise the voice when the telephone was answered. The woman wasn't Miranda, she sounded older, and she spoke so loudly that he had to hold the receiver away for fear of deafening his eardrums.

"Can I speak to Ian, please?" he asked politely, the voice commanded nothing less.

The voice replied. "Ian isn't here. He's taken Miranda out to the theatre, but I'm her mother. Can I help you?"

Of course, that explained it. She sounded just as formidable as Miranda. He was glad that the telephone separated them.

"I rang because he left work early today, saying that he wasn't feeling well."

"He will be back tomorrow. He came home, took some cold relief, and slept for two hours. He didn't want to waste the tickets that had already been booked, so he went out."

"Thank you for the information. Goodnight," said Clive, putting the phone down, relieved to give his eardrums a rest. He

118

felt disappointed that there was nothing he could prove against Ian. He had been looking forward to phoning Bob and reporting his favourite protégé, whose talents had been frequently rammed down Clive's throat, but Ian had been too clever for him.

Maybe he wasn't cheating on his wife. Clive wasn't sure either way now, but even if he wasn't, he had engineered getting home early with time to get himself ready to go out. The trouble was, it couldn't be proved, either way, and Bob would only say that Clive should have given him the time off anyway to go out for a special occasion, and he would be left with egg on his face.

He snorted with anger and downed his whisky in one gulp. Just watch out Ian Wood! I'm going to be breathing down your neck from now onwards until you make a slip, and then you're for the chop, and the thought of this gave him a certain satisfaction.

Chapter Seventeen

"Max, you must take me seriously! I need one ally, because when Mummy and Daddy find out, all hell will be let loose!"

Amy had just told her brother about Ian, their love for each other, and her intention to leave Peter. His reaction initially had been one of amusement, but when he realised that she wasn't joking, he changed, and his expression became incredulous. Like everyone else, he had assumed that Amy's marriage was happy, and Peter seemed a great brother-in-law.

"Why on earth didn't you tell me right from the beginning when he bullied you?" he said, frowning. "I could have stopped it right there and then!"

"I know the mistakes I made," said Amy, quietly. "I was such a fool. I wanted to keep him, at the time, and also I didn't want to admit that Daddy was right."

"Well sis, it's your life, so if it's what you want, you must go for it and to hell with everyone else! We only get one life," said Max, putting his arm round Amy's shoulder. She looked at him gratefully, and he realised how hard this must be for her.

Amy was a decent caring person. Peter had brought this on himself, in Max's opinion. He was close to Amy. His elder sister had helped him out of many scrapes when they were children, and had always been fiercely loyal to him. He was definitely with her whatever happened. His only misgivings were about Ian, and he voiced them.

"Are you certain that Ian is going to leave his wife? It isn't just talk, I hope." His friendly face looked worried as he looked straight into Amy's eyes.

"Absolutely certain!" said Amy firmly. "We love each other and neither of us are happy in our marriage." She held his gaze. He must believe that this wasn't just a romantic infatuation. It might sound like it, but this was special. She didn't want to tell Max about Ian's operation and how they had conquered his impotence, that was private. Only time would show their sincerity.

"OK sis, I'll put in a good word for you when the time comes, and please let me know your new address when you move out," he said, moving away from her. "I'd better get home now, Anna is waiting, we're out for dinner tonight."

"Thanks so much for listening, and do give my love to Anna," said Amy, hugging him.

She watched him from the doorway as he strode out to his car and sprang into the driving seat with ease. Her brother Max had been quite a catch, with his wicked green eyes and blond hair, which he always wore very short. He was tall like his father, and lean, with sturdy legs, the result of keeping trim and playing football to keep fit. He had vowed he would never marry, and Amy remembered the string of girlfriends he had, until two years ago, and then it had happened. He'd gone to Italy for a holiday and he'd met Anna, and it had been his turn to fall in love. He was very happy now, and he adored her, so Amy knew he would want her to be just as happy too. Now she had his support it helped and she was looking forward to telling Ian about it.

Ian could feel himself losing a grip on reality. These feelings he had for Amy seemed to rise above everything, and he knew his life was going haywire. He tried to keep a lid on his emotions, but it was hard. This love had taken him by storm and totally possessed him, both at home and at work.

Strangely enough, it was easier to cope at home because Miranda was so wrapped up in herself she didn't appear to notice anything wrong. She lived in a dream world, very similar to the ones she read about in her paperback novels.

He had temporarily stalled her demand for sex since the last dreaded encounter by telling her he had a small infection and the doctor had suggested abstaining for a while. She had accepted

f

this, knowing about the problem last year, but he knew he was on borrowed time. Soon, when he refused her, there would be a show down.

At work, he could sense Clive watching him. He had been aware of his changed attitude towards him recently and could sense he must be careful. But lunchtime was the only time they had together, and it was very hard to go nonchalantly out of the office to meet her, trying to hide his elation. It was even more difficult if one of the others asked him to go to lunch with them because he had to think up a plausible excuse.

Amy had restored his sexual confidence totally, and he now needed no help to make love to her. His response was immediate, and he found himself becoming aroused, not only in her company, but also when he thought about her.

All they had was the back of her little Fiesta, and small though it was, it was their private heaven. Every lunchtime they parked in a quiet spot, feverishly making love as if there was no tomorrow. He needed her so much, and he just couldn't keep his hands off this woman who had made him whole again, a complete man.

He had told Amy that he would leave Miranda, and she had said she would come too. She no longer loved Peter, but she had made it clear that she wanted the children and Jasper to join her.

Ian was getting so desperate for her now, that he was prepared to give up everything, even his girls, whom he loved so dearly, as long as he could see them sometimes.

He had to try and find them a flat. He had scanned all the papers, but it wasn't easy. He still had to maintain Miranda and the girls, so it didn't leave much money left. Amy was used to the good life, and he was well aware that he didn't have much to offer her. He was determined they would make it, he would find a way somehow. He had to, because nothing could douse the flames of jealousy that devoured him every time they parted. He couldn't bear to think about her returning home to Peter.

Once he had liked Peter, but every day he found his resentment of him increasing, and he knew that if Amy ever complained about his bullying again, he'd be round like a shot to stop him. Amy was now his whole life.

But she said very little about Peter, seemingly as wrapped up in their own happiness as he was, and just as sad as he was, every time they had to part.

Ian shook himself back to reality, and glanced at his watch. In ten minutes it would be time to go to lunch, and he would see her. He had done a good morning's work, so now he could wash his hands and smarten himself up.

When he emerged from the cloakroom, Clive eyed him with curiosity. He could see that Ian had combed his hair and had a wash, and there was an air of expectancy about him, as if he couldn't wait to get out. Clive was sure that he was definitely up to something. He decided that today he would follow him.

Ian was too immersed in his own happiness to be aware of much else. He was longing to see Amy, and he wondered if it would be possible to arrange another night together soon, without arousing any suspicions. He didn't notice the figure in the grey suit, who followed him across the road and through the car park, until he reached the corner where Amy was parked. When she opened the door to let him in, he made a rash move. He leaned over and kissed her, telling her how much he had missed her. She kissed him back, and he said urgently.

"Quick, let's go. We haven't got much time!"

Clive couldn't hear what they said, but he saw it all. He even recognised the pretty little piece with him. So he was screwing Peter's wife! He admired his choice, she was lovely all right, and this made Clive feel jealous because he knew she would never have looked at him.

Ian was young and virile, and was obviously giving her what she wanted. His resentment and jealousy festered, and the next time they met he followed them in his car.

They were so wrapped up in themselves that they didn't even notice him, and after parking just a little way away, he crept through the trees and near to the little car. His heart was pounding because of the risk he was taking, but a mixture of jealousy and the desire to prove to himself that he was right drove him on.

He needn't have worried about the risk of discovery. By the time he was near to the car, he couldn't see their heads, and his body prickled with anticipation at what he might see.

They were at it all right! As he peeped through the back window, he could see the blanket on which they lay. They had made use of the hatchback. He couldn't see much of Amy, but he could hear her groans, and he could see Ian astride her. He seemed to be very deep inside, and moving fast, and judging by their cries of joy, the randy little bugger was having a wonderful time.

Clive drew back in horror after witnessing it all. He felt very disturbed and shocked that Ian was screwing his friend's wife, and she, who had looked so winsome, was letting him.

When he got in his car he felt all steamed up with anger at their very public exhibition of lust. Anyone could have seen them! He was experiencing these disturbing images of them indulging their passion, so there, in a quiet place in the woods, he unzipped his trousers and relieved himself.

He felt much better afterwards, but still very shocked at their behaviour. There was only one thing for it. Miranda and Peter would have to be told, and so would Bob Martin. He regretted having to do it, and it would have to be anonymously, but Ian was getting to be a bit too much!

Peter sat staring at the typed piece of paper, the letters springing menacingly before his eyes. It couldn't be true, not Amy! He couldn't, and wouldn't believe it. Just a few words on a piece of paper, but enough to ruin his life.

JUST TO LET YOU KNOW YOUR WIFE IS HAVING AN AFFAIR WITH IAN WOOD.
FROM A WELL MEANING FRIEND

Now he recognised all the signs that he had been too blind to see, her indifference and lack of awe towards him, her excuses of being too tired all the time, and conveniently going to sleep before he got into bed. She didn't want him any more because she had Ian!

His anger rose. Ian who he had thought was his friend, secretly knocking off his wife, and he felt sick inside at the thought of it. He'd like to punch his head in! But Ian was strong and solidly built, and he would come off the worse and what good would that do?

As for Amy, he wouldn't have believed it possible. His own flings were of no importance, they had never threatened his marriage. He would never have thought Amy was capable of such deception. He should be feeling angry with her, but his anger was engulfed by fear. Fear that she might leave him, because Amy wouldn't go into an affair lightly. He knew that well enough. He couldn't live without her and the comfortable lifestyle he had married into.

"Daddy, can we go to the park with Jasper?"

Peter instinctively put his hand over the paper, but Sarah had only one thought on her mind. She was allowed to go to the park with Paul because they lived so near to it, and at seven years old, freedom was an exciting thing. Mummy was out shopping and Daddy rarely refused her anything.

He tried to bring his mind back to the matter in hand. "Yes, I suppose so, but stay in the park. I can see you out of the window," he reminded her.

"Thanks Daddy." Sarah kissed his cheek, and he smiled at her, feeling the pain shoot through his heart at the thought of losing his children. Amy would want to take them with her, and there was no way he wanted Ian Wood to have his children!

He clenched his fist to hide his agitation. Paul and Sarah were ready to go now, so he hid his anger by smiling as he opened the door for them.

To his absolute horror he saw Miranda on the doorstep, waving a piece of paper at him, which looked very similar to the one he had received.

"Peter, oh Peter, I must talk to you!" and then she sobbed in front of the children, loud enough for the whole neighbourhood to hear. Peter felt his dislike of her rise inside him. Trust her to be so melodramatic in front of them. Sarah whispered to him.

"Why is Linda's mummy crying?"

Paul didn't seem interested. Getting out was his priority. Peter pushed Sarah gently towards her brother.

"Go with Paul darling. Don't worry about the grownups. We have quarrels, just like you do."

To his relief, Sarah seemed content with that. Her curiosity now satisfied, she ran after Paul's rapidly disappearing figure, shouting, "Wait for me Paul. I'm coming too!"

Peter reluctantly asked Miranda in. He couldn't leave her weeping on the doorstep, and he offered her a chair whilst she continued to weep and wail, and wondered how much longer he would have to listen to her.

Eventually she stopped and produced some tissues from her handbag. Peter studied the typed piece of paper she handed him.

JUST TO LET YOU KNOW YOUR HUSBAND IS HAVING AN
AFFAIR WITH AMY JOHNSON.
FROM A WELL MEANING FRIEND

"Peter, I can't believe it! I thought Amy was my friend!"

"Well how do you think I feel?" he retorted bitterly. "I didn't expect Ian to make a pass at her, and he must have done because Amy just isn't like that."

Miranda could feel herself flaring up. She was defending Ian, heaven knows why. He didn't deserve it!

"So you're suggesting it's Ian's fault, are you? Amy's not stupid. She acted all helpless and innocent, just to seduce him, and Ian fell for it. He's never been unfaithful to me before!"

Even as she said these words, she wondered if it were true. She had never wanted to know, always believing that he loved only her. After all, he had married her, and they had the girls.

Their argument was interrupted by the entrance of Amy, who could see by the stricken look on Peter's face that he knew, and judging by Miranda's wails of misery, so did she. Amy felt her heart banging hard, the moment for recriminations had come, but she also felt a strange sense of relief that it was out at last. There would be no more lying and cheating. She didn't even question who might have sent the letters, and Peter also gave it no more than a fleeting thought. Someone else had known and thought it fit to tell them.

"I'm sorry you had to find out like this," said Amy awkwardly. She wondered whether she should tell them both of their plans to be together, but without Ian to back her up, it might not be a good idea. Miranda might prefer to hear it from him. Also she felt that they both needed to get used to it. The news, for both of them, had obviously been devastating, and she did regret the hurt they had caused.

Peter ignored her, and turning to Miranda, who was still sobbing loudly, he voiced Amy's thoughts.

"Where is Ian now?" he asked, feeling hatred deep inside when having to mention his name.

"Taking the girls out," sobbed Miranda. "I didn't receive this until after he had gone." She looked angrily at Amy, but then covered her face and broke into sobs again.

Peter wanted to talk to Amy, to try and sort this mess out, but he knew he had to get rid of Miranda. Maybe she was upset and shocked, and so was he, but this melodrama was making things ten times worse. He tried to make his voice sound kind.

"Did you come over in the car, Miranda?"

"No, Ian's got the car. I caught a cab."

The cab had been a bit expensive, she knew, but she had to make a fit entrance to deliver her heartbreaking news. Somehow, getting off the bus, and then walking up the road, wouldn't have made the same impact as alighting from a taxi in the drive and then breaking down with emotion on the doorstep. Miranda wanted to cause a stir, as she felt anyone would in the same situation. It wasn't the sort of thing she could keep quiet about.

Peter tried to make his voice sound soothing. He must get rid of her!

"Miranda, I think you should go home and wait for Ian, and when he comes in you can talk about it."

Miranda ignored him. Handing Amy the offending paper with a flourish, she retorted, "Read this! You know, of course, that this is what we have been talking about!"

Amy read it, and she was wondering who could possibly have known.

"Yes, it's true." Her voice was quiet, hoping not to inflame the situation any more.

"I thought as much!" said Miranda grimly. "Yes, call me a cab, Peter!" Now she wanted to get home. She needed to blame someone, preferably Amy. Ian was just as weak as all men. Oh how she hated Amy! If she went home now, she could phone Mum and Gwen and pour out all her misery to them. She'd make Ian sorry. He wasn't going to get off lightly!

Peter dialled the number of the taxi company and requested them to come as soon as possible. He would do anything rather than take her himself, even pay for the taxi. It would be well worth it. "It'll be five minutes," he told her, feeling such relief.

She turned towards Peter, pointedly ignoring Amy, who just sat there, wishing she had Ian to support her.

"Peter, have you got a biscuit? I always need to eat when I'm emotionally upset," she added, as way of an explanation.

Peter got up without a word, and went to find the biscuit tin. He offered it to her, and then sat there for the next couple of minutes watching her crunch her way through a packet of shortbread, in between gulping out her misery. Anyone else would have choked to death, he thought wryly, but not Miranda.

The taxi duly arrived, and Miranda kissed his cheek with great affection and then swept grandly from the room, leaving a pungent smell of lavender behind her. She paused at the door, her voice raised enough for the driver to hear.

"Amy, you'd better make sure you stay away from my husband, because if you don't, I won't be responsible for my actions!"

Peter had no doubt that Miranda could pack quite a punch, so he winced a little, noticing the cab driver's face alight with interest. Nosey sod! It was nothing to do with him.

"Don't worry, Miranda, I'll pay," he said grandly, purposely ignoring her last remark. He gave the driver a ten pound note and instructions on where to go, and his relief was tremendous when he waved her goodbye.

Now for Amy. What should he say and do? He had anger and jealousy raging around inside him, coupled with a feeling of failure, because until now he had always been very sure of Amy's love, but not any more.

When he entered the lounge, she was sitting in a chair, her shoulders bowed, and she was crying quietly. Jasper was sitting at her feet, his head on her lap, gently licking her trembling fingers. Peter felt a wave of jealousy rise inside him, but he resisted the urge to kick him away in disgust. It was no good telling her he was only a dog, she loved him.

Amy sat there, waiting for his explosion of temper. For once in her life she deserved it. If she had to she would leave right now, if he turned violent! But Peter didn't want to give her a reason to leave him, so he sat wearily in the chair and asked the question he had to have an answer to.

"What's going to happen to us now, Amy?"

She had to ignore the pain in his eyes. She had to discount everyone else's feelings, to go to the man she truly loved. If Peter was violent towards her she could justify leaving him and taking the children, but he was being so calm and reasonable. Her dislike and resentment towards him vanished, leaving this tremendous

128

guilt for what she'd done. It was easy to push it aside when she was with Ian, but in the cold light of day it returned to plague her.

Her love for Ian had not diminished in any way, and she felt the pain acutely at the thought of losing him. She thought about his brown eyes, full of tenderness and love, his gentleness, and his passion that matched hers and made her feel as if she had never known real love before him. He was like a drug that she just had to have. She faced Peter defiantly, determined to be honest.

"I didn't plan to fall in love with him, but I have, and I can't do anything about it . . ."

Amy stopped speaking as Paul and Sarah came bursting into the room. Peter would not want them to hear this, she felt, but this time she was wrong. She watched his face become dark with rage after her confession of her feelings, and he paid no heed at all to the children.

Peter felt something snap inside him. He had tried not to lose his temper, but his rage was so intense that he lost all sense of reason. For the first time ever his children were about to see the other side of him. He moved to grab Amy, but she was ready for him, her hand came up to push him away.

"You slut, I trusted you and him. I'll kill you both!"

Sarah was distressed hearing the father she adored raging at her mother.

"Don't shout at Mummy like that, Daddy."

She ran to her mother, and Paul stood protectively at Amy's side, eyeing his father in amazement. Just to complete the wall of protection, Jasper was there, growling low in his throat, warning him not to hurt her.

Peter looked at them all and realised that he was the loser. His wife was a whore, she'd destroyed their lives, and yet they all stuck by her! She'd turned them against him, his own children, and his love turned to hate, burning with a fierce flame that consumed him. All his rational feelings had gone. He wanted them all out of his life, the lot of them! He wrenched open the front door so hard that it crashed back against the wall and the house shook.

"Get out of my house, and take your children with you!" he spat venomously at Amy, and she saw his face so suffused with rage that she didn't argue. The children were crying by now, so she ushered them through the door, knowing he would bang it in their faces.

When they were in the car she felt relief. It was over now, the worst part. Peter might have possession of the house at the moment but that could be sorted out later. The next thing to do was to ring Ian on his mobile, and then to sort out where they could go.

Chapter Eighteen

David was eating his breakfast and feeling very pleased with himself. It was almost certain that he would be the next Tory candidate for Linton Green, so certain that a reporter from the local paper was coming to interview him this morning.

Everyone wanted to know about the successful merchant banker who was happily married with two grown-up children. Apparently he was a grandfather too, a very fit and active man, now retired, and played golf as a hobby.

This was the sort of information he planned to give to his interviewer, who was arriving in an hour. After he'd finished his breakfast, he would dress casually, but smartly, and ask Susan to put the coffee percolator on in readiness. He planned to take his visitor into the sun lounge, and they could admire the garden whilst they chatted. Henry, who had been their faithful gardener for years, was out there now, mowing the lawn. Now that April had arrived, the sun had condescended to shine, and a carpet of daffodils was bursting forth. The blossoms were appearing on the trees and bushes, and the garden was alive with pink, yellow and white. It looked really lovely at this time of the year, he thought complacently. All in all, life was pretty good, and he had a challenging future to look forward to.

The telephone rang, and he remained sitting, knowing that Susan would answer it and deal with anything that wasn't directly concerned with him. She didn't call him, so he continued eating his breakfast, enjoying the view out of the window. He had worked hard to become this affluent, so now he could enjoy it all, his lovely home, and everything he spent his money on.

Whilst he was finishing his tea, Susan came into the dining room and he could see by her expression that there was something on her mind. Her eyes were wide like saucers, as if she'd experienced a great shock. He noticed her hair, which was still blonde like Amy's, was neatly groomed. He thought fleetingly that she was still very attractive, and wondered again what had caused their love life to die.

"Your hair dresser's done a good job!" he commented, remembering that was the place she had just been.

"Yes . . ." said Susan absently. At that moment her hair was the last thing on her mind. She had news to give David that he wouldn't like, and what a day to have to tell him, but she couldn't keep it to herself.

"Who was that on the phone?" he asked, and this gave her the chance to broach the subject.

"It was Peter. He's very upset because he's just found out that Amy's having an affair."

She didn't mince her words, there was no point, and she watched his jaw drop with disbelief, and saw the hurt and amazement in his eyes. She had just destroyed his illusions of their daughter with those words.

"Are you sure there isn't some mistake?" asked David hopefully.

"No!" said Susan firmly, knowing that he would attempt to defend Amy. Peter had said that she had admitted it, and she was sure he wouldn't make up something as serious as that. He had sounded so upset on the phone. "Evidently it's his new friend, Ian Wood. Somebody sent Peter and Ian's wife an anonymous letter, and when Peter asked Amy, she admitted it was true."

David's heart sank. Just at a time when he needed his life to go on an even keel, this had to happen. He would have to hush it up or his election hopes were gone, and he didn't want all that to go to waste.

"I hope she's not thinking of leaving him," he said ominously, realising how bad it would look for him.

"Oh no," said Susan soothingly. "I'm sure it will all blow over. Peter says Ian couldn't offer her much. He lives in a small house on the other side of town, and he has a wife and two daughters to provide for. We know Amy's used to a comfortable life."

She didn't tell David that Amy had gone off when Peter had challenged her about it. There was no point in upsetting him any more with this interview coming up soon.

"Yes . . ." said David absently, remembering that he hadn't wanted Amy to get married as young as eighteen, but he'd given in after she'd coerced him, telling him how much she loved Peter. Then he'd imagined they were happy because the children came along. David had found his son-in-law to be an easy-going and friendly person, so he had assumed that Amy was very happy with him.

Why had she done it? Maybe it was his fault, making such a lot of her when she was a little girl.

"Well, I promised Peter we would talk some sense into her," said Susan firmly. She felt very let down. Hadn't she always set Amy a good moral example? It was very wrong what she'd done, but nobody seemed to care these days. Women had affairs just like men did, but she had thought that Amy wouldn't.

She put thoughts about herself and David experimenting before their marriage, and her resulting pregnancy, right out of her mind. Her sex life had ended after Max was born. His birth had been so painful that she'd feared having any more pregnancies. David hadn't argued or tried to persuade her otherwise. Maybe if he'd encouraged her to seek medical help, things would have been different, but her sexual feelings had died, and so apparently had his.

Knowing this about herself didn't make her feel sympathetic towards Amy. She had wanted to marry Peter at eighteen, they had consented to it, and now she owed it to them to stay faithful to him. She knew that David was probably feeling it more than she was. Amy had always been very special to him, and he wouldn't want any stain on her character. Apart from that, it would be most unpleasant if gossip about her infidelity was to get around. It would not help his future aspirations.

David wasn't sure which hurt the most, the knowledge that Amy had slept with her husband's friend, or the thought that all his ambitious hopes could be lost. "I don't know why she's done this," he said wearily, feeling very let down. "We've always taught her right from wrong."

He ignored the little voice in his head, reminding him of his

133

own secret life. Well, that was the difference. His life was secret and it didn't hurt anyone, including Susan. Amy didn't have the excuse he had. There was no excuse for her affair and he resolved to tell her so when he saw her.

"Daddy, can we go to McDonald's?" asked Linda.

"Yes, why not?" said Ian genially.

They had just enjoyed an hour or more in the swimming pool. The girls loved it when he threw them about and played with them, as he had made sure, right from infancy, that they didn't fear the water. Miranda couldn't swim and had always watched from the side, but he had always gone in with them and they could now both swim strongly.

He saw their happy faces looking expectantly at him, and he felt a wave of love towards them, his two lovely princesses. Was he doing the right thing by leaving them to the tender mercies of their mother?

He didn't doubt Miranda's love for them, but if he was only going to see them every other weekend, how could he stop them from growing up to lead a similar lifestyle to their mother? She never encouraged them to do any sport, fed them too many sweets and junk food, and was quite happy for them to sit round all day watching videos or being on the computer, as long as she was left in peace to read her romantic fiction.

Ian had a fear that they would end up being overweight and unhealthy if they didn't have regular exercise. So as well as swimming he planned to encourage them to do other sports as they grew up. Now they wanted to go to McDonald's, where they did those horrible skinny chips loaded with salt, that he hated. He decided on a compromise.

"You can have McDonald's on one condition, that is that you have some salad with it, and you share one portion of chips between you."

"I don't like salad! Mummy doesn't make us have salad," said Linda, pouting her lips mutinously at him. Ian knew she would be difficult. Linda always was, but he had to make a start somewhere. His expression remained firm. He wasn't going to spoil them in an effort to keep their love.

"Daddy, if I eat my salad, can I have a McFlurry ice cream?"

asked Sophie, hopefully.

Ian sighed to himself, but they were only children and if they were active, hopefully that would burn off the calories.

You can both have one if you eat your salad," he promised, winking at Linda, and she laughed happily, believing that she had almost won that argument.

"Race you both to the car," he said, allowing them a head start. He jogged up behind them, pretending to puff a little, catching up just as they reached the car.

"We won, Daddy," they shouted excitedly, and he laughingly agreed.

As they were getting in the car his mobile phone rang. It was Miranda. He felt his irritation rise. Could he never have any peace from her? He switched off his phone. Let her leave a message if she must. Sometimes it was better to be unavailable. As he was driving, Linda entertained him with a new song she had learnt at school, and he listened entranced to her clear little singing voice. Sophie joined in on the chorus, and he did too, causing them to laugh with delight. He found it much easier to be happy with them when Miranda wasn't around. Maybe they would cope with the separation. He did hope so!

After they had been to McDonald's he asked them, "Would you like to see Nanna this afternoon?"

Linda's face lit up. Her Nanna always played with them and read them stories. It would be nice to see her.

"Yes please," she said. "Has Nanna still got that book of fairy stories?"

"Probably," laughed Ian, delighted that they wanted to see Janet. She had always had less contact with them than Miranda's mother and Gwen.

Sophie looked at him in a puzzled way and then asked bluntly. "Why doesn't Mummy like Nanna?"

Ian looked at her in amazement. How did she know? He had never said anything. Maybe it was best to be honest.

"I don't think that Mummy dislikes her. They just have rather different personalities."

"She does!" interrupted Linda. "She told us, and she doesn't like us to go and see her."

Ian felt very angry. How dare she try and influence the girls! He had always taken pains to hide his dislike of Miranda's mother

135

and Gwen from them, respecting that the girls loved them, even if he found them tiresome. He could feel his dislike of her growing even more. Why on earth had he married her?

"I won't take you to see her if you don't want to go, but if you do, it's not up to your mother or me to tell you not to go. So what's it to be?" He knew his voice sounded cold, but sometimes they seemed to be against him too.

Linda was learning to manipulate adult emotions. It was a dangerous game, but one that made her the centre of attention, which, like her mother, she craved to be.

"We do want to see Nanna, but we won't tell Mummy," she said, conspiratorially.

"I will tell your mother," said Ian shortly. "We're not going to be dishonest about things."

"Oh no, then she'll have a temper," said Sophie, in a very matter-of-fact way.

"Well let her," said Ian firmly. "You girls are growing up, and you have two grandmothers who both love you very much, and you should visit them both regularly."

Linda saw his face set in a firm line. Daddy wasn't happy, and it seemed to be Mummy's fault. She was beginning to understand why they didn't get on.

Chapter Nineteen

Amy was feeling desperate. All attempts to contact Ian had failed. His mobile was switched off. She left him a message begging him to ring her soon. It was too difficult to explain everything in a message, especially with the children sitting in the car. They were already upset and confused by the events. She had destroyed their lives and she hoped they would forgive her. If only she could reach Ian and warn him about the anonymous letters. At least he would be able to go home prepared.

She debated where to take the children. Max would be sympathetic, but how would Anna feel? Was it fair to descend on them? Anna was expecting a baby soon and it might be too much for her. Her parents would be horrified at what she'd done and she didn't expect any backing from them. They loved Peter. Well hadn't she spent most of her life defying them and causing them grief? Nothing was new. If she went there, at least they would know, and they wouldn't turn their own grandchildren away. Surely Daddy would have to help her get the house back. He had helped to buy it in the first place!

David chose a casual outfit for his meeting with the reporter from *The Linton Green Times*. He had spent most of his working life dressed as a city gent, so it was a nice change to wear blue trousers with a white shirt and navy jacket.

He looked at himself in the mirror as he brushed his hair,

thinking that he could do with a tan. So maybe he could think about taking Susan for a cruise round the Greek Islands after this candidate business had been sorted out. Then he had an idea. Maybe if he paid for Peter and Amy to have a nice holiday, things would return to normal. Why not? It was worth a try, something to think about. But first he must let Amy know how disappointed he was with her.

"How long have I got before he's due?" he called to Susan, who was still titillating in their bathroom.

"About half an hour," replied Susan, appearing dressed in a cream suit with a mint green blouse. She knew that she would probably only make one appearance, to bring in the coffee and biscuits, but she still wanted to look her best. It was the housekeeper's week end off, but for once she didn't mind, because it gave her the excuse, at the very least, to be introduced. She wanted a small part in David's rise to glory. After all, she had stood by him, and encouraged him all the way, often assisting him in charity works and providing voluntary assistance to the local church. Because of her help he was a pillar of society and would make a very good Tory councillor, she was sure.

She stiffened at the sound of tyres outside. Was their visitor early? But as she looked out of the window, to her amazement, she saw Amy's car with the children in it.

She opened the door to meet them, noticing the strained look on Amy's face. Something bad had happened, and it couldn't be at a worse time.

"Come into the back room and I'll make some drinks for you. Daddy is expecting a visit from the newspaper, so we need to keep out of his way," she said quickly before Amy had a chance to speak. She hadn't meant to sound cold, but Amy really had turned up at a most inconvenient time.

Peter didn't remember how long Amy had been gone. The house seemed eerily quiet, and he had never felt so alone as he did at that moment. His wife and family were somewhere out there, driving around in fear. He had just blown his whole life away in his rage, and self pity took over, as he sat wearily in the chair, sobbing in frustration.

He went to the cocktail cabinet, and with shaking hands,

poured himself a whisky. As he gulped it down he felt the liquid burning the back of his throat, and then after, the surge of well-being it created seemed to subdue his misery a little. He lit a cigar and puffed on it, allowing the circle of smoke to waft around him and pervade the clean sweet smelling atmosphere of the room. He didn't usually smoke, only a cigar occasionally when socialising, but he felt he needed something calming now, and it seemed to help.

By the time he had drunk his third whisky, Amy, and the tribulations she had given him, were less painful to think about. The whisky had done its work well, by subduing his emotions, giving him a new confidence.

He decided to ring Derek, his good old mate. He would listen to his problems and only offer advice if asked to. When he thought about it, Derek might even know already, if Amy had told Gill. He picked up the phone and dialled their number, totally forgetting it was Saturday and they might be out with the boys.

Gill's husky voice announced the number, and in his present state he found it stirring his senses. She was a sexy bitch that one, enough to make him forget his reason for calling.

"Gill darling, is Derek there?"

Gill's voice quickened when she realised it was Peter. She was depressed and alone. Her two sons were away with their cousins for the weekend, and Derek had made use of their absence by going away too. She had been hoping they could have time to themselves without the boys, but her plans had backfired on her. He was with the partner that she tried desperately not to think about, the one who had usurped her. She had taken a dose of antidepressants, but still felt the rejection. The doctor had said she must cut down on them, but how could she cope with life, it was all too much.

She wondered briefly if he knew about Amy's bit on the side. He sounded very mellow, as if he'd indulged in a drink or two, but then he could be drowning his sorrows, like she was.

"He's away for the weekend darling, visiting an old school friend who doesn't much like children."

"Oh, so he's left you to baby-sit."

His remark was intended to make her feel she was missing out a little. As life had treated him so badly, he didn't want to think

139

he was the only one. But Gill was feeling glad that he had rung. She didn't have a beau at the moment. Why not Peter after all these years? She didn't have to worry her conscience about Amy, her attentions were elsewhere.

"No, the boys are with their cousin at Brighton, giving me a break. I didn't want to go." She had to let him know she had the choice. Now it was her turn to make a veiled comment. "How's Amy and the family? It's a long time since I saw any of them."

Peter's feeling of well-being was slipping away, to be replaced by anger. Gill had just reminded him of Amy's misdemeanours, and he was filled with a desire for revenge. There was Gill, Amy's best friend, on her own for the weekend, and here was he, eager for company and understanding. He also needed to know he could still pull a woman. After all, his wife preferred someone else, so her best friend was ideal; she'd chosen Ian to misbehave with, who until then Peter had counted as a good friend.

His hatred of Ian was so strong that he wished him all manner of harm at that moment. His mind dismissed these thoughts. It was no use dwelling on them.

"Well it seems we're both on our own. How about I come round and we share a drink together?"

Gill's senses tingled. She knew exactly what he wanted, and about time!

"I'll look forward to that," she said huskily.

Peter felt a surge of excitement as he put the phone down. She was ready, willing and able and so was he. This time it was Amy's fault. She had driven him into the arms of her best friend by her own behaviour, so he need feel no guilt. As for Derek, if he was visiting an old school friend, they could well have been out on the town woman hunting too. Gill wouldn't tell him or Amy, he was sure. He was now looking forward to screwing the woman he had fancied for a long time, but up until now, hadn't dared to go after.

He dialled himself a taxi, knowing he wasn't fit to drive. He had no desire for a brush with the law, so his car would remain in the garage. Amy wouldn't be back yet, if ever. He felt the anger and pain again. It was all her fault!

He put the answerphone on and picked up the bottle of whisky. His taxi would only be five minutes. No time to get changed or shower. Gill liked brandy, he knew that. She liked anything really, soaked it up like a wet sponge. He chose a good French one from his store. The results would be worth it. He was determined to prove himself, even if it meant screwing her all afternoon.

Ian switched his mobile back on whilst his mother was playing with the girls. Miranda had left a message in her usual, domineering fashion, ordering him to ring her immediately. He ignored that. Amy had too, and by the sound of her voice there was an emergency. He went out into the tiny kitchen to ring her back, feeling relief flood through him when she answered it.

"Amy, my love, whatever is wrong?" he asked, mystified.

"It's Peter, he's found out about us, and Miranda too. She came over, and he got wild, and I've left with the children and Jasper!"

Ian gasped with amazement. He could imagine Miranda's wrath. He would be the next to go, but maybe it was for the best. Now was not the time for debating, poor Amy was in a state. Don't worry Amy, just tell me where you are and I'll be there soon."

"Well I've just left my parents' house. They know, and they're not happy. They've told me to go home to Peter and say I'm sorry. What a joke!"

Ian felt fear and insecurity flood through his inside. He must ask, no matter how much it hurt, he had to know. "Are you sorry, Amy, are you going to make up with him?"

"Never!" said Amy emphatically.

Ian's heart lifted. She wanted him still. They had no money, nowhere to live, but none of this daunted him. They had each other, and they would make it, he was sure. But right now he needed to hold her in his arms and reassure her that everything would be all right.

He returned to the lounge where Janet was playing I spy with the girls. He could leave them with her for about an hour, after that they would get bored. Janet didn't have a computer or any modern games. But an hour should suffice because he needed to plan the rest of his life with Amy, and he couldn't wait.

"I've got to go out for a while," he said as casually as he could muster, but no one seemed that interested. Maybe the novelty of an adult playing with them made a change from the computer. Miranda bought them every new game that came out, as did everyone nowadays, the girls had to have the same as everyone

141

else. He didn't stop to debate this any further, but got in his car and went to find Amy.

As he drove, he thought about the situation they were in and where they could go from now on.

If Miranda wanted to divorce him, he certainly wouldn't stand in her way, but somehow he didn't think it would be that easy. He didn't want Amy mentioned in a divorce suit. As far as he was concerned, she hadn't broken them up. Miranda had done that, unwittingly maybe. Or maybe it was him. He had fallen out of love with her. She had not been there for him when emotionally he needed her most of all. Lack of communication was to blame. He realised that they hadn't been close enough to talk about and resolve this very real crisis in his life. He was as guilty as her. He should have been able to tell her how much he was suffering, but they were just not close enough.

His way of coping with the pain had been to try and forget all about love and sex. But then there was Amy, not his to have, and he just couldn't resist her. She had given him back his reason for living, his pride, masculinity, confidence and everything that made him a man. He only wanted her and the way she made him feel. His feelings overwhelmed him, and he knew life would mean nothing without her. Whatever had happened to him? No woman had ever moved him to tears before in his life, but they had something really special, something that only comes along once in a lifetime, and he was prepared to risk everything, even the loss of his children, just to be with her. He had to admit to himself that he didn't want her to be reconciled with Peter.

There was regret too, that it had been Peter, not himself, that had met and married her, and given her two children. If only he wasn't sterile. After the operation he had been tested, but his sperm count had been so low the doctor had said it was most unlikely he would be a father again, and at the time it hadn't seemed to matter. His dearest wish now would be to have a child of their own. As far as he was concerned, she was the woman he loved, admired and respected, and a child of their own would have been wonderful.

He came back to reality when he saw her car parked at the side of the road. Amy had the dog on his lead, and the children were sitting in the car looking very subdued. He felt a wave of pity for them, and guilt for his part in it all. He resolved that he would do his best to give them a happier life when they were together.

There she stood in front of him, the woman who had given him everything, and he felt his love burning so fiercely inside him. He looked into her eyes, those beautiful deep blue eyes that had enslaved him since the first day he had met her. She still had traces of tears in them, and he felt a mixture of anger towards whoever had hurt her and a desire to show her tenderness to ease her sorrow away.

Amy ran into his arms.

"Amy, please tell me what's wrong. Has he been bullying you?" he asked sternly, determined to confront Peter with it if he had.

He had expected her to be worried that the children had seen him, but she, too, didn't seem to care any more. He stood there, holding her closely, scarcely able to believe his good fortune. He kissed her gently, stroking her hair as she poured out details of Peter's anger and the way he had thrown them out, and his reaction was very angry.

"He's just too much, Amy! You can't trust him. One of these days he'll do something serious."

"I know," she said tearfully, "I just can't stay with him any more. Even the children are frightened of him now."

"I'm coming too, right now, after I've taken the girls home," he said quietly. Let Miranda rave at him, and he knew she would. His only regret was the girls, and his conscience bothered him about that, but not enough to make him stay.

"You won't have much of a future with me," Amy said miserably. "I went to see my parents and they virtually threw me out. They've taken his side, so I've lost the house, and he's so mean with money, I doubt he'll ever pay me any maintenance."

Ian held her close. Poor little rich girl was no longer, but it made no difference to him. It made them more equal. "I don't want to live in that house with you," he said firmly. "Give us time and we'll get our own. We can make it together, I know!"

Amy looked tremulously at him. Did he really mean it? "I intend to get a job," she said firmly. "I've wanted to be independent for a long time."

He looked at her admiringly. She was stoic, not a poor little thing who fell apart when she was no longer being cosseted. With her determination, and the strength of their love, they would

143

survive, he was sure.

One very important fact occurred to Amy, and she reminded him, holding her breath for his answer. This was a good test of his love. "I must have the children with me, and Jasper, and that will make it even harder to find a flat."

Ian kissed her tenderly again. Nothing was going to thwart him. Amy wanted him, and he was basking in the euphoria of that knowledge. "What's yours is mine, children and animals," he said smiling. "Amy, I know we can be happy." And as he stood there, he felt his love for her so strongly that he knew it would last a lifetime.

Chapter Twenty

Clive rubbed his hands with glee. He was going to enjoy this interview. Ian Wood's day of reckoning had come. It was common knowledge, thanks to Miranda, that he had left his wife and family, and was now 'shacking up', because that's what it was, with that tasty little piece with the big blue innocent eyes. Not that she was, hadn't he witnessed them at it in her car, so wrapped up in each other that they hadn't seen him? He couldn't admit it to anyone because he might be accused of snooping, but he had acted in the best interests of the bank, as always. He smiled with smug satisfaction. Now Wood was going to have to toe the line or get out, and Clive was looking forward to telling him so.

He jumped with nervous excitement at the sound of the knock on the door. The time to gloat had come.

"Come in!" he said sharply, enjoying the feeling of power his position afforded him. He watched Ian enter the room. The young whippersnapper was still holding his head high, with no sign of remorse on his face, and his eyes were unflinching as they stared back at him.

"You wanted me?" he enquired, and Clive felt his hatred of this confident young man, who had his whole future ahead of him and probably knew that he was now entering the lion's den, and yet showed no fear. His attitude made Clive feel a little less sure of himself, so he adopted a bullying tone. He had to be top dog.

"I hope you're proud of yourself Wood, sleeping with your

145

friend's wife. I don't know how long you think you can get away with it."

Ian felt his indignation rise, but knew that losing his temper was not the answer. They had to expect plenty of this, because until they became divorced, that was exactly what it looked like. But why did it have to creep into his working life? He was still working hard, more so since he had been with Amy. Things had felt a little more stable and he could concentrate. Miranda had made sure everyone knew about it, but now that he was away from her, life was calmer, and he had turned to Amy for the love that made it all worthwhile. Even without marriage they were as one person.

"My private life is my own concern, surely, as long as it doesn't affect my work?" he said firmly, struggling to keep his tone polite.

Clive's eyes narrowed. This jumped up bank clerk, because that's all he was, was standing up to him. He had no shame, and he certainly wasn't in awe of him. He felt he had lost, but he wasn't going to retire gracefully. That wasn't his style. His tone became menacing as he faced Ian over the desk.

"Never mind your work! We do not tolerate scandal in this organisation as you well know. You have left a wife and two children without a father. I suggest you do the decent thing and go back to them. You've been offered a position in Cornwall. Take it and get out, because if you don't, you're out of a job. We don't want you here!"

Ian stared at him, seeing the hatred in his eyes. He'd always sensed this man disliked him, but now he could see it was more than that. Why was he being so self righteous? What right did he have to condemn Ian for falling in love? The anger that he had fought so hard to control, rose inside him. He had to answer for himself, show this arrogant bully that he was not afraid of him.

His face was white with anger, and he could feel the suppressed rage inside him longing to be set free, and the quietness of his voice belied the turmoil deep inside. "I won't be bullied into going to Cornwall by you. My job is here, but don't worry, I'll resign anyway. I have no wish to work for you!"

He stared contemptuously back at Clive. What an oddball he was, and he reminded him so with his parting words. "You could never understand. That's why you're single!"

146

"How dare you!"

Clive's face was suffused with rage. This cocky upstart had hit a raw nerve! Clive was well aware of why he had never married, but how dare he remind him of it! This foolhardy young idiot had played right into his hands, and was about to lose everything, including his job. Clive had won.

"I'll write my letter of resignation now," said Ian coldly.

"There's no rush as long as I have it by tomorrow," said Clive, inwardly exulting in his victory. That was the trouble with the young. They were impetuous. Maturity taught you that sometimes you just had to go along with things to survive. But thank goodness he was like that. No longer would he have to live in the shadow of this promising young man who made him feel like a has-been. He watched Ian leave the room, his head still held high. There was something about his manner that contradicted the situation. Why did Ian, the loser, make Clive feel as though he was really the victor, and that Clive was the loser?

Amy drew a deep breath before she picked up the phone. She wanted to talk to Gill but she wasn't sure what her reaction would be. She must know by now that Amy and Peter had split up. Amy and Ian didn't even have somewhere to live. A motel was all they had found so far, because no landlord had been prepared to accept Jasper. Amy was beginning to feel rather desperate.

Every night they slept, locked in each other's arms, hanging on desperately to their love, which was being savagely attacked on all sides.

Peter was being difficult, threatening to remove the children because they did not have a proper home, and Amy was worried because she knew this was true.

Gill's familiar husky voice announced the number, and Amy cut in nervously. "Gill, it's Amy."

Gill recoiled with horror at the sound of her voice. She had no conscience about the affair with Peter that she had just plunged into. He had turned to her because of Amy, and the frenzy of animal passion he had showed her had matched the wild streak in her own nature. It was pure fun, and she hadn't had that much satisfaction for years. But being friendly with Amy was not an option now. She was very firmly on Peter's side, and avidly

147

looking forward to their next encounter.

"Amy, you've got a nerve, phoning me like this!"

Amy felt her indignation rise. Surely her best friend would understand when no one else did.

"I'm sure you know Peter and I have split up. I fell in love with Ian. I couldn't help it, and now we're trying to do the honest thing."

She didn't see why Gill should make her feel guilty. She was no saint, and she didn't appear to be much of a friend after all. Amy realised at that moment, how shallow Gill was.

"You're no friend of mine after what you did to Peter. You weren't content to have a bit of fun, were you? You had to get involved."

"But I love Ian!" protested Amy, angry with Gill's attitude, knowing all the things she got up to. Why was there one rule for her? She was such a hypocrite!

"Love!" scoffed Gill. "He's no different to any other man. He'll leave you when the going gets tough, and you'll have to go back! Don't tell me about it, because I don't want to know!" She didn't want to know, because when Amy went back to Peter she, Gill, would probably be dumped too, and all the fun would be over.

She banged down the receiver to accentuate her anger, and Amy was left angrily clutching hers, knowing that her best friend had deserted her when she needed her most. It really was Ian and Amy against the world.

Miranda was boiling with fury. Ian had moved in with that tart who pretended to be so middle class. If she was so rich, then she could support Ian!

Ian had made a mistake, which Miranda planned to use to her advantage. He had signed a form back in the early days of their marriage, allowing either his or her signature for the withdrawal of funds from their joint account.

After Miranda had blown her top, she had started to milk the account. It was now empty and this gave her a certain satisfaction. It was a way of paying him back for humiliating her. She'd show him what it was like to be poor. How long would love's young dream last then.

148

According to Clive, who seemed to know everything, he was shacked up in a seedy motel, it must be seedy if 'she' was there, the woman who was as different to Miranda as she could be, and he was acting so loopy over her. If it wasn't for that bitch, he would have come home by now, Miranda was sure.

She'd opened a building society account in just her name, and put the money in there, ready to spend when she wanted to. She wasn't going to let him spend any money on that slut! If he argued with her she would say it was for the girls, so he wouldn't have a leg to stand on. Let's see how long his precious affair would last now! Living on love wouldn't pay the bills, and she would make sure the girls didn't want to visit him whilst he was with that tramp!

Ian felt as if he had the whole weight of the world on his shoulders as he made his way back from work. Whatever had possessed him to give in his notice? He knew what, pride, and a refusal to curtail to Clive. But he knew that to throw his job in at a time like this was a foolhardy thing to do. They needed money to survive, and he must get out there tomorrow and find another bank to take him. He decided not to tell Amy at the moment. She didn't need any more stress than she had already.

He needed to draw some money out to pay the motel bill for the past week, so he stopped at a cash machine and took his turn amongst the queue of people.

Eventually he reached the machine, slipped his card in the slot and entered his pin number, pressed the button requesting cash, and waited patiently for the machine to deliver it. But he waited in vain. The machine flashed a message, 'insufficient funds', and he gave a perplexed frown. He knew that wasn't right. The mortgage was paid out of this account, and he always kept a surplus of at least a thousand pounds to cover any unexpected bills.

The machine continued to flash, and he could hear the impatient shuffling of feet behind him. He put in his pin number once more and asked for a total balance. When it showed minus fifty pounds, he stood there, the blood draining from his face as realisation struck home. It must be Miranda, no one else had access to this account. His dearly beloved wife had taken the lot!

Didn't she realise she was penalising herself and the girls too? She was obviously so angry she hadn't thought of that.

He moved away to let the man behind him use the machine. How could he go back to Amy without any money? He did have some pride.

He jumped into the car and drove off. Whatever could he do now? Did he dare take a chance and write a cheque for the motel bill? His wages were due to be paid in tomorrow. He had to, there was no other choice, but first thing tomorrow he was going to put a stop on that account and close it, once he'd received his wages. Miranda wouldn't be allowed a second chance to bleed him dry.

He had given her more than he could afford in maintenance money, or conscience money, as she referred to it, not just for the girls, but for her too. Why couldn't she get a part time job like other women? Amy was trying hard to get one. Today she had been for a job interview. Maybe she had got it. That would have been good news. Ian knew he must get another job quickly, otherwise it would look as if he was trying to live off Amy. He was still preoccupied with his thoughts as he parked the car, so he didn't immediately see the figure emerge from the clump of bushes outside the motel. The man looked sinister, his face was swarthy, his eyes very dark, and he wore a cap which covered his hair. His appearance was rough, and Ian knew instinctively, as their eyes met, that this stranger was hostile.

Vince pulled his cap a little lower over his face. He knew he had to be quick. It was still light, and people were not that far away. He'd been told, no real stuff, only a frightener. The girls' father didn't want the scandal of a divorce. He had said this bloke had turned her head, and there was a grand in it for Vince if he could gently persuade him to leave her.

" 'Scuse me mate, you're Ian I take it?" His tone was low, his voice a little sneering. Best to make sure, but he fitted the description perfectly.

Ian eyed him suspiciously. He looked a shady character. "What's it to you?" be demanded.

The man's voice became a growl as he grabbed the front of Ian's jacket and pushed him against the wall. "If you value your health, you'd better leave your pretty little lady friend and go back home. If you don't, things will get really nasty, I promise you!"

150

"Get your hands off me!" shouted Ian in retaliation, pushing back at him. His anger, at once again being told what to do in his life completely overshadowed any feelings of fear he might have otherwise had. This took Vince by surprise, and he loosened his hold. People usually trembled with fear when he threatened them. Why was this man so different?

It was now Ian's turn to mock. "Clear off before I seriously damage your health," he said in retaliation.

No one had ever stood up to Vince before, and he was at a loss for words. He knew he couldn't lose this grand, he needed it to settle some pressing debts, otherwise someone else would be dishing out punishment to him. He flinched at the thought, thinking desperately of how he could make this man take notice of him. His adoration of his daughters was well known. Maybe through them was the answer.

"How would you feel if one of your girls was to have a nasty accident?" he asked slowly and menacingly.

Ian's rage knew no bounds. This bastard was threatening the girls now, and this made his guilt even harder to bear. He lashed out wildly, not caring whether anyone else could see or hear. "Leave my girls out of this. I'll kill you, I swear I will!" His fist caught Vince on the nose.

Vince felt blood spurting out and a sensation of numbness. This guy was a nut! Never mind his grand, he wanted out, right now!

He turned to run, but Ian was so incensed with rage, that he went after him. Vince saw the car coming as he turned the corner, and just managed to jump out of the way, but Ian wasn't so lucky. Vince watched with fascinated horror as the woman driver tried desperately to brake, the tyres slid on the gravelled car park, and the offside wing caught Ian, tossing his body up in the air like a rag doll, until it came to rest on the gravel with a sickening thud, with blood pouring from his head.

Chapter Twenty-one

"Mrs Wood, could you please come round to the General Hospital? Your husband has been involved in an accident."

Miranda felt her blood run cold. She could hardly bear to ask. "What sort of accident?"

The voice was controlled. "He was hit by a car and has head injuries."

"But he will be all right?"

"We hope so, but he's still unconscious at the moment."

Miranda felt her hysteria rise. Another drama in her life. Maybe Ian was dying. Would it be too late for him to tell her how sorry he was for leaving her? Tears of self pity pricked at her eyes.

"I'll be there soon. Please don't let him die!" she sobbed.

"I don't think it's as bad as that." The calm voice tried to reassure her, but Miranda had her own ideas.

She lost no time in ringing her mother. Her story was colourful. She said that Ian was fighting for his life and she needed to be with him right now. Her mother sympathised, agreeing to come round immediately to stay with the girls.

Miranda debated whether she should tell them the grim news, but decided that their distress would only make hers worse. There would be time for that later.

She didn't have long to wait. Her mother arrived in minutes, and Miranda stopped the taxi from leaving and directed it onto the hospital. She didn't feel she could drive herself. Her nerves were in pieces. What sort of state would she find Ian in? Maybe the soothing voice was wrong.

It didn't take her long to find the casualty department. There were other people waiting to be attended to, some more patiently than others, but Miranda could no longer control her grief. She wailed with misery at the surprised man at the reception desk. "Where is Ian Wood? I'm his wife. He has head injuries and he needs me."

The man signalled for a passing nurse to pacify Miranda. Her performance was loud, and it was having an adverse effect on other patients.

Sister Kerry Martin took pity on her. This unfortunate lady was obviously fearing the worst, and she tried to reassure her. "Mrs Wood, your husband has had various tests to see if he has suffered any brain damage, or any blood clots, but nothing sinister has been found. He did wake up for a while, but is asleep again now. We have to keep him in for observation, but you must look on the positive side of things."

"I want to go and sit with him," said Miranda, now convinced that the blow to his head would make Ian see the error of his ways, and then he would fall back into her arms again, once he was better, of course.

"Yes you may," Kerry smiled gently, trying to ignore the dominant tone of her voice. "Don't worry about the equipment you see attached to him. We're just ensuring that his heart and pulse rate remain normal. He has suffered a shock too, so we must watch him carefully."

Miranda shuddered at the thought of it. Hospitals were places of drama and death, and she would have such a tale to tell everyone. She thought wildly that she would keep a day and night vigil by his bed to stop that slut Amy from coming to see him. She was the one that counted, his wife, the one they had telephoned!

"Do you know what happened?" she asked Kerry, wondering where it had happened. Had he been with Amy, and did she know about it?

"No," said Kerry. "You'll have to ask him when he wakes up."

Kerry pushed the door open leading into a side room, and Miranda was aware of a middle-aged woman in a grey suit hovering nervously outside. She turned towards Miranda and spoke.

"Excuse me for asking, but are you the wife of that poor man in there?" There was concern written all over her face, and Miranda wondered why she should care about Ian.

"I am Mrs Wood," she said proudly, "but who are you?"

The woman wrung her hands in agitation. "Mrs Wood, I'm so sorry, I'm Beth Davis. I was staying at the Greenview Motel. I don't live this way, and my company sent me down to take part in an exhibition of the products we sell; perfume and jewellery you know . . ." her voice trailed off when Miranda interrupted her.

"How does this affect Ian?" asked Miranda coldly. She had no wish to be reminded of that dratted motel!

"I pulled round the corner in the car park, one man ran across, just missing my car, I wasn't going that fast really, and your husband literally appeared from nowhere. I tried to brake to avoid him, but he ran straight at me and was caught by the offside wing. It was so awful! I called the police and ambulance straight away, and we found your home phone number at the front of his address book, the rest you know."

Even through her grief, Miranda's mind was working overtime. "Was anyone else contacted?" she demanded briskly.

Beth gave her the answer that she wanted. "No, not until they check with you. You are his next of kin."

Miranda could feel her triumph inside. She wasn't going to let Amy Johnson anywhere near him. He was all hers. She regretted her hysterical outburst to her mother now. Mum could also be dramatic, and this needed to be kept under wraps.

"Well, Mrs Davis, I suggest you leave now, or we might take legal action against you!" she said cuttingly. She had no sympathy for the woman, who by her own admission, had caused Ian's injuries, and she felt a certain satisfaction at her discomfiture. Someone had to pay for all the misery that Miranda had suffered.

"Are you coming in here, Mrs Wood?" Kerry asked as pleasantly as she could. She had heard the exchange between the two women and could feel her dislike of Miranda growing, not that she could show it. People often said things they didn't mean in the midst of their grief, but this woman almost seemed to be enjoying the situation. Seeing her husband seemed to come second after making the car driver feel solely responsible for the accident. She had watched her pacing up and down ever since he

154

had been admitted, waiting for someone from his family to arrive. It's not as if she had been drunk or anything, the police had checked all that.

Miranda tried to steel herself for the sight of him. "Yes, but I can't look if his injuries are too horrific!" She gave a strangled sob, just to let everyone know what an ordeal it was for her.

She followed Kerry into the room, her attention was immediately drawn to the still figure, asleep in the bed. His face looked pale, and there was a dressing on top of his head. She could see that some of his hair had been shaved round the affected area. His face was completely unmarked, to her relief. There was a drip attached to his arm, a machine monitoring his heartbeat, and a nurse hovering nearby. Miranda once again dissolved into tears, clutching at his still hand. "My love, I'm here! Please get better, don't die!"

The two nurses exchanged glances, and Kerry said briskly. "Your husband is doing very well Mrs Wood. We have every reason to be optimistic."

Miranda savoured the feel of his hand. It had been a while since she'd had physical contact with him. Why shouldn't she make the most of this situation? Especially while he was in this defenceless state. These nurses, luckily, had no idea that they were parted.

"Is there any other family of Mr Wood; mother, father, brothers, or sisters, that you feel he would like us to contact?" asked Kerry's companion.

Miranda's mind whirled. She didn't want Ian's mother down here, showing her dislike and then stealing all the limelight. That would never do! His brother would make some excuse not to come. He only cared about himself. Ian's family were no good, he was better off without them.

"He's an only child, his parents are dead. He only has me," she said, without a twinge of remorse, dabbing at her eyes again.

"How sad," murmured Kerry, privately thinking that this woman was such an exhibitionist. Anyone who could put up with her must have the patience of a saint.

As Amy drove back from the doctor's she was experiencing a turmoil of emotions. She was elated because she had been told

155

she was pregnant, anxious because the timing wasn't right, and apprehensive because the future was so uncertain.

Once she saw Ian and told him, she knew she'd be able to cope. It had been a shock because he had believed he was sterile, but more than once he had told her how he would have loved to have a child with her if it were possible. Maybe they were down on their luck at the moment, but things would change. Dr Seymour had been very professional and not shown disapproval of the situation. He knew it wasn't Peter's baby because he had performed his vasectomy operation. Amy had swallowed her embarrassment, but when he had asked her if she was considering a termination, her denial was vehement. She guessed, as the family doctor for many years (in fact he had brought Amy into the world), he was like an old friend.

After she had picked up the children from school she headed back to the motel and she noticed that Ian's car was already there. Good, that meant he was home! She was looking forward to telling him the news that he was about to become a father again. Their own baby, she could hardly believe it!

As they got out of the car, the couple from the next room along appeared at the entrance. The woman, who had spoken to them in passing before, called out, "Excuse me love, if you're looking for your man, he's down at the General Hospital. He was hit by a car. I don't know how serious it is."

"What!"

Amy's face whitened. The shock of this news made her feel weak at the knees. Not Ian, it just wasn't fair. Surely he wasn't badly hurt?

"When did this happen?" she asked faintly, conscious that Paul and Sarah had stopped arguing after hearing this news.

"About an hour ago. We came along just after, and we saw the ambulance and the police."

Amy made a supreme effort to remain calm. She felt panic inside her at the thought that she might lose him, but outwardly she remained in control. She politely thanked the woman, and then urged Paul and Sarah to get back into the car.

They had resumed fighting again, causing her even more stress. "Stop it you two! Ian's been knocked down by a car, and all you can do is argue. You're absolutely pathetic!"

"Sorry Mummy."

They both sat still, suitably chastened, and Amy sped along the road as fast as the rush hour traffic would permit her to. She knew they must be getting tired and hungry, but right now seeing Ian was her priority. This pregnancy was making her feel so nauseous, and the worry on top of it wasn't helping, but her mind was full of Ian, so she paid no heed to her complaining stomach.

Her one hope, when she got there, was that she could see him. She wasn't his next of kin, if he was awake he would ask for her, but if not, the hospital would call Miranda. She couldn't deny that Miranda had a right to know, but Amy could think of nothing worse than a confrontation with her.

"Clive, it's Miranda. I'm at the hospital. Ian has been knocked down by a car."

Clive put on his most sympathetic tone of voice. "How terrible! Will he be all right?"

"Yes, I think so, but you must keep this all quiet."

"Of course, Miranda."

Clive wondered what she had up her sleeve, and he wasn't kept in suspense for long.

"That position you told me about in Cornwall. Ian wants to take it. Can you arrange for the bank to move us straight away. He may have to recuperate for a little while, and we won't wait for the house to be sold. The estate agents can do that, but the sooner we go, the better."

Clive was startled, especially after Ian's verbal resignation earlier that day. If Ian moved, it would be much better for him. "Has Ian agreed then?"

"Yes, if you have the transfer papers drawn up, he'll sign them," she said.

She felt no guilt about the lie she was telling. Her only thought was to get him away from Amy.

"How long will he be in hospital?" enquired Clive.

"Only a few days the doctor says. He hit his head, but it's not a serious injury, and he's now recovered consciousness."

For once in her life she played down the drama and told the truth. If she exaggerated Ian's condition he wouldn't get the promotion, and then her plan would fail.

"That's good news. I'll sort things out tomorrow and phone

you," said Clive. He wanted to be rid of Ian, so he welcomed Miranda as his ally.

As Miranda put the phone down she turned, and there approaching, was Amy. She stiffened with anger, somehow the bitch had heard, but there was no way that Miranda was going to let her past. "What do you want, whore?" she shrieked wildly, hoping that everyone could hear her.

Amy bit her lip, knowing she had to expect this. Thank goodness the children were sitting out in casualty. She didn't want them to hear. "Miranda, I need to know how Ian is. I wasn't there when he was knocked down!"

Miranda's eyes bulged with rage. Was this woman never going to take no for an answer! She stamped her foot, and the floorboards reverberated under her less than dainty touch. Her shrill voice had the desired effect of arresting the attention of everyone within earshot. "If he'd been with me this would never have happened. Well he is with me now, and he's staying with me. He doesn't want you any more!"

The triumph in her eyes annoyed Amy. She was lying, she must be! "I don't believe you!" she said firmly.

Miranda laughed mockingly, pointing towards the door of the room. "They won't let you in, try asking them. I'm the only one who can go in."

Amy was angry! This wasn't fair! In the eyes of everyone else she was nothing, not even a relative. If Ian didn't ask for her, she had no way of seeing him. Miranda was still his wife, even though they were separated.

The nurse standing by the door couldn't fail to hear everything that had been said, just like everyone else around, and she now addressed Miranda.

"Could you please keep your voice down Mrs Wood? This sort of scene will not help your husband to recover."

Amy moved quickly, in desperation. She just had to see him! He was inside that door. She tried to enter, but it was no good, Kerry barred her way.

"Please tell me how he is," Amy said, desperately. The only way to get past Kerry was by pushing her, and she didn't think the hospital staff would take too kindly to that. "How is Ian?" she asked in desperation.

Kerry felt sorry for her. With a wife like loud-mouthed

158

Miranda, who could blame him for having another woman. Miranda seemed to have a way of getting under everyone's skin.

"He will he all right soon, but he's suffering from shock. I think it may be better if you don't see him. This dispute between you and his wife will only cause him stress."

"I know," said Amy miserably. Now she really did feel like 'the other woman', someone without any rights, and of no consequence. The gloating look in Miranda's eyes sickened her, and she watched with misery in her heart as Miranda entered the room and shut the door behind her. "They are separated you know, and Ian is living with me," she told Kerry, who looked at her sympathetically.

That information explained a few things for Kerry. Ian had now regained consciousness, but he seemed a bit foggy, couldn't remember too much, but that wasn't unusual after a head injury. He might have temporarily forgotten that he'd left his wife. He hadn't questioned her being there, but he hadn't appeared pleased to see her either.

"Ring up in the morning at eight o'clock, and ask for me, Sister Kerry Martin. I'll let you know how he is before I go off duty," she said kindly.

She wasn't supposed to get involved really, she knew that, but she could imagine how Amy felt. She didn't look like a bimbo, she seemed nice, and not being able to see him at a time like this must be pure torture. Maybe after a night's sleep Ian's memory would be clearer, and he would ask to see her, and if seeing Amy would help his recovery, then so be it, because ultimately that was all Kerry cared about.

159

Chapter Twenty-two

Amy telephoned the hospital promptly at eight o'clock the following morning, more anxious than ever for news of Ian. She had suffered a disturbed night, with very little sleep, not helped by the feeling of nausea which continued to plague her. She asked to speak to Kerry, and was relieved when her soothing voice came over the line.

"Sister Kerry Martin here, can I help you?"

"It's Amy here, please can you tell me how Ian is?" Would she remember their conversation yesterday? "You did tell me to ring at eight," she reminded her.

"Yes of course, Ian is much better today. He is awake, but apart from a cut head, he has no physical injuries."

Amy's heart felt just a little bit lighter, but her need to see him was urgent. "That's wonderful! Can I come and see him today?"

Kerry swallowed uncomfortably. It had been wrong of her to get involved in the first place, just because Amy seemed nicer than his wife. If she came head to head with Miranda again, who knows what might happen.

"I'm afraid it's not up to me, Amy. Miranda's still here, and Ian hasn't asked her to go. Perhaps you should wait until he leaves hospital."

Amy felt as if the bottom had just fallen out of her world. Could Ian have gone back to Miranda? Why hadn't he phoned her? So many questions she wanted to ask him. Well she had been told she couldn't visit, but this time she would go anyway. If he had finished with her she wanted to hear it from Ian's lips. She thanked Kerry and put the telephone down.

She told herself not to worry about it, but she couldn't help it. There was such pain inside her at the thought of losing him, and there was anger too. What a fool she'd been, giving up everything to be with him, and now she was carrying his child and he might never know.

She told herself not to judge him until she knew for sure. If she was alone, she must cope with it, not only for the sake of Sarah and Paul, but also for the new little life that was growing inside her. She made up her mind that if she lost Ian she would still survive, because of their child.

David sat with his head in his hands, trying to see his way out of his impending doom. He'd always thought of himself as very tough and strong minded, made of stern stuff, a typical politician. But he knew he was caught like a rat in a trap, he was desperate and there was no way out.

Sally had found him, God only knows how, and she had made his life a nightmare. Blackmail was her game. He had been forced to drop out of the local election because she had threatened to reveal their relationship to the local press. He had hoped a few thousand pounds as a pay-off would get her out of his hair, but Sally had other ideas. She had told him she was pregnant, she wanted money for an abortion, and then a regular allowance for the rest of her life.

He had been hounded by her, it wasn't love, but she had an obsession which caused her to stalk him, and then the incessant telephone calls and demands for money. The strain of trying to keep it from Susan was driving him mad, and he could see his future in tatters unless he could rid himself of this little whore.

She needed to be got rid of but Vince had refused to help him. His job in frightening Ian off had gone wrong, and he no longer wanted to work for David. Ian was in hospital, but still alive, but Vince had told him he'd had enough. David was desperate!

The telephone was ringing again. It was her, it always was these days, perfectly timed as usual, Susan was out and he'd have to answer it! He couldn't risk her leaving a message on the answerphone. He picked up the receiver with shaking hands.

161

"Yes," he said curtly.

"Hello David. I need some more money from you." Her voice grated on him, to think that once he had been so attracted to her. She was a blood sucking vile creature, and he knew she wouldn't rest until she'd sucked him dry.

His tone became begging. When would she leave him in peace?

"Sally, I've already raised a great deal of money to help you. You'll bankrupt me soon. What are you trying to do, finish me completely?"

Sally smiled with satisfaction on the other end of the telephone. She had him just where she wanted him. Not only had he dropped out of the election, she had also reduced him to a mental wreck, as she had intended. This man was power seeking and totally selfish. He didn't care who he trod on to get where he wanted, and Sally wanted revenge.

She had watched her best friend change from a happy person, full of life, to an alcoholic, and all because she had fallen in love with this man. He had used her for a while and then dumped her. Escort girls were not supposed to fall in love, but Jenny had been beautiful and vulnerable, only in the job because she needed to get away from her stepfather who had been sexually abusing her for years.

Her naturally happy nature had helped her to survive her ordeals of childhood, and David had seemed like a knight in shining armour. Jenny had naïvely believed he would leave his wife and make a new life with her.

After he had ended it, she had never been the same. Being betrayed by a man once again was too much for her, and then the drinking started. Sally had tried to get her to go to work, and go out and meet new people, but Jenny would have none of it. She drank anything and everything she could lay her hands on, even resorting to stealing from Sally to finance her addiction.

One night Sally had come home to find her unconscious, laying in a pool of vomit, and although this was not unusual, there was something about her stillness that frightened her. She couldn't find a pulse, and she knew, even as she dialled for an ambulance, that Jenny was dead.

The post-mortem had revealed such a large quantity of alcohol and pills inside her, that it made it impossible to know whether she tried to take her own life, or whether she had just choked on her own vomit and died. The inquest had recorded an open verdict, but as far as Sally was concerned, David had killed Jenny, as surely as if he had stabbed a knife through her heart.

"Well, if you prefer that I have this baby, it's up to you. I can't look after it, so you would have to, and I would need much more money over the next few months because obviously I can't work." Her tone became sneering. "How do you feel about being a daddy again David, and how would your wife feel about the new addition."

"Leave my wife out of it!" shouted David wildly, and then made an effort to compose himself. How could he let her get to him like this! She probably was only bluffing, there was no pregnancy, but he couldn't take the risk.

"I will meet you at the car park on the common as before, but £10,000 is all I can let you have. After that Sally you must disappear out of my life for good, or else I will contact the police."

"I don't think you will," said Sally, enjoying the feeling of power she had over him. He might be upper class, and she was nothing to him, but oh how the mighty doth fall!

"Be there at eight, when it gets dark," said David commandingly. This little tart might think she'd got the upper hand on him, but he wasn't going to let her win. He would fight back!

Ian tried not to glare at Miranda, wondering just how she had come back into his life again. He remembered the events, but as it was now Wednesday, he seemed to have lost a day somewhere. He remembered being told by a thug to leave Amy, but nothing and no one would make him do that. He also remembered the pig had threatened the safety of the girls, and that had made him flip. He'd chased him, and that's how he'd been hit by the car.

Well it would have either been Peter or her father that would have hired someone to do that, but it made no difference. He felt no fear, life without Amy would have been no life at all, foolish or not, it made no difference to his intentions. He tried to keep the irritation out of his voice when he spoke.

"Miranda, I appreciate you coming to see me, but I want to see

Amy, and it's better if you go soon so that you don't have to see one another."

Miranda gave him a hurt look. After all she'd done! She was prepared to take him back, even start a new life in Cornwall, sell the house, uproot the girls from school, and still all he could think about was that slut!

"That's not what you said to me yesterday," she said, allowing a sob into her voice, and dabbing her eyes with the clean handkerchief she had kept in her bag ready for use.

Ian tried very hard to remember yesterday. He thought he must have spent most of it asleep, and certainly didn't remember any conversation with Miranda. "What did I say?"

Miranda drew a deep breath. This was her last chance, and she knew it. She felt no guilt about lying to him. Ian hadn't been capable of making a rational decision ever since he'd met that tart in her opinion. "You told me you wanted to take that post in Cornwall that Clive told us about a while ago. I've gone as far as making enquiries about schools for the girls, and Clive has drawn up the transfer forms all ready for you to sign today. Ian, I will take you back, and it will be a new start for us."

Ian looked intently at her. She was lying, he knew, and he didn't want to be taken back. He remembered his last conversation with Clive, the way he had spoken to him, and his resignation. Miranda and Clive were trying to get him away from Amy, but they were wasting their time.

"No Miranda, I may have had a knock on the head, but I never wanted to go to Cornwall when you asked me the first time, and now my life has changed even more. My future is with Amy, and I shall eventually want a divorce from you."

He tried to be kind but firm, she was so thick skinned, it seemed the only way. But Miranda's reaction was as he had thought it would be. She let out a howl of rage, and picking up the nearest thing, which happened to be a jug of water on the locker beside his bed, emptied the contents over his head.

"I hate you so much Ian Wood! You've ruined my life and abandoned your children. I wish that car had killed you!" and then she collapsed on the floor, sobbing and screaming, just like a toddler who has just had an ice cream taken away from them.

Ian took the towel from the radiator and dried off his face. He just wanted to get away from her, and to his relief he found some shoes inside the locker. He quickly put them in a carrier bag, and was only just in time, as Miranda's outburst had caused a couple of nurses to come running in.

"My wife is feeling faint," he said, knowing how much Miranda would enjoy them fussing over her.

They both went to help her up from the floor, and Ian took the opportunity to leave the room, explaining that he needed to go to the toilet. Whilst he was temporarily forgotten about, he put on the shoes and slipped his slippers into the bag. Thank goodness he had been allowed out of bed to get dressed today, otherwise this would have been harder. He had been told that he would have to see the doctor and then he might be allowed home, but he couldn't wait for that. His idea of home was anywhere with Amy, not Miranda.

He slipped quietly into the corridor, he did not look out of place now that he was dressed, and headed for the door and freedom. But just as he stepped outside, he realised he had no money, nor had he any idea where his wallet or mobile was. But that seemed a minor detail right now. He ignored the slight feeling of dizziness in his head, and the chilliness of the wind, so unexpected for mid-May. He would walk back to the motel to find her if he had to.

It was now mid-morning, so Amy decided to go to the hospital. Ian obviously didn't have his mobile phone any more. He must have lost it. She had tried ringing it so many times, but although she left a message, he never came back to her. She knew he would if he knew. Maybe Miranda had it; if she did, she'd be sure to delete all Amy's messages.

The buzz of the entry phone disturbed these thoughts, and she hesitated, hope flooding through her that it just might be Ian.

"Yes, who is it?" she enquired. To her amazement, her brother's friendly voice answered.

"It's Max here, sis."

Amy pressed the button to release the door for him, wondering if he was coming to lecture her on the folly of her ways. She had told him she was going to do it, and now she had.

He stood in the doorway and his face bore its usual friendly smile. Amy ran to hug him, feeling not so alone now.

"Come in, I'll make some coffee," she said. "After that I have to go out."

"It's lovely to see you, Amy," he said warmly.

"I'm glad to see someone is pleased to see me," said Amy, wryly.

"Well, I had to come and see you when you told me you'd done the dastardly deed. This man must be something special if you've given up everything to come and live in a motel!"

"This is only temporary. We want to get somewhere else, but it's not easy with Jasper."

Amy felt conscious of the bare surroundings as Max looked around. He, too, had been helped by their parents, and had a nice house. For the first time in her life, Amy felt embarrassed about where she lived. She could see disapproval in his face, and being Max, who was so open and honest, he would speak his mind.

"Is there anything I can do to help? Why is Peter still in the house? You should be there with the children, surely?"

"Well I left him," said Amy, wondering why she was defending Peter. It was true, but she knew he wouldn't give it up without a fight, and her conscience still bothered her about taking the children away from him.

"Mummy and Daddy have virtually disowned me, and according to the papers, Daddy's dropped out of the election. I expect the scandal ruined it for him. It's all my fault!"

Max put his arm around her shoulders, soothingly. "Like I said before, you have to do what's right in this life, and if you're not happy with Peter, then you must get out. Mater and Pater will accept it eventually. If the fact that you and Peter have split up affects his election chances, I'd be amazed. Look at all the things we hear about MPs in the House of Commons. They still manage to stay on top."

Amy wanted to believe him, her conscience weighed very heavily on her, so she explained.

"I tried to tell Mummy and Daddy about Peter's temper, and his roughness, but they don't believe me. It gradually destroyed my love for him."

The merry smile vanished from Max's blue eyes, to be replaced by a look of concern. He said stoutly. "Well no one bullies my sister. Our parents are snobs, and it's no good ignoring things like that just to save the family from scandal. You aren't

166

the first person to be divorced, and you certainly won't be the last. They just need to come into the twenty-first century, and stop worrying about what their neighbours think!"

Amy hugged him in gratitude. "How wonderful you think that. I thought everyone was against us."

Max looked directly at her, holding her away from him, smiling grimly. "The problem is, Peter has told our parents that he is going to try and get custody of the children, and quite frankly sis, whilst you are living here, he stands a good chance."

Amy felt the blood rush to her head. Fear and anger coursed through her at the thought of it.

"Oh no, he mustn't. As soon as we can get somewhere we will!" she exclaimed, trying to ignore the possibility that she might be fighting to keep her children alone. She then proceeded to tell him about Ian's accident, and her thwarted attempt to visit him in hospital.

"Come on, I'll take you there. Two heads are better than one," joked Max, and Amy felt relief coursing through her. She did have one ally after all.

Chapter Twenty-three

"I'm going to let everyone know just what a rat you are! My best friend would be alive today if it wasn't for you!"

"If you think a tramp like you would be believed, you're crazy! I'm not going to let you ruin my life. You're just as self destructive as Jenny was!"

Even as David uttered these words, he knew this wasn't true. There was nothing self destructive about Sally. She was a survivor, and she knew enough about him to ruin his life. She'd already done it politically, and soon his family would know about his other life that he'd been so careful to conceal for all these years. Once again he felt the hopelessness sweep over him.

Sally's anger flared at his mention of Jenny. He hadn't even expressed regret on hearing of her death. She turned and slapped his face hard, shouting, "That's from Jenny!" She could feel herself shaking with anger, and in the heat of the moment, fervently wished she had a knife in her hand to plunge deep in his heart. Watching him die in agony in front of her would be retribution for what he had done.

David put his hand to his stinging cheek, and the ridiculousness of the situation struck him. He, a self-made, and very rich man, was under the thumb of this little tart, who was nothing. Her life was valueless, she made her money out of fools like himself who needed sex. He felt a great rage rising inside him, unlike anything he had ever known before. His hands went round her throat, and they tightened. He saw the fear in her eyes, as she tried to struggle, but his grip was like a vice, and he felt no conscience. She wanted to cause so much damage in his life. She was choking now, and the colour had gone from her face, but David was triumphant, she was dying, and so he had won.

Clive saw the car in the woods just as it was getting dark. He felt himself get hard at the thought of it. Everyone at work thought he was a bit of a flirt. There was speculation as to why he was single, but he wasn't gay. He'd tried sex, but it had been nothing for him, no enjoyment, just plain boring! What was wrong with him? It was great for everyone else, and it made the world go round. He didn't like being different from everyone else, so he kept it a secret. They would only say he was odd. He lived in a fantasy world. His fantasies involved watching others have sex, this turned him on greatly, the sight of women without clothes on excited him, but only towards himself, and he frequently imagined how nice it would be to have a woman go down on him, and to be teased with her mouth and her lips until he came.

Clive spent his free time in the woods. He enjoyed exposing himself to women, watching their horror at the sight of his penis was a real turn-on, and also viewing couples in cars having sex. He spent his time masturbating. During the daytime he was a respectable Office Manager at the bank, and at night he was out satisfying himself. He didn't think there was anything wrong with it, he wasn't a pervert, and this was the only way he could express his sex drive.

He managed to get nearer to the car by dodging through the trees. It wasn't quite dark yet, so he approached carefully, keeping low. The car was parked by a dense bush, which enabled him to get a very good view without much chance of being seen.

Excitement rose inside him, and his hands undid the zip to free his bulging erection. As he peered into the car, he heard their voices raised, the woman was leaning close to the man, and he saw her hand come up to slap him. So they were arguing, that meant a passionate session afterwards! Clive waited with eager anticipation.

Then he saw the man put his hands round her throat. He couldn't see her face, but he could hear the choking noises. Fear at what he was witnessing rushed through him, and all sexual

169

h

thoughts vanished. He was trying to murder her, and Clive had no wish to be a party to that.

He turned to run, forgetting his trousers were round his ankles, and he tripped. Making a frantic attempt to remain upright, he grabbed at the bush, and there was a loud sound of twigs breaking. At that moment he saw the man's face, the manic fury that was possessing him, and terror flooded through him. Would he be next?

The next events happened so quickly that he felt as if he was in a dream. The car door was flung open and the woman was pushed out onto the ground. Clive stood rooted to the spot, watching her choking, whilst the man drove the car off wildly, tyres screeching leaving behind a cloud of dust.

Clive took the cowards way out. No one must know he had been there, his good name was more important to him than knowing whether this woman lived or not. He ignored her choking on the ground, and with shaky hands he pulled up his trousers and did up the zip. Then he ran, as fast as he could, out of the wood and back to his car. He was going back to the safety of his home, away from the man with the manic eyes.

Ian propped himself up against the side of the telephone booth and tried to ignore the dizziness that was threatening to overcome him. He was trying to remember the name of the motel they were staying at so that he could ring and get Amy to come and pick him up, but his head was so fuzzy he couldn't think straight. He had no money on him, so he couldn't get a bus, or a cab. A feeling of helplessness, which he wasn't used to, swept over him. He knew he had been wrong to leave hospital so suddenly, but he needed to be free of Miranda and that had seemed the only way to achieve it.

He passed his hand over his aching head, and then brightened. Mum, there was always Mum, she would send a taxi. She couldn't drive and had never owned a car. He frowned whilst thinking of her number. His brain was just useless today, but this number he'd known since a child! He told himself to calm down, his heart was thudding, and he could feel himself sweating with stress. Whatever was it? 0323 at the beginning, but what about the rest. Oh yes, 1233 sounded right, he fervently hoped so, because he wanted to make a reverse charge call.

He called the operator, he couldn't get her to check if it was correct because his mother was ex-directory, and he was the one who had suggested that years ago to protect her from his violent father. Ian had worried that he might return one day, so he hoped this had made it too difficult for him to find her.

The female operator answered after what seemed a lifetime to Ian, and he quoted the number to her. "Who shall I say is calling?" she asked, in a bored voice.

"I'm her son, Ian Wood, please tell her it's urgent?" His tone was almost begging, and he prayed that Janet would be in. He felt ill and tired, and everything seemed so difficult to cope with right now. He longed for the warmth and comfort of Amy's arms again.

The operator's bored voice came back on the line, interrupting his thoughts. "You're through, speak now," and to his intense relief, his mother's familiar voice was saying hello.

"Mum, it's Ian, I'm out of hospital with no money, can you send a taxi to pick me up please?"

"Hospital! Whatever is wrong? No one told me!" Janet bristled with indignation, but concern for Ian took over. "Where are you? I'll come and get you right away."

"I'm down Mortimer Street in a call box, about five minutes walk from the hospital going towards the town centre."

"Right son, hang on, and I'll get there as quickly as I can."

Janet was amazed. How often had Ian asked for her help? He was the one who usually looked after her. Something was up, and she felt worried. Why wasn't he with Amy, and what was he doing in hospital? No doubt he would explain when she saw him. He had told her she would be meeting Amy soon only last week, but why wasn't she bringing him back from the hospital?

Janet never used taxis, but this was an emergency. She dialled for one, and then she tried to ring him on his mobile to tell him, but it didn't seem to be on. She intended to go in the taxi. Whilst she waited for it she tried, without success, to make some sense of the situation. It was beyond her, but no doubt when he saw her, Ian would explain all.

"I'm afraid Mr Wood left earlier today. He discharged himself without seeing the doctor." Myra Andrews omitted to tell Amy and Max the circumstances of Ian's departure. She had already been hauled over the coals by Sister for not noticing his escape, being too busy administering to Miranda. She had been told that this could be very embarrassing for the hospital if it leaked out.

"Was his wife here when he went?" Amy asked, anxiety churning inside her at the dreaded answer. Myra swallowed uncomfortably. The scene with Miranda had made it clear that the Wood marriage was not a happy one, but it was none of her business, although like everyone else, she couldn't help being curious. Miranda's outburst had set the tongues wagging. She would love to tell Amy how Miranda had left the hospital in a major strop, blaming everyone for his escape, who wouldn't want to escape from her?

But common sense prevailed, and she said quite truthfully. "Yes, Mrs Wood was here."

She saw the bleak look in Amy's eyes, and wondered if she was the cause of Miranda's anger. If she was, who could blame Ian. No wonder he had tried to escape, but obviously his wife had found him again, because this young woman hadn't. She felt a fleeting pity for her.

Max took charge of the situation. Amy's face was pale and distressed. Perhaps this Ian was not the man she thought he was, and if so she would definitely need his, and Anna's, support.

"OK, we'll go back to the motel to check if he's there, and if he's not, you're bringing the children to stay with us until you decide what to do!" he said firmly.

Amy was grateful for his strength. She felt as if she was falling apart. The situation was bleak one minute, and then there seemed hope, but each time it had been dashed by circumstances. She was unable to cope with this yo-yo of emotions, and the all too familiar wave of nausea swept through her once more, causing her even more distress.

Max had noticed her pale and wan look, so he tried to keep up his cheerful manner during the journey to the motel. Amy seemed to be in a world of her own, and he was aware that his merry banter was falling on deaf ears.

As he had feared, the room was empty, and the receptionist confirmed that there had been no sign of Ian. Max could see that Amy had given up hope when she collapsed sobbing in his arms, and confessed her pregnancy.

The first seeds of doubt were sewn in his mind as to whether his support of her was the right thing to do. Anna had only recently had their first baby, a boy they had named James, how would she welcome a pregnant sister-in-law, and her two children?

"Has Ian taken his clothes and belongings?" he asked quietly, passing her a handkerchief to wipe her very red eyes.

Amy tried to speak normally. Her throat felt as if it had a huge lump in it, and she couldn't stop shaking. She had never felt so alone in all her life. She hated Ian as much as she had loved him, for leaving her to face all this alone, she was homeless, penniless and pregnant, but of course he didn't know that, and now he never would.

"He only had a few things, we were planning to get the rest when we found somewhere else to live." Her voice was quiet and controlled, which was amazing, because she could feel a tidal wave of emotions coursing through her inside. If she had been alone she would have screamed and shouted, but she had no wish to share her anger and grief at this time, it was locked away inside her.

Max helped her to pack the few things that belonged to herself and the children into the car, and they returned the key to the receptionist and booked out. The first thing they did was to go and pick the children up from school. Max welcomed this diversion, his jokes were laughed at, and they seemed very happy when told they were coming to stay with Uncle Max and Auntie Anna for a while. There was also the attraction of their new cousin they had not yet seen. He glanced every so often across at Amy, but she sat still and preoccupied, seemingly in a world of her own. He could see she had taken this really badly. He had a feeling that when they arrived home, he was not going to be Anna's favourite person. But, he reasoned with himself, he couldn't just turn his back on Amy like their parents had, she was his sister. He did hope Anna would understand.

173

Chapter Twenty-four

David watched Sally's contorted face with evil satisfaction as she fought for her life. He was like a man possessed, all sense and reasoning had deserted him, and he worked silently, his sole aim being to silence her permanently.

He came back to reality when he saw the man's face, and heard the sound of twigs snapping. Now panic set it. Not only had he got a witness to this murderous act, she could still live to tell everything about him. Whatever had made him act like this? This scheming blackmailing bitch had reduced him to this mental wreck, who would stop at nothing to try and keep his good name intact.

But he had failed, she had outwitted him. Gone would be the respect he had worked so hard to build up during his life. He would lose the love of his wife and family, never again could he hold his head up high. The newspapers would be full of his frolics with escort girls, and worst of all, he would be exposed to his family as the biggest hypocrite ever. At that moment, David Lee, self made man, always prepared to tread any difficult path, even a slightly crooked one at times, gave up, he had reached breaking point.

He opened the car door and pushed out the choking figure. If they caught up with him it would be at least attempted murder, but they wouldn't. He would make sure of that. Prison was not an option, he wanted to have the last say in his future.

He was panting as he drove wildly out of the car park. Sheer panic made him drive at double the speed limit along the country road, narrowly missing cars coming the other way. He could feel the exhilaration of freedom as he roared up Gallows Hill. No one could catch him now. He was invincible! This was his last conscious thought as he reached the top and deliberately, without stopping, drove his car straight over the precipice.

Janet made a cup of tea. Ian was asleep on the sofa in the front room. It was now early evening, and he had slept for about three hours. She decided not to disturb him. He had told her all about his accident, and the trip to hospital and the invasion by Miranda. Now she understood why he had discharged himself so quickly. She felt the all too familiar dislike of Miranda rise inside her again. That woman really was the limit! Not only had she made Ian's life a misery, she also hadn't had the decency to tell Janet that her own son was in hospital. How much lower could she get?

She put the television on quietly to watch the news, doing her best not to wake him. Her thoughts wandered again. What about Amy? Why hadn't she been with him at the hospital? Was this woman he had given up everything to be with as genuine as Ian thought she was? He seemed to be blinded by love. Maybe she didn't feel the same.

Ian opened his eyes, momentarily confused as to where he was. So much seemed to be happening to him at the moment, but at least he didn't feel so dizzy now. Of course, he was at Mum's.

"Oh tea, I could drink the pot dry." He grinned, pointing at her cup.

Janet brightened. He looked better now, that was the main thing, he had given her quite a turn earlier, and she had been tempted to call her own doctor, but Ian had pointed out that he might be sent back to hospital, and he didn't want that.

She poured him a mug full, putting in extra sugar to give him some energy, he certainly seemed to need it. "You look better now son, are you?" she enquired anxiously.

"Much better," agreed Ian, seeing his mother smile with relief. "I've just remembered Mum!" he said excitedly. "Greenview Motel is the name of the place we stayed at, we can ring Amy now and she'll come to fetch me."

Janet felt a stab of jealousy, which she knew was unfair, so she

175

hid it. It had been nice having him at home, if only for a few hours, just like the old days when he was a boy. Well if this young woman was half as genuine as he thought she was, she would be round to pick him up soon. That familiar feeling of loneliness swept over her again. She could never seem to get used to it. This time she made up her mind she wasn't going to interfere. He had to make his own life. She picked up the telephone book to look up the number for him.

Amy lay in bed at Max's house thinking of all that had happened. Her initial grief at once again losing Ian had passed, a numbness had set in, but she was aware of the pain inside, which she knew she would have to learn to cope with. She had taken a gamble, and lost, no matter how much she tried to dress it up in her mind, it was just an affair for Ian, and no doubt, with his new found sexual confidence, he could make a go of his marriage. She had to face up to it no matter how much it hurt.

She touched her stomach, thinking of the new life that was growing inside her. She could never regret that, because as far as she was concerned this baby had been conceived in love. This child would be just as loved as her other two children, and she resolved, at that moment, to pick up the pieces of her life and build a future worth having.

Seeing Anna, still beautiful from childbirth, with her glowing cheeks and sparkling eyes, nursing her new born son James, had roused all her maternal instincts. She wanted, and needed, this baby. She realised that staying here could only be a temporary measure, even Max's big house was over full with herself and the children, and she had hastened to assure Anna that it wouldn't be for long. Max and Anna were entitled to their own privacy. But going back to Peter was not an option, she would find a solicitor, file divorce proceedings, and then maybe the house could be sold. With her half she could buy another, even though it would obviously have to be much smaller and more modest. With these thoughts in her mind, she turned over, tried to put the turmoils of the day behind her, and went to sleep.

She got up early the next day to get the children ready for school, thankful at least that it was term-time. She planned to go job hunting. Her interview the other day had been cancelled, the job had gone before she'd even got to the interview. It was disheartening, but she resolved that she wouldn't give up. She pushed thoughts of how she would cope when her pregnancy became apparent out of her mind. That was just too negative to think about.

She showered and dressed quickly in the en suite room attached to the guest bedroom which she was occupying. This was a real touch of luxury after the last three weeks at the motel. The double bed had been very comfortable, and Anna, with her flair for beautiful and elegant things, had pink draped velvet curtains at the windows, cream carpeting on the floor, and a satin bedspread. The walls had pictures of country scenes in spring, and an elegant full length mirror. The fitted wardrobes had gold handles on the doors, and inside they were the size of a dressing room, surrounded by even more mirrors all round. She decided to enjoy her brief stay there, because she realised that it would be a long time before she would stay in such nice surroundings again.

Paul and Sarah were sharing the room next door. It had two beds, one fitted underneath the other when not in use, and it was reserved especially for all children that visited and stayed. The room was light and airy, decorated in bold colours, red and green, with green carpeting, apple green walls and curtains with splashes of red and green on them. The quilts matched the curtains, and the whole room seemed bright and alive. There was a television and video, with shelves full of books, and a desk. The built-in cupboards were full of toys, so it made an ideal playroom. Amy thought wryly that Paul and Sarah would not want to leave here in a hurry.

She went in to wake them up, urging them to get dressed and come down for breakfast.

"Mummy, can we stay here again tonight?" asked Sarah. "I want to hold James again."

Paul didn't share her enthusiasm. "He makes a lot of noise when he goes to sleep," he said, ruefully.

"Just like you used to," said Amy, finding him a clean shirt from the suitcase. "Hurry up now, I must give this a quick iron."

She went down the stairs to the large and spacious kitchen, just like mine at home, she thought wistfully. It was another bright room. The walls were painted in lime green with predominately white tiles interspaced with larger ones with fruits on. The units

177

were in limed oak, as was the kitchen table and chairs. The curtains complemented the tiles with more fruit on a lime green background, and the white floor tiles shone with cleanliness. It was beautiful, just like a show home. Anna did not have any animals, and did not share Amy's love of them, so Jasper had not been allowed outside the kitchen, and he had slept in the utility room, which was large and warm, plenty big enough for his bed to fit in.

Amy had expected this, as when they had visited in the past he had always been left at home, but she was grateful that at least he was able to come. She patted him gently, whispering, "Soon we'll have a new home old boy, I promise you."

Anna followed her down the stairs, rubbing her eyes. Even with her long black hair tousled, and no make-up on, she was still very beautiful. She was tall and very slim, childbirth had added a few curves to her normally boyish figure, and it suited her. She was breast feeding, and the fullness of her breasts, and the bloom of motherhood only added to her attractiveness.

"Amy, I'm sorry I haven't done any breakfast yet. James woke up at five for a feed. It seemed to go on for ever, and then I must have fallen back to sleep. I didn't even hear Max get up and go to work." She was privately wishing that she could have the house to herself, and then she could sleep around James's feeds. She had been feeling very tired since the birth, only a month ago, and had agreed to put up Amy and the children for Max's sake. He felt so sorry for his sister, but Anna wasn't comfortable being involved. She wanted to maintain a good relationship with her in-laws. This lovely house was courtesy of them. She was well aware that Max's wages as an insurance clerk wouldn't have run to it, and she had only been a shop assistant before they married, and at the moment was thankful that she didn't need to return to work.

Amy felt guilty. She remembered how tired she had felt after giving birth. Elated yes, but totally exhausted. Max probably didn't realise. Men never did, but she hadn't forgotten, no matter how much a baby was loved, the demands it put on a woman in the early days, especially the first one, were tremendous.

"Oh Anna, don't be so silly! You only need to worry about James. I can prepare breakfasts. I'm just so grateful for your support!"

Anna looked relieved, and Amy carried on.

"Once I've taken the children to school I shall be out job hunting, and if there's any housework or shopping I can do that for you too." She was about to remind Anna they wouldn't be staying for long, but the telephone rang, and she took the opportunity to iron Paul's shirt whilst Anna answered it.

When Anna returned to the kitchen her dark eyes were wide with shock and she was pale and trembling. Amy jumped up to put her arms round her, wondering whatever could be wrong. Anna's voice was scarcely more than a whisper.

"Amy, I don't know how to tell you this, I can hardly believe it myself . . ."

Amy's first thought was Ian, even now she couldn't help herself. Her heart was beating so fast she felt she would faint with fear, but still she had to know. "Can't believe what, Anna?"

"It's your father, he didn't come home last night. Your mother said he had been acting oddly since he dropped out of the election, so she didn't worry too much at first, thinking he had just wanted to go somewhere to be on his own . . ."

"But he's home now?" Amy asked anxiously.

Anna swallowed awkwardly, and tried to moisten her dry lips. How could she tell Amy this? She rushed on quickly, anxious to get the ordeal over with. "No, I'm afraid the police have just been to tell your mother that the remains of your father's Rover were found in a ravine at Gallows Hill. As yet, his body has not been recovered, but it's not surprising . . ." her voice tailed off.

Amy could feel a voice screaming inside her, berating her for all the harm she had done to everyone, and she tried to put her hands over her ears to shut it out. "Don't give me the details," she sobbed. "There's no way he could have survived all that."

She sat there burdened with guilt. It was because of her, she was sure. First he'd dropped out of the election, and when he couldn't take the disgrace she'd heaped on the family, he'd wanted to end it all. She hated herself so much at that moment, the burden of guilt just seemed too much to bear. Why, oh why had she fallen in love. It had done so much damage. She put her hands over her face and sobbed for the man who had loved her so much.

"Please forgive me Daddy. You were angry with me, and I never had a chance to say goodbye. I love you."

179

Chapter Twenty-five

Susan slowly put on the black dress she had bought especially for the funeral. It was made of silk, a simple straight design with short sleeves and a high neck. She planned to wear her crystal necklace and earrings with it, they should set it off perfectly, and it would be most suitable for the occasion. There were many relatives coming today, she had to look her best, and maintain her dignity. To the outside world it appeared that David had suffered a fatal accident, the coroner had recorded death by misadventure, but Susan had her own thoughts on this.

There was no doubt in Susan's mind that Amy's behaviour had contributed to her father's death, she hadn't blamed her in so many words, but then she didn't have to. Amy was so full of remorse that she would do anything to ease her conscience. Susan had requested that she moved into her house with the children and stayed there until her divorce was sorted out. She now grudgingly accepted that Amy could not be reconciled with Peter. She had heard that he was having an affair with Gill, and Susan didn't approve of that, with Amy's best friend who was married, so it seemed that a divorce was best all round.

She brushed her neat blonde hair into a bun, which seemed right for the occasion. She did miss David after all their years together, but she couldn't honestly admit to herself that she had loved him. Once he had stirred her to the very depths with his passion, but soon after she had suffered a very painful miscarriage. After that she had been afraid to let go in their love making, Amy was born, and then Max, but his birth had been so painful that she had never wanted David near her again.

His acceptance of no love life had surprised, but also relieved, her, so she put it out of her mind, assuming that over a period of time his sex drive had diminished. In return for the fact that he made no sexual demands on her, she gave him her loyalty and companionship, and assumed that they had a reasonably good marriage.

His behaviour recently had been very strange, firstly dropping out of the election, and then being jumpy and moody every time someone came or the telephone rang. She knew he was hiding something from her, and then she found a telephone number in the pocket of his suit when he came back from the business conference. She had rung it, and when it was answered a woman's voice had announced, "Maria's Escort Agency." Susan had put the telephone down in horror. She didn't want to know anything about that and she had never asked him.

She was glad she hadn't asked him. Whatever had been going on had died with him. Susan never wanted to give her neighbours a chance to gossip about her. Amy had a right to feel guilty about adding to his stress, but Susan didn't feel the need to confide in her or Max about the agency. It was too personal and private, as well as humiliating, for her to mention.

"The car is here mother."

Max appeared at the door, his face showing his concern. His mother was a remarkable and courageous woman. He was proud of her. She looked beautiful and very dignified. It was so sad to be widowed at fifty-three. It was no age. Privately he couldn't believe that anything Amy had done had caused his father's death. He was a rising politician and made of sterner stuff than that. Even though there was no evidence to support it, Max was of the opinion that it had been a fault with the car, brakes or something similar. No one could prove it, the car was a burnt out shell.

He helped her into the waiting car. Amy was sitting on the other side of her, and Anna sat on the large seat opposite, holding baby James, with Paul and Sarah beside her. He glanced at Amy, who said nothing, her face was controlled, but he noticed her lip tremble slightly. He squeezed her hand gently. She had such a burden of blame on her shoulders. She gave him a half smile of

181

appreciation for his loyalty. "Let's say goodbye to Dad," he said softly, and the car moved slowly off.

Ian didn't tell his mother that he was going to the church. She was convinced that Amy had gone back to Peter because she had moved out of the motel. Ian guessed she would be staying at her mother's, and this would be her first public appearance. The only thought in his mind was to get her back.

He had read of David's death in the local newspaper, which also gave details of when the funeral would be. As expected, it was in the local church at Linton Green and members of the public were invited. As far as David was concerned, Ian suspected that he had arranged to have him attacked, but Amy wouldn't have known that, and he had no wish to blacken her memory of her father. He was sorry for her sake that she had lost her father, but he didn't stop to ponder about his death. There could be any reason when he had contacts with dubious characters like Vince. He only hoped, knowing Amy as he did, that she wasn't blaming herself.

He hadn't wasted the time spent at his mother's between David's death and the funeral. He had followed up an advertisement in the paper for a couple to run a toy shop. An elderly aunt had left it in her will to Simon Dean, a young city broker, whose whole life revolved around stocks and shares. He had tried to sell it without success, and was now looking for a woman to run the shop, and a man to do the buying. All he wanted out of it was a profit without any worry or hassle, and in return he would pay a small wage and provide free accommodation. There was a maisonette above, where his aunt had lived, with three bedrooms. Ian had even talked him into allowing Jasper there too for added security. It was all in need of decoration, but Ian was not deterred about that. They now had a chance of a future, and he couldn't wait to tell Amy.

She must still want him, but because of Miranda's interference at the hospital, she probably thought he had left her. As if he could! And if she'd only realised he was coming back to the motel, because his car was still there. But by the time he'd come to fetch it, she was gone. She had to be with her mother, because of her father's death. He understood, and had waited patiently until now. He had missed her so much, and was longing to see her.

Peter would have got out of going to David's funeral if he could have done, but Susan had telephoned and made it clear he was invited. His affair with Gill had become a little out of hand; news was leaking out, she was beginning to rely on him too much and had started following him around. For him it had only been a bit of fun to get back at Amy, and he didn't want a commitment, but Gill was persistent.

In the beginning he had enjoyed her wild streak, but when he realised she was on antidepressants, and suffered mood swings, the fun seemed to go out of it all. He could handle her getting drunk, and sex with her was great, but when she threatened suicide if he ended it, he realised what an unstable person she was. One night, when she was drunk, she told him that Derek was gay, he had only married her to have children, and then a lot of things made sense. No wonder Gill and Derek went their separate ways. Gill was searching for someone to fulfil her, and Peter was now worried he might be that person.

He put on his dark suit and tie. He would see the children today, and maybe they would be upset at the loss of their grandad. Although he wanted to back out, he couldn't. He didn't want them to think badly of him. He regretted losing his temper that day. He would now have to work hard to regain their respect. He wasn't looking forward to seeing Amy. Maybe she knew about Gill, and he realised that this time he had bitten off more than he could chew.

He finished getting ready, put on a pair of black shoes, and then surveyed himself in the mirror. He looked smart, in his opinion, he hoped Paul and Sarah would think so. He might soon not be a part of this family, but he was still their dad, nothing could alter that.

The telephone was ringing, it was Derek. He felt a slight pang of guilt, but only a little.

"Would you like to come with us to the funeral? Parking won't be easy, and there's no sense taking two cars."

Peter hadn't realised they had been invited. He had declined riding in the limousine with the family because of facing Amy, but arriving alone was a bit daunting. Maybe this wasn't such a bad idea.

"Why not," he said. "I'm ex-family now you know," he said sarcastically.

"Well friends can stick together," said Derek genially. "We'll be round for you in about fifteen minutes."

"Is Gill OK about it?" asked Peter, cautiously.

"She's just as apprehensive about it as you are, she parted on bad terms with Amy too, but for today we must forget all that," Derek reminded him.

"Did Susan invite you?" he asked.

"Yes, that's what made it so difficult to say no. From what I've heard she's invited most of the town. She wanted to give him a good send off," explained Derek.

"I see," said Peter. He swallowed awkwardly. This was like a farce. He was knocking off his best friend's wife, who knew, but was pretending he didn't, because he was gay, and now they were all going to a funeral together as a cosy threesome. This would certainly give everyone something to talk about.

Sally had read about David's death with great satisfaction. She had been laid up with a very bruised neck for several days. It had been very painful to eat and swallow, but her life had been spared, ironically, by the snooper in the woods. She didn't remember much, only his terror stricken face, and then the coward had taken off, leaving her choking on the ground, she must have fainted. When she came to it was pitch dark and she had been scared, but had managed to stumble to her car and drive home.

She had decided to go to the police and report him, but the only trouble was her past. She had grown up in care, and had convictions for shop lifting, and soliciting. She had been a prostitute before she became an escort girl. She wanted to forget that, and they would bring it all up. She was trying to be respectable now, especially with the baby on the way. It was amazing her baby had survived all this. She wanted this child. It was the first time in her life she would have something of her own. It didn't matter who had fathered it, David or whoever. She didn't want to know who it was, but she did want her child to have a future. She decided to go to the funeral and mix with the people at the church. She wanted to see what his wife was like, and then when the time was right, Mrs David Lee could make a donation for a better future for Sally and the baby.

Amy walked on one side of her mother, and Max was on the other. They both held her arm, but Susan was in control. Her head was held high, her manner was dignified, and she hid her grief as they followed the coffin into the church.

Amy felt overcome with emotion, scarcely believing that the big, strong person who had always been her father, could be packed away inside the wooden coffin, dead. "Dead, he was dead." The words echoed in her head as she tried to remain composed. She vaguely registered the sea of faces, turning towards them as they walked slowly down the aisle. This very aisle that she had glided down on his arm when he had given her away on her wedding day.

The vicar was turning towards them with a smile on his face. She felt anger inside. How dare anyone smile. Didn't they know her father was dead? He saw her distress, and held her hand gently, murmuring, "God be with you my child." And then turning to her mother, he gently clasped her hand, and Amy saw the mistiness in her eyes, and realised how hard she, too, was fighting to keep her grief private.

They were shown to their seats, and momentarily forgetting her own pain, she hugged Sarah and Paul to her, knowing what an ordeal it must be for them. She had wondered if it was right to bring them, but they had both said they wanted to say goodbye to Grandad.

The service had not been too long. Max had elected to say a speech about his father. It was a résumé of his life and achievements, spoken in such a warm and caring way. When his work as a carer of the community was mentioned, Amy felt the guilt that she could never be free from course through her. All that was gone because of her.

She felt the tears in her eyes as the coffin disappeared behind the curtain. She blinked them away, trying to match her mother's composure. Paul and Sarah stood silent, totally overawed with the whole thing. She put a protective arm around them, wishing she could spare them all the sadness of life at such a tender age.

The strains of *My Way* by Frank Sinatra filled the church, and she glanced at her mother. Susan was now dabbing her eyes, and Amy, too, could feel her cheeks wet with unshed tears. Didn't that just sum her father up? He was a good man, and he had done everything in his life his way. How poignant this was for her mother, who had carefully chosen this song in memory of him.

They knelt in prayer for the last time, and Amy inwardly prayed for the umpteenth time for forgiveness for what she had done. She was then aware of the Vicar signalling them to lead the congregation out.

Susan had requested that Amy and Max should join her to meet all the guests and thank them for attending. It was only relatives that were going back to the house, and Susan knew that with all the publicity, there would be many people. They had come for David, and she wanted to show her appreciation.

"Can I stay with you, Mummy?" asked Sarah, as they stood waiting. Amy had planned for the children to go in the car with Anna and baby James, and she hesitated, trying to decide what would be best.

"Oh, there's Daddy," said Sarah delightedly. By now she had forgotten her Dad's outburst. She hadn't seen him for quite a few weeks, and it seemed like a lifetime.

Amy noticed Peter's face light up, and both the children ran to be hugged by him. She could see he had missed them. She stood awkwardly as he gently hugged her mother, offering his condolences, and then shook hands with Max, quietly congratulating him on the birth of his son. He nodded briefly at her, not attempting any contact at all, and she could see he had not forgiven her.

"Are you coming back to the house?" asked Susan warmly, and Amy remembered that her mother had always liked him.

Peter hesitated, avoiding Amy's eyes, "I'm not sure."

"Please Daddy, do!" clamoured Sarah and Paul.

Now Peter wished he hadn't come with Gill and Derek. He was finding it difficult facing Amy in case she knew about his affair with Gill, but he was torn. He was still family, and he wanted to see his children.

"I haven't brought my car. I came with friends," he explained.

Amy spoke up, aware of the awkwardness of the situation. She was the problem, but the children weren't, and they were obviously very pleased to see him. She had kept them away from him until he cooled down. But now he had every right to see them.

"Do come back, Peter. We have to greet a lot of people and thank them for their support. You could go in the car with Anna and the children, and then we'll arrange a taxi for you later."

Peter forced himself to look at her. She was pale, but just as beautiful as ever. The long black dress she wore really suited her. He wished he'd never got involved with Gill. Even though he'd heard she'd split up with Ian, she'd never come back to him now. He could sense it. She was polite to him, but that's all. She was divorcing him, and it hurt so much.

He hugged the children close to him again. "Yes, I will come," he said simply, smiling at Sarah, who was clutching his arm tightly. Susan pointed them in the direction of the car, and then she moved on to the next person.

Amy looked up to see Gill and Derek standing there. Derek was his usual self. He spoke to her mother and Max, and then he hugged her warmly, when he offered his sympathy. Gill, on the other hand, stared straight through her and barely spoke to her. When she did, she did not meet her eyes, and Amy guessed her sympathies were still very much with Peter.

Well Gill was of no consequence now, Amy had heard the rumours of an affair between Peter and Gill, but with all the trauma in her own life, she hadn't thought about it much. If they were, it didn't bother her, but she did hope Derek wouldn't be hurt by it. He had always been such a nice person, in her opinion. He didn't deserve to be hurt. Was that down to her too? She couldn't take much more blame, but if she was still with Peter, it would never have happened.

But this time her conscience argued back with her. It was working overtime at the moment. It reminded her of Peter's treatment of her in the past, at the party. That night he had destroyed her trust. She knew it didn't excuse her affair, but maybe it explained it. Her heart argued back too. It wasn't just an affair, she had fallen in love, and once again she felt the hopelessness of the situation sweep over her.

She spent the next hour greeting people and going through the procedure expected of her. Some were relatives, some were friends, and even more of them were just ordinary people of the

187

community, but they had all showed they cared. Her father had cared about the people, this is why he had tried to lead the local Conservative party.

Susan greeted the last person. Her hand was getting tired with all the shaking she had done. This young woman was alone. She didn't know her, but she was struck by her similarity to Amy in looks, with her blonde hair and blue eyes. She wore a simple black skirt with a white blouse, and a black silk scarf tucked into her neck. Susan wondered if she had hurt her neck, because she seemed to be moving it a little awkwardly. She wondered who she was.

"I'm so sorry for your loss Mrs Lee," murmured Sally.

Now she could see her close up, she noticed how proud and dignified this woman was, even in the midst of her grief. She felt jealousy flood through her. No wonder she had breeding, she had money! It wasn't fair, she thought angrily, she should have had a life like mine!

"Thank you," said Susan graciously. "Your face is so familiar to me, I feel I should know you."

Sally had her lie very well rehearsed. "I met you when your husband opened the Church Summer Fete last year. I was running the lucky dip stall. It was thanks to him we raised such a large amount of money."

"I see." Susan smiled at yet another reference to David's good works. He had certainly left his mark on this community. She had met so many people in her support of David and his charity works, she was totally convinced by Sally.

Sally had heard snippets of murmured conversation whilst sitting unobtrusively in the back row, even that Susan was looking for a new housekeeper, and all sorts of new ideas were forming in her mind.

Amy smiled too, and shook her hand. The smile froze on her face as she looked over her mother's shoulder, and saw those oh so familiar brown eyes boring into hers, compelling her to look back and acknowledge him.

Ian had appeared from nowhere, and he stood, a few steps away, willing her to come over to him. He had never met her mother or her brother, and this didn't seem the right time to do it, but he was determined that Amy would speak to him. He was stirred as always by her beauty, those hypnotic blue eyes, that stared back at him, and he exulted inwardly when he saw her reaction to him. He could see she still loved him, not that he had any doubt, in spite of what his mother had said.

Amy's heart was thudding madly. If her mother and Max realised who this was, their reaction would not he a good one. She didn't want to cause any more stress to her family. She knew she should ignore him, walk away from this situation, but she knew she couldn't. Her heart, as usual, was ruling her head, and there was nothing she could do about it.

She turned to Susan, passing her hand over her forehead, "Mummy, I have a headache. Do you mind if I follow on in a minute. It's only about a ten minute walk, and it might help to clear my head."

Susan was startled. How would it look if Amy didn't ride back with them? "We can't just leave you here . . ." she started to protest.

"Yes you can!" said Amy, firmly. "I want to be alone!"

"Very well," sighed Susan. She knew her daughter's strong will only too well. It had been a long morning, and she knew there were more people to greet at home. She wanted to sit in the car and relax for a few minutes before it all started again.

Amy waited until her mother and Max were right out of sight before she went up to Ian. All the words of anger and recrimination died on her lips, and she waited, her heart beating so loudly, for him to speak.

Ian's arms went round her. "My God, Amy, I've missed you so much. I'm so sorry to hear about your father. It's terrible!"

Her anger towards him flared, as the guilt she had tried so hard to subdue reared its ugly head. "Yes, it is terrible, and it's all thanks to me he killed himself!"

Her body had gone rigid, and he held her away from him, looking deep into her troubled eyes, trying to make some sense of her words.

"Whatever do you mean?"

All the composure that she had struggled so hard, for so long, to control, deserted her. She pushed him away from her, and shouted angrily.

"I'll tell you what I mean! Because I allowed myself to fall in love with you, I've lost my home, my children have been dragged around from one place to another, my husband is having an affair

189

with my best friend, and I've hurt my family so much that my father not only dropped out of the election, but when the disgrace became too much for him, he committed suicide!"

She stood there sobbing, but warding his hands off, knowing how she would soften towards him if they went round her again. Then she would be forced to tell him about the baby, and once again he would talk her into submission until the next time he let her down.

Ian digested her words. He felt angry too. He had been threatened by a nasty character, knocked down by a car, he too, had lost his home and the respect of his children, all in the name of his love for Amy, but he knew that he would still do it all again if he was given a choice. He struggled to keep calm otherwise he might say things he would regret.

"Amy, let me remind you, I, too, have lost everything, including my job, because of our relationship, but I don't regret it. Can you imagine how awful it was for me being stuck in hospital without seeing you. They called Miranda, they didn't know we were split up and she didn't tell them. Even my mother didn't know until afterwards that I was there."

Amy dried her eyes. Was he telling her the truth? She couldn't take much more of this emotional see-saw. She was tempted to run into his arms, and then she remembered her conscience.

"I have to end this once and for all for the sake of my father's memory," she said quietly, trying not to weep at the thought of it.

"Utter crap!" expostulated Ian, unable to contain himself any longer. He knew her father was no plaster saint. He could denounce him now, but it would only drive a wedge between them. David wouldn't have ended his life because of a little bit of scandal about Amy that would be forgotten in time, he wasn't that sort of man. But if she wanted to believe that, he would have to go along with it to keep her. He stepped forward and put his arms round her trembling body, stroking her hair, and he felt her body relax against him. He put all his heart and soul into his next words.

"Amy, I understand how you feel, and I know how much your father loved you. He would want you to be happy, but if you can honestly look me straight in the face and say you don't love me, and you'll be happy without me, then I'll let you go."

Amy was weakening, and she knew it, she couldn't tell a lie.

190

Life without Ian just wasn't worth contemplating. She was still on this emotional roller coaster, and she couldn't get off. She tried to be strong, pointing out, "My conscience will always get in the way of our happiness. Not only that, I have got to go through hurting my family yet again by leaving my mother at this sad time."

Ian looked straight into her eyes, seeing the uncertainty there. He hadn't won her yet, and his heart was lurching in agony in case he lost her.

"Amy, the only thing I know is that we have a very special love. Many people have suffered along the way, we know, and we are very sorry, but to make it all worthwhile we must have the courage of our convictions and carry this through, then our families will understand how much we do love each other, and your father's death will not have been in vain."

Amy looked at him and was lost. The love in her heart was just too strong to deny. This man was all she ever wanted, and as she clung to him, she prayed that Daddy would understand and forgive her, because she really couldn't help herself.

Chapter Twenty-six

Eight months later . . .

Sally lay in bed contemplating her future with great satisfaction. Never again would she need to be an escort girl, she was respectable. A mother, living in a beautiful house, which she intended to make her own.

Her son, Daniel was sleeping in a crib next to her bed. She glanced lovingly over at him. He was six weeks old, a beautiful baby, with a mass of tightly curled black hair and very dark eyes. He had just a hint of mixed blood, with negroid features and thick lips. Not that it mattered to Sally. He was the most precious thing in her life. For the first time in her life she cared about someone, and she knew she would do anything she had to, just to give him a decent life.

So it had turned out that David wasn't his father, not that this would alter her plans. His real father was just another punter, who wouldn't have wanted to know about him, and even if he had, Sally had no intention of sharing her son with anyone.

She smiled to herself when she thought of what a pushover Susan had been. She had taken her into her home as a housekeeper so trustingly. It had been easy to get a couple of forged references. Sally did know how to cook, having spent most of her adult years living alone and looking after herself. Cleaning the house had been a bore, but she knew she had to gain Susan's confidence, and it hadn't taken long to achieve that.

Susan had overlooked her inexperience. She was vulnerable after being so recently widowed, and also losing Amy, who had taken her children and moved out to be with another man. She wanted companionship, and the normally very private person that she was changed, and she had confided to Sally how much she missed her daughter, and her husband.

Sally had bided her time. She had needed somewhere to go until her baby was born, but being respectable was boring. She was tired of putting on the pretence of being a caring person. Secretly she hated Susan, thought her such a snob. She couldn't understand why people like her had everything in life without having to lift a finger, while she had struggled all her life, always working, trying to keep out of prison, without much hope of a decent future.

Well that was going to alter. She wanted this house, and the only way to get it was to get Susan to alter her will in Sally's favour, and then she was going to suffer a fatal accident. Sally had to make it look good, and she hadn't finished working out the details yet. Luckily Susan was estranged from her daughter Amy, but there was still her son Max. No doubt they'll all come sniffing round for their share of everything, she thought angrily. They might be middle class, but they're just as greedy for money as anyone else. They won't like it that I'm the new mistress of this house, their inheritance, so they thought, and Daniel will inherit after me. Tough, I'm the one that's been with her since David popped his clogs, and I'm going to enjoy the rest of my life here, after she's altered her will.

So far thinking about it was as far as she had got. Sally was none too bright, having been brought up on the wrong side of town. She was streetwise but uneducated, unlike Jenny. Poor Jenny! As she thought about her short life, she came to a decision. Soon, very soon, she must make her move to secure her future.

Susan lay tossing and turning in the room next door to Sally. She had made a bad decision and she knew it, and now she had to do something about it before things got out of hand.

For the first time in her life she had acted rashly. She had made a decision that she greatly regretted, and now she had to put the situation right. Sally must go. Initially she would be upset, but

193

j

eventually she would understand, Susan hoped. After all, she wasn't family, not her daughter, and Susan had a conscience about Amy. She knew she hadn't been fair to her.

She had blamed her for David's death because she was so angry about Amy's marriage breaking up. His death may have been an accident, she preferred to think so, and knowing David as she did, Amy's marriage break-up would not have driven him to suicide.

When Amy had left to be with Ian, Susan had been devastated. She had expected her to stay until she had got used to being without David. She had even hoped that after the divorce, Amy and the children might choose to live with her. She had told her that she no longer had a daughter, but she hadn't really meant it. She wanted to hurt her as much as she was hurt at that moment, but she had been the loser all round. Not only had she lost her daughter for eight months, she had also lost her grandchildren. She had hoped that Peter might bring them round to see her sometime, but so far it hadn't happened. She had found being alone was unbearable.

Sally had applied for the job at that time, and Susan had remembered her face, she was the girl at the funeral, the one who looked like Amy. It was her resemblance to Amy that made her take her on. At that time, feeling as low and lonely as she did, whether she was a good housekeeper or not didn't seem to matter to Susan.

Susan had found someone to unburden herself to, someone who wasn't family and didn't know the family, and she found it a great comfort. Sally, too, seemed able to confide in her. She told Susan about her life. Her parents had died in a car crash when she was a baby, she didn't remember them, there were no close relatives, and she had been brought up in an orphanage. Susan felt so sad for her.

A month after being there she told Susan about her pregnancy. Evidently her fiancé had walked out on her, and Susan offered to let her live in and stay until her baby was born. Susan added that if she could still cope with the job after her baby arrived, there was a home here for her.

That had been her worst mistake of all, she realised. Not only had Sally not been up to the job, she had also taken advantage of her kindness, Susan could see that now. She had used her, abused her home, not cleaned it properly, put things on her beautifully polished tables without mats and marked them, ordered expensive food and then wasted it, the list was endless. Susan had never had a housekeeper like it, and when she found her taking over and answering the telephone without telling her who had called, she made up her mind, Sally must go. She sat up in bed and plumped up her pillows again. If only she could sleep! She resolved to give Sally her notice tomorrow, and then sort out her life by contacting Amy.

When she woke up in the morning, she got up and made herself some tea. She didn't really feel like eating breakfast, too much on her mind, so she got dressed and waited for Sally to appear. When she had first come, Sally had been the first to get up and get breakfast, before getting on with her other duties, but since Daniel had been born, he had taken up all her time, and Susan was doing everything herself. Susan realised it just didn't work. She would give her a month's notice, and next time she would vet her housekeeper more carefully.

She looked out of the window at the grey January day. It seemed to echo her sombre mood. She was sure Sally could get a live-in job elsewhere, even with the baby. Susan no longer felt comfortable with her around, and she wasn't her responsibility. It was eight months since David had died and she knew she must learn to cope alone. She heard the sound of Daniel crying, and Sally appeared to get his bottle ready.

"Good morning Sally," she said, trying to sound bright, and Sally only responded with a curt nod of her head.

Susan inwardly seethed with anger at her bad manners, but she had always controlled her emotions. It was the way she had been brought up, it was supposed to show good breeding, and she couldn't change now. The ludicrousness of the situation hit her. Her house had been taken over by this young woman, who had no breeding at all, through no fault of her own it was true, but it had reached a stage now where she was not only taking it all for granted, as her right, but also taking advantage, and it had to stop.

She heard her go upstairs to her crying baby in the bedroom, and then all was quiet, so she presumed she was feeding him. An hour went by, it was now ten o'clock, and there was no movement from upstairs. Susan came to a rapid decision. She would tell her now.

She went upstairs and tapped on the door of the bedroom, but there was no response. She opened the door quietly and saw that they were both asleep. She realised how stupid she had been to get involved. This girl was just using her. She shook her gently.

"Sally, it's ten o'clock. Will you please get up, I want to talk to you."

Sally sat up, growling, "What do you want? I'm tired!"

Susan looked horrified. How could she have ever thought she was like Amy? This girl was ill-mannered and ignorant. She spoke quickly to her, "I am giving you one month's notice. I will, of course, give you a good reference . . ."

These words to Sally were like a red rag to a bull. She sprang out of bed with her eyes blazing. She was tired of being nice to this middle class bitch.

"If you think you're going to sling me out in the street you're wrong. You owe me and my son for all the misery your dear departed husband gave me."

The blood drained from Susan's face. The thought that David could have any connection with this creature was abhorrent to her. She felt faint, and she didn't want to hear any more. She went to turn away. "Get out of my house," she said simply, and the baby stirred and started crying again.

"Look what you've done you bitch!" choked Sally. Her eyes stared at Susan with a demonic glint in them and she became scared. Was this woman mad?

Sally's mind flashed back to over ten years ago. Those were the words her mother had uttered. She had never been loved, not like her sister, she had always taken the blame for everything. No wonder she had done bad things. Then she had done the worst thing of all. She had torched the house and taken off after they went to bed. She hadn't wanted to kill her mother and sister Lucy, but they had asked for it, in her eyes. Now this woman was doing the same.

She was surprisingly strong for such a slim person, but anger lent strength to her arms. She wrapped them round Susan's neck in a vice like grip.

"I could choke you to death," she said cruelly, thinking of what David had done to her.

Susan could feel everything spinning around her, and then merciful blackness. Sally kicked her body as if it was a rag doll as she lay on the floor. She tied her arms and legs with the rope she had found in the garage, and stood waiting for her to come round.

She only had to wait for five minutes. Susan was groaning on the floor, and trying to move; panic set in when she realised she was tied up. This woman was mad, she tried to humour her.

"Sally, your baby is crying. Untie me, and I'll help you to look after him."

Sally glanced nervously at Daniel. She was hard and indifferent to anything other than him. He was special, and she didn't know what was wrong. She had already fed him.

"Shut your row!" she said viciously. "You've upset him, and you've upset me! I'm not going to untie you until you alter your will in my favour, and if you don't do it, I'm going to leave you there and torch your house, so even if I don't get it, no one else will either!"

Susan spoke slowly and clearly. She was aware that her life was in the hands of this creature, who was totally insane, so she did nothing to antagonise her. Her voice trembled as she tried to control her fear.

"If you untie me, I'll get some paper and do what you ask."

Sally slowly untied her, and from the end of Daniel's cot she produced a gun.

"Don't do anything silly!" she said, her eyes shining with passion, and at that moment the telephone rang.

Chapter Twenty-seven

Amy was two weeks overdue, and Ian was worried. The baby was quite big now, certainly big enough to be born, so why hadn't it come? He had watched over her lovingly all through her pregnancy, supported her in every way, and he couldn't wait for it to be born.

This baby was really special to him, it was a gift, he felt. He had thought he was sterile, but this was his proof that he could still father a child. The mother of his child was the girl of his dreams, and this made his happiness complete. He just wanted it to be safely born now and then he could relax.

"Ian darling, I have a doctor's appointment at nine o'clock. You haven't forgotten?" Amy asked him when they got up that morning.

"As if I could!" said Ian, putting his arms round her ample frame. He touched her swollen stomach gently, and then put his ear to it, laughing.

"Is there anyone in there? Don't you think it's time you came to meet your family."

Amy giggled too. "Don't do that. I might have it here and now," she threatened him.

Paul and Sarah were still on their Christmas holidays from school and were spending a few days with Peter. The divorce was going through, and the house would eventually be sold and the money divided. In the meantime, Amy and Ian had worked very hard to make the maisonette into a home for them all.

Peter had told Amy that he would be moving away, not too far because of the children. She had heard that Derek had left Gill to live with another man, so although he hadn't said it, Peter was trying to escape Gill's clutches. Now Amy understood why Gill's life was so haywire, and the true reason for her depression. She felt a fleeting pity for her, but it had been Gill's choice to drop her, so she didn't waste too much time thinking about it. It was funny really how everyone else had condemned them for falling in love, when they should have looked at the flaws in their own marriages.

The toy shop was thriving, business had really picked up thanks to Amy's organisation. She had a way with customers which no one could resist, and they just kept coming back to buy. Ian did the buying, and together they ran the business and coped with the children. He busied himself with unpacking stock and organising the window, leaving Amy to serve, knowing she was competent.

Simon Dean's first reaction when he knew of Amy's pregnancy had been dismay, but when she showed her determination to do a good job, and Ian lent his support, Simon had been very impressed to see the takings go up. He returned her loyalty by hiring a temporary sales lady to cover her for the last two weeks of her pregnancy. He had wanted to do it for the last month, but Amy had insisted in carrying on until Ian had put his foot down. She was now two weeks over, and the doctor had said that if nothing happened today, she would be admitted to hospital to be induced.

Ian had repainted the maisonette, and that was all he could do with the limited amount of money they had. It looked clean, but the furniture was old, and the carpets too, so Amy had made new curtains to brighten it up. The children had chosen their own bedroom colours, red and cream for Paul, and pink and turquoise for Sarah. Ian and Amy had laughed at the brightness of it after settling for white in their own bedroom, and neutral colours everywhere else.

Amy hadn't cared what colours they had really, as long as they were happy. They seemed to he coping with the separation as long as they saw Peter sometimes, and after some initial distrust of Ian, they now accepted him as their mother's partner. This relieved her considerably. As soon as the divorces became final, they would marry, they both knew that. Amy longed for that day.

"It's very cold out today. Jasper didn't want to go far," remarked Ian, as Amy was putting on her coat. It didn't do up over her enlarged frame, but she had refused to buy a new one for such a short time. Money was tight enough as it was.

"I'll be OK Ian. I only have to step quickly out of the car, so don't nag me!" she said grimacing. There was a look of horror on his face. He was such a fusspot these days, but it was nice to know how much he cared about her. She felt a warm glow of love go through her.

There were only two things to spoil their happiness, and she hoped that time would heal these. Firstly her mother's refusal to accept them, and then Linda and Sophie hadn't wanted to come and see their Dad. He had to take them out on his own. Amy felt guilt run through her again. She was, it seemed, the villain of the piece, but sorry as she was, she knew if she had the time again, she would still have wanted his love and all the heartache that came with it.

Ian was doing his best to remain amicable with Miranda. She had moved her mother and Gwen into the house because she didn't like being alone. Now she had plans to have a conservatory built and add another bedroom. She wanted Ian to foot the bill, so it looked like he would have to sign over his half of the house to her.

As Ian was helping her into the front of the car, the silver MG belonging to Simon Dean glided smoothly into the drive. He smiled over at them, and then with the ease of movement that his regular trips to the gym permitted, he swung his legs over, and jumped out of the car. "I'm glad I've caught you folks." His eyes rested on Amy, quizzically, and she knew why. "I wasn't sure if there'd be another one yet," he quipped, and she smiled back.

"There will be soon," she promised him.

Simon was about six feet tall, with brown wavy hair, which he continually pushed out of his eyes, and very brown eyes. He was tanned all the year round, sometimes from his holidays always spent in very warm countries, but more often than not from his regular sessions on a sun bed. He lived his life on the edge of his seat, being heavily involved in the rise and fall of world stock markets. Although only in his late twenties, stress lines were beginning to appear on his forehead, and his face, although good looking, had fine lines appearing too, so he could really be

200

described as rugged. He had so far managed to avoid any commitment with a woman, preferring to live this fast life on his own.

He had often privately admired Amy. Ian was a lucky guy! He had never up until now met anyone he had wanted to settle down with, but there was something very special about Amy. Not only was she very beautiful, she looked positively blooming today, in the late stages of her pregnancy, she was also loyal and hard working, never using her condition as an excuse to give less than a good day's work.

He shook himself back to reality. She was Ian's woman, anyone could see how close they were, and he was here on business, to put a proposition to them. Running backwards and forwards from London to the country was a chore he could do without. When he had a day off from work, he wanted to spend it in his yuppy penthouse on the river Thames, not coming down here.

"I know you're just on the way out, but when you come back can we have a chat? I was wondering, as sitting tenants, whether you would be interested in buying the freehold, at a realistic price of course," he added quickly.

Amy glanced at Ian, knowing that at the moment, it was a financial impossibility. When their divorces were settled she would get some money, but not yet. The idea was tempting. It was their chance to achieve something, and she had enjoyed running the shop and watching the takings rise every week. If only they had the money now.

Ian's eyes met hers, and she could see he was having similar thoughts. It was a chance for them. He addressed Simon.

"We will discuss it after we've been to the doctor, Simon. As you know we are in the throes of divorce at the moment, and we have no spare cash. If it's something that Amy wants to do, and we certainly need to think about that, then we'll let you know."

"Yes," agreed Amy. "We will think about it!" she smiled at Ian. "We must go now, or we'll be late."

Ian started the car, and as he did so, she felt a sudden twinge inside. Was it indigestion? Ian was talking as they pulled away. "What a time to grab us!" he moaned. "Everything has to be instant with Simon. What do you think of the idea, anyway?"

"You know I'd love to own the shop, when we can afford it.

It's a chance to show everyone what we can do as a team."

"Yes, we're a great team!" enthused Ian, and then rather desperately, he said: "We'll have to try and get the money from somewhere. We don't want him to sell to anyone else."

"Well we are sitting tenants," Amy reminded him.

Ian allowed his mind to wander a little. He loved working alongside Amy. With hard work they could make their own future, show everyone just how determined they were. He glanced at her. She was suddenly very quiet.

"Are you all right?" he asked anxiously.

Amy tried to bear it as another, even fiercer pain, shot through her. "No," she said, gasping, when it had subsided. "Don't bother with the doctor. Take me straight to the hospital. The baby's coming!"

Chapter Twenty-eight

Max was sitting reading the Saturday newspapers, when a small paragraph caught his eye. It simply stated that Clive Calloway had been found guilty of indecent exposure at Wolseley Park. Not in itself riveting news, but there was a photograph of him, and the part that caught Max's eye was that he was the Finance Manager of Linton Green Municipal Bank. He wondered, idly, if Peter knew him. Something like that would finish someone's career.

It was a very dark January day and the wind was cold. The sort of day that no one would go out on unless they had to. He could hear the wind howling down the chimney as he put another log onto the fire, and moved his chair even closer to it.

Anna was upstairs dressing James, and then she would bring him down for Max to watch him whilst she had a shower. He put the fire guard carefully in place. Their son was now nine months old, on the move, crawling everywhere. He had certainly changed their life. He knew he would have to put the paper down soon. The little monkey would push it out of his hand.

The telephone rang and he sprang up to answer it, remembering that Anna had her hands full right now. It was Ian's voice, and he sounded very agitated. Amy was in labour, but there were complications. The baby was laying in a difficult position, and the cord was caught.

Max's heart missed a beat. "But she will be all right?" he asked fearfully.

"My God I hope so!" said Ian, almost in tears of anguish. "I've

203

got to go back to her. They've given her some drugs to help with the pain, but the reason I've phoned you is because she keeps asking for her mother. Do you think she will come? I've never seen Amy like this, I'm really scared!"

"I'll make her come, and I'll be there too!" said Max vehemently. "It's time our mother stopped snubbing Amy. I keep telling her, and this will certainly shake her up!"

"Thanks Max," said Ian gratefully. "I must go now!"

He cleared the line on his mobile, and switched the handset off before he went back into the hospital to be with Amy.

She was in the labour ward, with a doctor and a midwife in attendance, and Ian dutifully washed his hands and put the robe and mask back on, as had been stipulated in order that he could attend the birth. He looked anxiously at the doctor, working silently; Amy was panting with pain, the sweat clearly visible on her face. He had been to the classes with her, but somehow hadn't expected it to be like this. He wished he could do something, he felt so helpless.

"Squeeze my hand, Amy, go with the pain," he urged. "Hold on in there, your mother and Max are coming."

He saw relief in her eyes, and hoped that Max would be successful. Only a mother could know how she was suffering. He was a mere bloke, but oh how he felt for her!

"Don't worry Mr Wood. The baby is no longer in distress. We've managed to free the cord. It won't be long now," smiled the midwife, as Amy let out another yell of pain, and panted.

Ian mopped the sweat off her brow, feeling both elated and concerned at the same time. "Are you sure?" he said wonderingly, as Amy screamed again.

"Quite sure!" said the midwife firmly. "Amy, now start to push!"

Hope flooded through Susan when the telephone rang. Until then it felt like there was no one else in the world except herself, the innocent little boy in the cot and this maniac, who was now waving a gun at her.

"Can I answer it. I won't tell," she begged her.

"Don't be mad. Do you think I'm stupid!" shouted Sally, her agitation rising as Daniel started to cry again.

Susan counted the rings, six of them and then the answer machine kicked in inviting the caller to leave a message. Max's voice, sounding concerned, came over the line.

"Hi Mother, it's me. Just to let you know that Amy's in labour, and having a pretty bad time by the sound of it. Forget all your bad feelings. She's asking for you, and you really need to get over to the hospital, right away. It is urgent, or else I wouldn't be phoning! Where are you anyway? Shall I come and get you. Please call me back as soon as you get this message."

Susan glanced fearfully at Sally, expecting a strong reaction. The butt of the gun was pressed into her head, and she felt the dizzy feeling again, she was in fear of her life, and at that moment, she realised just how precious life was. She had wasted the last few months of hers being angry with Amy, and now she might not live to see her again, to tell her she was wrong.

Sally's voice was slow and measured, her eyes glittered as she said, "Now you can ring your precious son back and tell him you're not going to the hospital. Tell him you never want to see Amy again."

The look of horror on Susan's face made her feel exultant. This middle class bitch was completely in her power. Sally's mother hadn't cared about her, so there was no way she would allow Susan to settle her differences with Amy.

Susan's heart lurched with pain. She thought of her own horrendous confinement when Max was born. Amy shouldn't have to face that ordeal without knowing her mother cared about her!

"Please Sally, if you have any compassion, let me go to her!" she begged, all middle class self control gone now, only desperation left. Sally scooped up her crying baby in her left arm, holding the gun in her right.

"Compassion? No one ever had it for me in my life! You think just because you've got money, you can do as you like, well you can't, just do it!"

Susan looked at her. She was almost a comical figure with the gun and the baby, just about out of control. Well, heartbreaking though it was, she would have to go along with her, and then maybe later she might have the chance to get free.

She went into her own bedroom and dialled Max's number, and the butt of the gun was once more pressed against her brow. Daniel had stopped crying, unfortunately for her, although Max

205

did know of his existence. Every time he cried, Sally became nervous, and that might be when she could slip up, but there again, reasoned Susan, if she got too nervous, she might shoot her, and she felt terror for her life, which suddenly seemed so important again, rip through her. She spoke her words quickly, anxious to say her piece, and hoping he would realise something was wrong.

"Max, it's Mother here. I have no wish to visit Amy in hospital. You go. Furthermore, I have no wish to see you again, or your wife Elizabeth, or your son Jim."

She put the phone down before he could answer, hoping he would realise her deliberate mistakes. Max knew she didn't have a faulty memory. Sally, on the other hand, didn't know their names.

Sally smiled with grim satisfaction. She needed Susan to be estranged from her family. Now to sort out this change of will.

"Well done!" she said, feeling triumphant. "Now find some paper."

Susan did meekly as she said. An unwitnessed change of will would not be legal, she knew. She just hoped that Max would think about what she had said to him.

Max was dumbfounded by her words. He couldn't believe his mother was so heartless that she would turn her back on Amy in labour. He would have staked his life on her forgetting all her grievances and going straight to the hospital. She had intimated several times lately that she would like to see Amy and Ian. Not only that, she was disowning himself and Anna, and baby James. He was absolutely flabbergasted!

The trouble was she had made such a fuss of her new housekeeper, and her baby, she just didn't seem interested in her own family. A wave of hurt shot through him. What had he done? Only tried to act as mediator, and where had it got him?

He got in his car to go to the hospital as promised, feeling heavy hearted at the news he had to give to Amy. Something was niggling inside that his mother didn't seem quite right. She never forgot names. Why had she called Anna. Elizabeth? and James had been Jim. Mother had been the person to say that she hoped no one would ever shorten his name, so why had she done it? Well he had such a lot to worry about at the moment, there really wasn't time to ponder on it, so he pushed it to the back of his mind.

*　　　*　　　*　　　*

Amy sat up in bed glowing, her baby daughter in her arms. She didn't feel at all tired, the pain was all forgotten, she felt ecstatically happy as she held the warm bundle of love close to her. Natalie Jane stirred making little noises in her sleep, and Amy stroked her downy head, which was covered in a little cap of silver blonde hair.

"I'll hold her, you must be tired," said Ian, his love and pride for both of them showing in his face. He couldn't wait to hold her either. She was safely here and Amy was fine too. Life was just so wonderful!

Amy carefully handed her to him. Ian had cried when he saw her, not just with the wonder of the moment, but also the realisation that they were both OK. She felt just as moved. The bonds of their love would never be stronger, and the bond between father and daughter would always be close. It had been so wonderful to have him with her when she delivered. It was an experience neither of them would forget.

She had been moved back into the ward with other mothers. Amy didn't mind at all, though Ian had commented that if they could have afforded private care she would have had a room of her own. Amy had told him that she preferred not to be alone, and anyway, she was going home tomorrow.

She lay back on her pillows. She didn't want to admit it, but maybe she was a bit tired. Then she saw Max and her heart lifted, Mummy would be with him, he had promised to bring her. Amy couldn't wait to be reconciled with her. She had missed her mother, and it was always great to see Max.

But she could see by his face that he hadn't been successful. He admired Natalie and congratulated them both, and then chatted about all sorts of mundane things, and all the time Amy was thinking of her mother, who couldn't forgive her and didn't want to see her new grandchild. Was she to carry this guilt for the rest of her life?

Suddenly, without warning, she felt the heavy feeling of depression sweep over her. Even the sight of her beautiful new baby couldn't prevent it, and the tears started to roll down her cheeks. She sobbed, and a concerned Ian put his arms around her, knowing the cause, without even needing to ask.

207

Sister came bustling in. "That's enough everyone for now. Amy needs to rest."

Amy didn't want Ian or Max to go, but they promised to come back again in the evening, and Ian reminded her he was taking her home tomorrow. They kissed her goodbye, and Ian promised to bring Sarah and Paul in to see her later. He hoped that would cheer her up.

After they had gone, she dutifully took the painkillers she was given. They could ease the pain in her body, but they couldn't ease the pain in her heart of being rejected by her mother.

"I don't know what's got into our mother!" exclaimed Max. "How could she be so cruel to Amy?"

"Yes, I hoped the birth of Natalie would bring them together," sighed Ian. He knew how hurt Amy was, and he wished he could have made things right for her. Surely now it was time to put the past behind them. Why couldn't her mother move on?

They had walked out to their cars, and Ian came to a sudden decision.

"I'm going to ring and tell your mother about Natalie. Let's see what happens then?" he said firmly, switching on his mobile phone.

"OK," said Max. "You can't do any worse than I did."

Max told him the number, and Ian dialled it. It rang a few times before it was answered. He expected Susan's voice to be clear and strong, but she sounded very quiet and subdued. Obviously upset, he decided.

"Mrs Lee, it's Ian here. Just to tell you that you have a new granddaughter, Natalie, mother and daughter are doing well."

There was a pause whilst she digested the news, and his heart pounded with expectation, waiting for her response. When it came, all his hope was crushed.

"I don't want to know about you, Michael, or my daughter, or your son," and then he heard the telephone go down, and he stood there in amazement, unable to comprehend her reaction.

Max looked at him sympathetically, his face showed the misery he felt.

"Didn't you fare any better?" he said feelingly. "If I didn't know better, I'd say she was losing her marbles. She even got our names wrong, calling Anna, Elizabeth, and James, Jim."

"Yes, she did with me," agreed Ian. "She called me Michael, and then referred to Natalie as my son. Do you think she forgot?"

"No, not my mother. She is as sharp as a needle! I know this sounds bizarre, but maybe it isn't her. I've got a gut feeling that something's wrong."

Ian's mind whirled. An impostor, but why? They must go round there. "Let's check it out," he suggested.

They both drove their own cars, and Ian parked his at the end of the road, whilst Max drove right through the gates and up to the house. He made a lot of noise getting out of it, and pretending to look under the bonnet, to enable Ian to slip quietly round to the rear of the house without being seen.

Max rang the doorbell several times, and when it was finally answered, his mother reluctantly appeared, with just her head round the door, making it clear she didn't want him to come in. Max felt hurt, so there was no mistake, his imagination had been playing tricks on him.

"I can't believe you could do this to Amy, your own daughter!" he said pleadingly, but Susan appeared to be unmoved, so he turned wearily to go home. He had tried and failed!

By this time Ian had managed to get to the kitchen door, but it was locked. He tried to peer through the window. She was out in the hall talking at the door, and he could hear Max, trying to persuade her to let him in. When he looked through, he could see her reason for not doing so, a young woman was standing behind her with a gun pressed into her back.

Ian crept away slowly and joined Max as they went out. When they were out of sight, he explained what he had seen.

"My mother being held at gunpoint! But why?" burst out Max. This was serious! "She's in danger! What can we do?"

Ian thought carefully. "She doesn't know me. I'll knock at the door and try to keep her talking whilst you go round the back."

His mind was working frantically, trying to formulate a plan. This woman's life was in danger, and they couldn't afford to get it wrong. He walked determinedly up to the door and rang the doorbell.

"Who is it?" her voice sounded irritated at being disturbed again, but he remembered what he had seen. She had no choice but to send people away with a gun pressed into her back.

"I'm sorry to trouble you, but I'm trying to find my way to

Linton Green. I need the town centre," said Ian, hoping she would at least open the door and give Max time to try and get in. His heart sank when, after a pause, she replied, without opening the door:

"You'll have to ask someone else. I simply haven't got time to speak to you."

By now, Max had arrived at the window and seen his mother's predicament. He remembered that Ian had said the back door was locked, but what about the utility room door, which was round the side? He tried it, doing his best to be quiet, and to his immense relief, it opened, and he glided noiselessly in.

He peered through in time to see his mother standing in the kitchen. The young woman had her covered by the gun, and had her back to him. She waved it at Susan, menacingly. "Now everyone's gone, it's time for you to start writing!" she spat out, and he saw his mother's terror-stricken face.

Max didn't stop to think. He launched himself from behind, straight at her, intending to knock the gun right out of her hand, but at that moment Sally panicked, and fired. The gun went off in her hand, the barrel was pointing at her own stomach where Max had deflected it from Susan. He watched with fascinated horror, as she crumpled up slowly, the blood gushing out of her stomach, and then within a very few seconds, although it seemed like a lifetime, she lay on the floor, completely lifeless. And then came the sobs of relief from Susan, as she ran into his arms, realising her own life had been spared.

"Oh Max, thank goodness you came!" she said over and over again. She was choked with emotion, and couldn't seem to stop shaking. The relief she felt was too great to express.

Max released her and went to open the door to let Ian in. "Mother, this is Ian," he said, and there was a pause. Ian wondered what her reaction would be.

Susan stared at him wonderingly. What had she expected to see? This man she had thought of as a marriage breaker. Someone with two horns, and breathing fire like the devil himself. Instead she saw a pleasant faced young man. He had kind eyes, and somehow she knew she would like him.

"Ian, I wish we had met in happier circumstances," she murmured, and they all stared in horror at the body on the floor.

"She was utterly mad!" said Susan. "She was trying to get me to alter my will or else she would kill me."

"But she was your housekeeper!" said Max in amazement.

"I know!" said Susan. "I was trying to give her notice, and she flipped."

The strain of the situation became too much, and she sobbed. "Oh what a mess!"

Max put his arms round her. "Don't worry mother, we'll call the police. It will be self defence."

"I'm just so grateful to be alive," sobbed Susan, and Max couldn't help noticing, that for the first time that he could ever remember, his mother had showed her emotions, and he liked it. It just showed she was human after all.

Max held her close whilst Ian called the police. Susan explained how she had felt sorry for Sally and given her a home. "Her baby Daniel is in the cot upstairs. How terrible he's lost his mother," she said sadly.

"Maybe he's better off, if she was mad," pointed out Max. "She might have harmed him."

Ian put the telephone down. "The police are on their way," he said quietly.

Susan gently extricated herself from Max. "I'll tell them what they want to know, and how you tried to get the gun. They will understand that you were defending me." Then she added, "After that there's something very important that I want to do." She smiled at both of them.

Whatever David had been doing, she wasn't interested in it, or his connection with Sally. She could guess really, but it was too late for that now. Her loyalty to David would remain, and the children didn't need to know. The memory of their father would remain untarnished, but she now knew that his death had nothing to do with Amy; he had probably been the author of his own misfortune. She would tell Amy it was an accident. It wasn't fair that Amy should take the blame. The truth had died with him, and now she was ready to move on.

"Yes, I want to see Amy and tell her I love her and I've missed her, and I want to see my lovely new granddaughter. Isn't Natalie a beautiful name?"

Ian smiled with relief. He could see that he was going to get along with Susan very well.

211